Storm Testament I

Storm Testament I

Lee Nelson

Council Press
Springville, Utah

ISBN 13: 978-1-55517-544-3

Published by Council Press, an imprint of Cedar Fort, Inc., 2373 W. 700 S., Springville, UT, 84663
Distributed by Cedar Fort, Inc. www.cedarfort.com

LIBRARY OF CONGRESS CATALOGING-IN-PUBLICATION DATA

Nelson, Lee.
[Storm testament]
The Storm testament I / by Lee Nelson.
p. cm.
Originally published: Storm testament , 2001.
ISBN 978-1-55517-544-3 (alk. paper)
1. Rocky Mountains—Fiction. 2. Ute Indians—Fiction. I. Title.

PS3564.E4675S76 2007
813'.54—dc22

2007026687

Cover design by Nicole Williams
Cover design © 2007 by Lyle Mortimer
Edited by Annaliese B. Cox

Printed in the United States of America

10 9 8 7 6 5 4 3 2 1

Printed on acid-free paper

Prologue

By Sam Storm

My great-great-grandmother, Caroline Storm, would never allow anyone to read her husband's handwritten journals. His name was Dan Storm, and he filled eight volumes with his life story. Caroline would read parts to her children and grandchildren, about her husband's involvement in the Far West persecutions in Missouri, his living with the Ute Indians before Mormon pioneers came to the Utah territory, and his involvement with the Mormon Battalion and one of the handcart companies. But she would never let anyone else read the journals. She promised that after she died everyone could read the secret parts.

After her funeral in 1905, the journals could not be found. She had been living with her son, Joseph, in American Fork, Utah, and the house was searched from top to bottom, but the journals simply were not there.

For the next seventy-four years, every time the family got together for a reunion, wedding, or funeral, the favorite topic of conversation was what became of Daniel Storm's journals, and after his death, why Caroline refused to let anyone read them. Some speculated that they contained juicy tidbits about early polygamy. Others suggested that they might contain criticisms of Joseph Smith or Brigham Young. Perhaps there were accounts of revenge against Missouri mobbers or Utah Indians that, if made known, would bring shame to the family. But only Caroline knew the real reasons for keeping the journals secret, and she didn't tell.

The family was divided into two camps, those who believed she had destroyed the journals before her death and those who believed that she couldn't have destroyed them, that they must be hidden, or perhaps stolen.

I personally was tired of hearing about the journals. There wasn't any sense worrying about them now that they were gone. Someone should have been more concerned while Caroline was alive, and not have let them disappear.

This is how I felt on that fateful afternoon in June of 1980 when I was having lunch with Grandma Storm at the old house in American Fork. She was talking about the journals, the same old stuff I'd heard a thousand times.

I was in no hurry to go anywhere, so with an occasional nod, I encouraged her to keep talking, even though there was nothing new or particularly interesting in what she was saying. Having just graduated from Brigham Young University with a degree in English literature, I was unemployed and not very interested in becoming an English teacher. I was in limbo, trying to figure out what to do with the rest of my life.

"I just know she wouldn't have destroyed them," said Grandma, with conviction. "Too many times she said how grateful she was that Grandfather had written his history for posterity."

I didn't respond to her statement. There was nothing to say. Family members had been searching in vain for over seventy-five years, and never had a single clue been found as to where the journals might be.

Grandma stood up slowly and, with the help of her cane, hobbled into the bedroom. She was gone for what seemed a long time, but finally returned carrying an old blue box under her arm. I cleared a space for her on the table so she could set it down.

"Maybe somewhere in these old papers there's a clue," she said.

"You're a little old to be playing Sherlock Holmes," I said.

She ignored my remark and handed me a handful of yellowish wrinkled papers. Most were letters from relatives and friends, homey stuff about someone getting married or breaking an arm or buying a new flush toilet. I had read most of the letters before and wasn't particularly interested in reading them again.

Near the bottom of my pile were some old advertisements, probably torn out of magazines or catalogues. These never failed to interest me. One of the ads showed a pen and ink drawing of an upright organ, the kind you pump with your feet, priced brand new at $27.95.

While thumbing through the ads, I discovered another letter, a short one, just a few sentences, written on the letterhead, "Sears & Chadwick, Philadelphia, Pennsylvania." The contents were as follows:

Dear Mrs. Storm:

Mr. Chadwick has retired, and the material which you sent to him has been referred to me.

Regards, P. K. Stein

The letter was handwritten and rather hard to read. Sears & Chadwick seemed familiar, but I couldn't recall where I had seen the name before.

Suddenly I remembered a cold wintery day the previous January when I was browsing through some old books in the university library. I'd found an old black wrinkled book, titled something like, *Ben Franklin, Father of American Publishing*. It had been published by Sears & something, maybe Sears & Chadwick. Yes, that must have been the publisher.

I wondered why no one in the family had ever said anything about Caroline corresponding with a Philadelphia publisher, a possible clue to the whereabouts of the journals. I held the letter out to Grandma and asked her what she knew about it.

"Oh, I don't know," she said. "Grandmother was always writing to this or that mercantile company complaining about one thing or another. I suppose Sears answered one of her letters."

"This letter is not from Sears & Roebuck, but Sears & Chadwick," I pointed out. I could tell by the blank look on her face that she had never before noticed the distinction I had just made; neither had anyone else in the family.

"Do you know what Sears & Chadwick is?" I asked.

She shook her head.

"It is a Philadelphia publishing house." I jumped up in my excitement. "And I can only think of one reason that your grandmother would be corresponding with a publishing house."

I watched Grandma's hands tighten their grip on the arms of her chair. The loose skin was almost transparent, exposing blue veins and white sinew. She tightened her grip even more in an effort to control her shaking body. I looked at her face. Her jaw was firmly set, her blue eyes blazing intently, exposing the feelings that swelled up inside her. Those clear blue eyes didn't look old and tired like the rest of her body.

Finally she let go of the chair and took the letter in her hand. She looked at it a long time, then asked, "Do you suppose Grandmother sent the journals to Sears & Chadwick?"

"I know she did," I answered with conviction, "and I'm going to find out what happened to them."

I reached for the telephone dialed the number for the operator.

"Information. What city?" responded the operator.

"Philadelphia."

"Go ahead."

"Sears & Chadwick, a publishing company."

After a brief pause, the operator said there was no such name listed.

"Thank you anyway," I said as I hung up the phone.

I told Grandma that Sears & Chadwick had apparently gone out of business, because there was no telephone number. I asked her if there were any other letters from Sears & Chadwick, Mr. Chadwick, or Mr. Stein. She was sure there weren't, but we went through the letters again, just to make sure. We didn't find anything.

I had never been very interested in family histories, genealogy, and those kinds of things, but finally, after seventy-five years of fruitless searching, coming on a clue to the whereabouts of Dan Storm's journals really got me excited.

I told Grandma that I was going to Philadelphia. The journals had probably been lost or destroyed after so many years, but maybe not. Perhaps they were collecting dust in the attic of what used to be the Sears & Chadwick publishing house. I was determined to find out.

Upon arriving in Philadelphia, I went to the University of Pennsylvania library and found a city directory for the year 1905. Just as I had hoped, the Sears & Chadwick publishing company was listed. The address was 315 South Warsaw Street.

After obtaining a city map, I headed for Warsaw Street. It was across the river in the older section of town. Except for a few drab-looking stores with old paint and faded Coca-Cola signs, the street was lined mostly with brownstone apartment buildings. The address I was looking for turned out to be one of the stores.

"Tony's Delicatessen" was written in red and black letters on the big yellow facade. In the single window was a piece of clean, white butcher paper announcing fresh ravioli every Thursday.

Friendly bells jingled on the back of the door as I entered the delicatessen. I was engulfed in a rich assortment of smells—salami, dill, and yeast were the most distinct.

Behind the counter, three young, strong Italian men were busy making sandwiches. I watched the one closest to me as he quickly sliced open a hard-crusted bun with his wide-bladed knife. His strong, brown hands were almost quicker than the eye as he piled the bread high with slices of salami, turkey, and boiled ham. Next he heaped on slices of dill pickles, cheese, diced tomatoes, chopped peppers, and shredded lettuce. He sprinkled the entire sandwich with a generous supply of spicy garlic oil, then wrapped it in waxed paper and passed it through a little window in the wall to the waiting hands of a waitress at neighboring Bill's Diner. The young Italian then turned to me and asked what I wanted.

"One of those," I responded, pointing to the little window where the sandwich had disappeared.

"No can do. Bill needs her to serve lunch," he laughed. "One hoagie coming up," he continued, without waiting for me to respond to his little joke. He quickly sliced open another bun and began to assemble my sandwich.

"What do you know about Sears & Chadwick Publishing Company?"

"Who?" he asked, without looking up.

"The publishing firm that used to occupy this building."

"That was a long time ago. My father bought this place in 1910, and it's been a deli and sandwich shop ever since. That's all I know."

He handed me the sandwich. I paid, and as he turned away to wait on another customer, I asked, "Did they leave any old manuscripts behind?"

"Any what?" He turned back to me, somewhat annoyed by my persistent questioning.

"Man-u-scripts, pieces of paper with writing on them."

He looked at me like I was crazy, slowly shaking his head with a negative response.

"Do you know anyone who might be able to tell me anything about Sears & Chadwick?"

"Just before the building was paid off, before Papa died, he made the last payments to a woman who lived across the river up by the university. I think it was her father who sold us the building. Her name is Barbara Wharton. That's all I know." He turned to wait on the next customer without giving me a chance to ask more questions.

"Thanks," I said, as I headed out the door toward the university in the hopes of finding the Sears's daughter. The telephone book listed only one Wharton family in the area near the university, a Mrs. Barbara M. Wharton.

The red brick house was located in an old, established, rather plush neighborhood. It was of colonial construction with a steep pitch roof and plenty of ivy on the gables. It was surrounded by spacious, well-manicured lawns and flower gardens.

I felt a tinge of excitement as I walked up the brick walkway, realizing it was perfectly possible for someone in this house to give me a clue as to where my great-grandfather's secret journals had been hidden for the last seventy-five years.

Before I could ring the bell, the door was opened by a tall, stately, good-looking woman, probably in her mid-sixties. She had a vibrant, healthy look, uncommon in women her age. I guessed she probably exercised regularly—tennis or jogging—and was careful about her diet.

After introducing myself, I got directly to the point and told her I was looking for a manuscript that had been sent to the Sears & Chadwick Publishing Company around 1904, the year before my great-grandmother's death.

I wasn't surprised when she gave me a blank, questioning look, as though she hadn't understood what I had said. I repeated my question.

"Oh, I don't think I can help you," she responded in a tone of voice that indicated a genuine concern. "So many years have come and gone. But please come in. I'll tell you everything I know."

She led me to an informal dining area on a partially enclosed patio with many potted plants. She asked me to be seated at an oak table, and she poured each of us a glass of cold apple juice before sitting down across the table from me.

She explained that the old publishing house on Warsaw Street had been sold before she was born and that the family hadn't been engaged in publishing since that time. She couldn't recall having ever seen any manuscripts among family belongings.

My heart sank. Her explanation seemed so final. She gave me a little background about the company, that it was a partnership founded by her grandfather, Henry Sears, and John Chadwick in the 1830s. It had thrived until the partners became old. The sons were not able to keep the business profitable, and there was a gradual decline until 1910, when the decision was made to sell out. At first the family had tried to sell the company and its equipment, copyrights, and inventories, but there were no takers. Eventually they sold the machinery to a printer across town and the building to Tony Bentino, who opened the delicatessen and sandwich shop.

I asked her about Mr. Stein, the fellow who had written to my great-grandmother in 1904. She vaguely remembered him as an eccentric editor who was fired after driving one of their most successful writers to another publisher. She guessed that Stein was probably the one responsible for losing my great-grandfather's journals.

Eventually there was nothing more to be said about the journals, or Sears & Chadwick. I thanked Mrs. Wharton for her time and the apple juice and then left. As I walked down the path to the street, I thought how foolish I had been to come all the way to Pennsylvania on such a thin bit of evidence. It occurred to me that I might try calling all the Steins in the telephone book, asking if they had any manuscripts lying around that had been removed from a floundering publishing house by an irresponsible grandfather. It was a dumb idea.

I spent the night at the YMCA. It was a restless night, with visions of hoagie sandwiches, apple juice, brownstone apartments, and red brick mansions. Behind the Philadelphia scenes, I could see the pleading face of my grandmother, begging me not to let the family down, telling me not to come home without the journals of Dan Storm. Gripped tightly in her fist was the Stein letter, our family's first piece of real hope in seventy-five years that the journals had not been destroyed or lost forever. But I just couldn't think of what I ought to do next. I kept thinking that I had tried and failed. There was nothing else to do.

The next day, for the lack of something better to do, I decided to see some of Philadelphia's historical attractions. There was no sense in just turning around and heading back home after I had come so far. I visited Ben Franklin's house, saw the Liberty Bell and the statue of William Penn. Grandma's pleading face kept flashing before my eyes. I was miserable.

About noon I headed back over to Warsaw Street to Tony's Delicatessen, with nothing more in mind than to buy another hoagie sandwich.

As I entered the store, Tony was busy trying to get rid of a red-haired salesman wearing bright green trousers, a blue and orange sport coat, and yellow-lensed glasses. The man was trying to sell Tony insulation for his building, but Tony didn't want any. The salesman claimed that his insulation would save Tony at least forty dollars a month on his winter heating bill.

Tony bent over and retrieved a tattered shoe box from under the counter. Without a word, he opened the box and handed a small piece of paper to the salesman.

"That's my January heat bill."

"But it's only eighteen dollars," responded the surprised salesman.

"And it's about half that much in the summer," said Tony with finality. "I don't need insulation!"

The salesman departed without another word. I felt sorry for him as I ordered my sandwich. Tony gave me a nod of recognition but didn't offer any conversation as he prepared my sandwich.

"Do you have cold drinks?" I asked as he handed me the sandwich. He nodded toward the little window, telling me I could get a cold drink at Bill's Diner next door. The diner had tables, and I felt like getting off my feet for a while, so I went next door, ordered a large root beer, and settled into a booth near the counter.

The red-haired salesman was sitting at the counter, nibbling on potato chips and drinking a beer. Bill, the owner, was behind the counter, drying glasses.

"What does it cost to heat this joint in the winter?" asked the salesman, as if he were more interested in making conversation than selling insulation.

I listened with interest to see if he would have better luck this time. Bill asked the salesman why he was interested in heating bills.

"If you'll tell me what you are spending, I might be able to show you how to save some money," responded the salesman.

"About eighty dollars a month, but I can't afford any insulation," answered Bill, guessing he was getting set up for a sales pitch.

The salesman reached into his briefcase for sales material, and I turned my attention back to my hoagie and root beer. I didn't feel right about going back to Utah without the journals, but I had already followed all of my clues to dead ends, and I couldn't think of anything else to do. Out of frustration, I let my mind be drawn back to the insulation conversation between Bill and the salesman.

I began to wonder why Bill was paying eighty dollars a month to heat his building, when Tony next door was paying only eighteen dollars a month. The two buildings were side by side, the same size, identical construction, probably built at the same time.

Tony hadn't said anything to the salesman about having already purchased insulation. That would have been an easy way to get rid of the salesman. Perhaps Sears & Chadwick had insulated the building before Tony's father bought it. But certainly there was little need for commercial insulation at the turn of the century, when coal was practically as cheap as dirt.

Suddenly I had an idea, too fantastic to be true, but . . . I gulped down the last of the root beer, wrapped the remainder of the sandwich in the waxed paper, shoved it in my pocket, and headed back over to Tony's.

"Another hoagie?" asked Tony, as I closed the door.

"A few more questions," I said, my voice sounding more earnest than I intended for it to sound. Tony didn't say anything but gave me an annoyed look as he waited for my question. I knew my hunch was a long shot, and probably another dead end, but then again, maybe I was on to something.

"What kind of insulation do you have in your ceiling?"

"I don't have any, I don't want any, and if you are mixed up with that red-haired salesman . . ." He pointed to the door, indicating the direction I ought to be headed.

I assured him I had no intention of selling him anything, especially not insulation. But if Tony didn't have any insulation, I was very curious to know why his January heating bill was only eighteen dollars, when Bill next door paid over eighty dollars in January.

I explained that since Tony or his father hadn't insulated the building, it had probably been done by Sears & Chadwick. And certainly a struggling publishing house wouldn't purchase insulation when there were plenty of unsellable books and manuscripts around—items that would make excellent insulation when one considered the solid construction of the ceiling, certainly able to support the weight of books and manuscripts.

Tony shook his head in disbelief, but he still couldn't tell me how the building was insulated. He finally agreed to take me up to the attic for a quick inspection. We went into the back room, and he led me up a creaky stairway after grabbing a flashlight from a window ledge. There were no electric lights above the heavy trapdoors at the top of the stairway.

The rafters and joists were rough-hewn, which dated them back to a time before planed lumber was used in building construction. Between the joists was a soft gray-brown dust, the accumulation of over fifty years, maybe longer.

Tony aimed the light down as I brushed away the dust between the two nearest joists. The dust was light and powdery, but a few inches down my fingers brushed against a solid object. It was a thick brown magazine-size envelope. I opened it and removed a stiff, yellow manuscript. The title page read as follows: "The Abolishing of Slavery and the Resulting Economic Disaster, by Nathan Sanders III, 1860."

I carefully slid the manuscript back into the envelope. Tony didn't say anything.

"I've got to look for my great-grandfather's journals. Can I use your light?"

"The extra weight of you walking around up here might cave the ceiling in on my meat counter," he complained without much enthusiasm. I sensed he was giving in and would let me make the search. I assured him that I would keep my weight on top of the joists to prevent a possible cave-in. He handed me the flashlight and disappeared down the stairway.

Systematically, I began working my way through the long dusty rows. There were more books than manuscripts, books that the company had been unable to sell. Some of the manuscripts were in envelopes, some were wrapped with string, and some were loose in disarray, with missing pages. I couldn't help but ponder all the work that had gone into these lost manuscripts, the dreams and aspirations of dead writers collecting dust in the attic of a delicatessen.

About halfway down the second row, I found nine hard-bound volumes tied firmly together with a piece of twine. They were heavy, maybe five or six pounds. I brushed off the dust, exposing the smooth green leather underneath. Printed clearly on the front cover of the first volume were the words, "Daniel Storm, Number 1."

Quickly I pulled the bundle close to my chest as if I were afraid someone would take it away from me. Tears welled up in my eyes and began streaming down my dusty cheeks, leaving streaks of brown mud. My chest ached with the joy of finding a priceless treasure.

I don't know how long I sat there hugging the dusty journals, trying to comprehend the significance of my find, but eventually I worked my way back to the stairway with the journals clutched tightly under my arm.

At the foot of the stairs there was a wash basin with a cold water tap. Quickly I washed my face, hands, arms, and neck, and wiped off the journals with a damp rag.

After showing them to the amazed Tony and his helpers, I placed a long distance call, collect, to Grandma in American Fork. At first she thought I was kidding, but when I described the journals as bound in green leather with black lettering, and tied up with yellow string, she finally believed I was telling the truth, and she began to cry. I promised to hurry home as quickly as possible.

During the next several months, I devoured the journals, realizing that even though they were of overwhelming significance to family members, they also contained sufficient depth, intensity, and historical significance to be valuable reading to most anyone. After reaching that conclusion, and using the journals as my guide, I put together the following book, which, by the way, is based only on the contents of the first three volumes. Hopefully I will be able to publish the contents of the other journals at a later date.

Chapter 1

My name is Dan Storm, and I was only sixteen years old when I met the Ute warrior. It was in the fall of 1839, and I was heading south along the Green River. The old trapper I had been traveling with had been killed by some renegade prospectors. Later my horse and supplies were stolen by the Blackfeet. The old trapper and I had been looking for Ike, an escaped slave who had come up the Missouri River with me, but when I was unable to find him, I supposed he was dead too. I'll tell more about that later.

I was going south more in an effort to get away from the Blackfeet than for any other reason. In the back of my mind, I was toying with the idea of following the river all the way to the Pacific Ocean, where there were civilized Spanish settlements. Maybe there I could find a new life for myself. I certainly couldn't go back to Missouri. Every sheriff west of the Mississippi was itching to get their hands on me. I would rather die in this Rocky Mountain wilderness than give those Missourians the satisfaction of seeing me punished for what I had done. I'll tell more about that later too.

I realized there was a good chance that I would die in the wilderness. In escaping the Blackfeet, I had left everything behind except my knife and clothing—a buckskin shirt, leggings, and moccasins. The fall frosts had already turned the grasses gold, a beautiful contrast to the deep blue of the mountain sky. But I didn't have any inclination to enjoy the scenery. With winter coming, I had neither food nor the weapons needed to obtain food.

I hadn't eaten anything but serviceberries in almost three days and had been walking most of the night when I came upon a fairly large beaver dam backing up the waters of one of the small tributary streams feeding into Henry's Fork. From the grassy hillside above the pond, I could see fat brook trout sunning themselves in the quiet backwaters or swimming lazily among a forest of partly submerged and sharply pointed stumps where beavers had gnawed down a grove of young trees—like a forest of sharpened pencils pointing skyward out of the water. My mouth watered at the thought of one or more of those fish roasting on a stick over an open fire. I didn't have any hooks, but maybe I could figure out a way to trap or spear some of them. From the hill where I stood, most of the pond appeared to be shallow enough for wading.

On the opposite side of the dam there was a thick growth of willow and young cottonwood trees, providing an excellent hiding place. I hadn't seen any sign of Blackfeet for several days, so I believed they were not on my trail. This would be a good place to rest, make some weapons, and hopefully gather some food.

The icy mountain water felt refreshing on my weary feet as I waded into the pond. I had lashed my knife to a willow staff and had what appeared to be an effective weapon. Unfortunately, the fish wouldn't hold still long enough for me to spear them. I was weak from lack of nourishment and soon abandoned the spear, deciding that I must figure out a better way to catch the fish. As I explored the shallow headwaters, I discovered a hole where fish could be trapped if the water surface could be lowered five or six inches. There were already a number of fish in the pool, waiting to be trapped. I waded back to the dam and located a narrow place, where I succeeded in tearing away enough sticks and mud to increase the water flow sufficiently to lower the water line enough to trap the fish.

An hour later, I was exhausted and soaked from chasing fish around that little pool, but I had three beautiful trout resting side by side in the grass. Before coming out of the water, I refilled the gap in the dam with sticks and sod so the water would return to the original level, allowing more fish to enter the little pool, fish that would feed me the next day.

After hanging my buckskin shirt and leggings over some bushes to dry in the midday sun, I began gathering materials for a fire. I had lost my flint with the rest of the supplies and would have to build a fire with a bow and drill. I had seen this done many times but had always had trouble doing it myself. If I failed, I would have to eat the fish raw and shiver through the night in damp buckskins. Since escaping the Blackfeet, I had been traveling without the benefit of fire.

First I fashioned a bow from a green willow and a buckskin lashing cut from inside of my shirt. Then I found a flat rock with a natural indentation on one side, which I picked a little deeper with the point of my knife. I carved a spindle and bottom piece out of dry cottonwood, then fashioned a tinder nest out of ruffled cottonwood bark. There hadn't been any rain in recent days, so I felt confident the materials were dry enough to work.

After carefully cutting a *V* in the bottom piece, I looped the bow string around the spindle, which I set firmly between the socket rock and the bottom piece, held firmly in place by my foot. First slowly, then faster and faster, I worked the bow back and forth, pushing the whirling spindle firmly down upon the point of the *V* in the bottom piece. Soon little puffs of gray-white smoke began drifting away from the bottom of the spindle, and hot black particles began falling down through the *V* onto a piece of bark, forming a little conical pile, or the spark.

As soon as the spark was about the size of a small pea, I dropped the bow and spindle, careful not to jar the spark, which might fall apart. Carefully I picked up the bark with the spark on it and dropped it into the nest of ruffled bark. Then, pushing the nest gently around the spark, I began blowing ever so gently, coaxing it to life. Gradually I puffed harder and harder as the amount of smoke increased. Soon I was blowing almost as hard as I could, and there was lots of smoke. Suddenly, the nest burst into flames. I dropped it on the ground and began piling on dry twigs. For the first time in days, I smiled. My mouth was already watering in anticipation of eating those fish.

After cleaning the fish, leaving the heads on, I cut a willow stick for each trout, sharpening both ends. I pushed the sticks into the soft ground next to the fire, the top ends leaning over the fire, then secured a fish to the end of each stick, heads down with the fleshy backs closest to the fire.

I didn't realize how hungry I had become until the fragrance of the roasting flesh entered my nostrils. The first fish was only half cooked when I began eating it. My hunger was so intense that even the cold, uncooked parts tasted absolutely delicious.

My body was weakened from long hours of walking with little nourishment, and by the time I finished the second fish, I swear I could feel strength surging back into my weary muscles. And my hunger was becoming more intense with every bite. By the time I finished the third and last fish, I longed for a dozen more and felt strong enough to go chase them down in the little pond, but first I wanted to make a bow and some long split-tipped arrows, which I thought might make the fishing a lot easier.

My buckskin leggings and shirt were still wet when I put them back on. I thought they might dry faster if I was wearing them, and they would protect my skin from scratchy bushes when I climbed the hill to cut a staff for my bow. There was plenty of green willow and cottonwood around the pond, but the best bows are made from serviceberry or chokecherry, woods preferred by Indians for their bows.

There appeared to be a healthy clump of serviceberry bushes near the top of the hill, across the pond. I picked my way along the beaver dam and started climbing the hill, enjoying my new strength.

For the past three days, I had been constantly looking over my shoulder and searching the surroundings for Indian signs. Catching and cooking fish had provided a welcome diversion, but with food in my stomach and the warm afternoon sun on my back, I neglected the usual cautionary measures essential for survival in the hostile wilderness.

I was so busy inspecting bushes in my search for a bow staff that I didn't see the mounted warrior until I was nearly upon him. If his impatient horse hadn't attracted my attention by pawing the ground, I would probably have walked right into him. As it was, I couldn't have been more than fifteen or twenty yards away when I saw him.

He wasn't wearing paint like the Blackfeet had been wearing, and unlike the Blackfeet, his hair was fashioned into two long black braids, one behind each ear. I had heard that Ute warriors braided their hair, and concluded I was face to face with a Ute. His only clothing was leggings and moccasins. He carried a short bow, and a quiver full of arrows hung loosely over his shoulder. He was riding bareback on a dapple gray horse, bigger than most Indian ponies. The warrior's chest and shoulders were well-muscled, his chin firm. He had a comical look on his face, as if he were quietly laughing at my lack of caution.

I had heard other things about the Utes too, that they were the strongest tribe in this south country, and that they frequently captured slaves, which they sold to the Navajos and Mexicans. They also liked to take scalps.

I turned and raced back down the hill toward the pond, the mounted warrior close on my heels. I knew there was no way I could outrun a horse in the open country, but perhaps I could hide, or at least better defend myself in the thick brush on the other side of the beaver pond.

It was lucky for me that the slope of the hill was fairly steep, preventing the Indian's horse from lengthening its stride to a full gallop. I ran with wild abandon, fast enough to maintain a thirty- or forty-foot gap between me and the Indian, but not fast enough to widen the gap any further.

I expected at any moment to receive an obsidian-tipped arrow in the middle of my back, but taking a quick glance over my shoulder, I could see that all of the arrows were still in the quiver. It seemed clear that his intention was to capture me alive. Then he would have a choice of either torturing me to death or selling me into slavery, so I could spend the rest of my life in a Mexican silver mine. Maybe he thought a white boy would bring a good price.

The hill dropped off sharply at the water's edge, creating an eight- or ten-foot bank above the water. I didn't even break stride as I reached the edge of the bank. I pushed off from the edge and flew out over the pond, instinctively aiming for an open place between two of the beaver-sharpened stumps. My legs were churning wildly through the air as if I were still running when I hit the water at the intended place, the momentum of the fall forcing me to my knees in the shallow water. I lunged forward, half swimming and crawling in my mad efforts to get out of the way before the Indian pony plunged over the bank and landed on top of me.

Realizing the water was little more than a foot deep, I scrambled to my feet, looking over my shoulder as soon as I had my footing. Having just noticed the steep bank at the water's edge, the Indian was trying to pull his pony to a stop, but the momentum was too great. The pony sat back on its heels in an honest effort to stop, but it was too late. At the edge of the bank, the Indian made a mistake in trying to turn the horse to one side by pulling its head around. If he hadn't done that, the horse would probably have maintained its balance and lunged straight ahead into the pond. As it was, both horse and rider lost their balance and tumbled head over heels toward the pond, the unfortunate Indian hitting the water just ahead of his pony.

I was only sixteen years old and rather skinny, certainly not yet skilled or confident in the art of hand-to-hand combat. Nevertheless, I realized that if I was ever going to have to fight this Indian, there would never be a better time than the present. I drew the knife from my belt and readied myself to advance on the Indian, offering a quick prayer that I would have the courage to do what needed to be done.

The horse was about ten feet in front of me, on its side in the water, its back toward me, its hooves thrashing wildly in a desperate effort to regain its footing, the wild-eyed head splashing back and forth in the water. The Ute warrior was not in sight. I hoped he was under those thrashing hooves.

Suddenly the Indian's head broke the surface of the water, a foot or so from my side of the horse's back. He looked straight at me, a grim expression on his face. I took one step back, bracing myself for the attack which I suspected would be coming. Suddenly I realized, however, that in order for the warrior's head to be where it was, in such shallow water, his body had to be extended horizontally on its belly beneath the thrashing pony. I relaxed my grip on the knife, realizing that the Ute warrior was pinned beneath his pony. I knew too that once the pony got over on its stomach, it would probably trample the warrior as it scrambled to its feet.

I waited a few moments, expecting the horse's hooves to do my fighting for me, but the animal's violent thrashing quickly subsided, and its head fell limply back into the water. The horse was either dead or dying and would not be getting up again.

The warrior, who had been waiting for his mount to scramble to its feet, now realized that the horse was not going to be getting up and began to squirm back and forth in an effort to get out from under the horse. I bit my lip and made myself move in for the kill, realizing that if he wiggled free, the odds would again be in his favor. He was older and much stronger than I was. My intention was to drown him by holding his head under the water or, if that failed, to cut his throat with my knife. It was a matter of kill or be killed, survival of the fittest, and if I acted quickly, I would probably be the survivor.

Holding my knife out in front, in a half-crouch I waded carefully toward the helpless Indian. Seeing me coming, he stopped wiggling and stared directly into my eyes. There was no fear in his expression; his black eyes were intense and fierce. It was clear he intended to fight me with his teeth if necessary. My courage began to melt, but I forced myself to move one step closer.

Suddenly a brown, muscular hand broke the surface of the water like a large trout rising for a fly. The fingers grabbed the edge of my shirt. The seemingly helpless Indian was suddenly the aggressor, and I fell backward in an effort to get away from him. Fortunately, my buckskin shirt was soaked and, as wet buckskin is about as slippery as an eel's tail, I was able to pull away from his grip. I wasn't about to get that close again and take the risk he would drown me. I would have to kill him from a safe distance with a spear or club.

I waded over to the beaver dam in search of a weapon, and soon located a perfect bludgeon, a young sapling about three inches in diameter, about six feet long, and bark chewed off by beavers. It had been cut recently and was green and solid, a perfect weapon.

The thought occurred to me that if I climbed out of the pond and started running, I might be able to get away before the Indian could wiggle free. It seemed likely, however, that he would come after me, and maybe get a few friends to help. I didn't much like the idea of the Utes and the Blackfeet coming after me.

No, the best thing to do was to kill him. Then he couldn't tell his savage friends about me, and I would have the benefit of his clothing and weapons during the tough winter months ahead. I waded back to the Indian, the club firmly in my hands.

The sun had dipped behind the western hill, and a brisk October breeze felt icy cold against my wet buckskins. My feet were numb in the frigid pond water as I neared the Indian, who had been almost totally submerged for a number of minutes. His teeth were chattering loudly from the cold. He didn't look nearly as threatening as before, but there was still no fear in his eyes as he watched me approach with the club.

I suppose if I had a rifle, I would have been able to squeeze off a round into the warrior's skull, but to beat the life out of a defenseless person with a club was more than I could bring myself to do.

I don't know how long I stood there, watching him, trying to figure out what to do. I was afraid that if I helped him get free, he would still try to kill or capture me. When his face twisted in a grimace of intense pain, telling me that he was hurt, I was finally able to decide what to do.

I raised the club high above my head, then threw it down into the water in a dramatic gesture to tell the Indian that I no longer had any intentions of beating him to death. I held out an open hand as an indication that I wanted to help, and smiled. At first there was distrust on his face, but then he smiled. That was cut short, however, with another grimace of pain. His face fell back into the water. It occurred to me that the straining to keep his head above water could be a very tiring task.

As soon as his head appeared above the water again, I waded to his side. With my back to the horse, I stepped over the warrior's back, straddling his body. Bending over, I reached around his chest with both arms, then leaned forward trying to pull him free. He didn't budge. Apparently, the weight of the lifeless horse was pushing him down against something hard, possibly a submerged tree or rock. I tried pulling from a number of different angles, but with no success. And whenever I pulled, it caused him intense pain.

Suddenly I had a better idea, and I was angry with myself for not thinking of it sooner. Instead of pulling on the injured man, all I had to do was pull the horse to one side. The buoyancy of the water should make the horse easy to move.

Taking the dead animal's head in both arms, I twisted, pulled, pushed, and jerked back and forth. Nothing happened, not the slightest movement of the body. Something was wrong. I ran my hand over the horse's side, trying to figure out what the problem might be. I noticed a hard, pointed bump just behind the shoulder. There was another on the flank. I drew the knife from my belt and pressed the sharp blade down on the hard part of the flank. The moment the blade touched the hide, the skin parted and the beaver-sharpened stump pushed into the open air. I touched the knife on the hard spot behind the shoulder. Again a small sharpened stump pushed through the hole into the open air. The horse had fallen on the pointed stumps like a piece of meat on skewers. No wonder it had died so quickly.

Now I understood why I couldn't move the dead animal to one side or the other. The only way to move it would be to lift it off the stumps. I had already noted that the animal was larger than the normal Indian pony. I guessed its weight at around nine hundred pounds. There was no way I could lift it off the stumps.

A few minutes earlier, I had been determined to kill this Indian and had not been able to do so. Now I wanted to keep him alive, and it appeared that I would be unsuccessful in that endeavor too. It was getting harder and harder for him to keep his head above the cold water. He was getting weak, and it would soon be dark. It was apparent he had been hurt from the fall, but how badly I couldn't tell, because his entire body, except for his head, was pinned underwater by the dead horse.

It occurred to me to go over to the dam and remove some of the sticks and mud in an effort to let more water escape, resulting in a lower water level. As I waded to the dam, I realized that a lowering of the water level would increase the weight of the horse on the injured man. If his injuries were internal or back-related, such a move could be fatal. Without the water to buoy up some of the horse's weight, he would be pinned down more tightly than ever.

I grabbed the pole that I had intended to use as a club and wedged it under the horse in an attempt to use it as a lever to lift either end of the body, but the bottom end of the lever kept sinking into the soft mud, making the pole useless. After a number of unsuccessful attempts, I tossed the pole to one side, wondering if there were any earthly way I could help this poor Indian. It was almost dark, and it didn't look as though he would be able to hold his head up much longer.

I knelt down beside him and helped hold his head up. His eyes had a faraway look, as if he were going to pass out at any moment. The thought occurred to me that maybe I ought to put him out of his misery. As numb as he was from the cold, he probably wouldn't even feel the blade of my knife if I pulled it quickly across his jugular vein. As I thought about this act of mercy, I realized that no matter how desperate his condition, I wouldn't be able to do it. But as I looked at the side of his strong neck, thinking where the knife would have to go in to most effectively reach the jugular, a related but different idea emerged from the depths of my mind.

Suddenly I knew exactly how to save the Indian. I wished I had thought of it sooner. I slapped his face to revive him and let him know that he would have to hold his head up by himself for a while. He seemed to understand. I let go of him and drew the knife from my belt.

The answer was so simple. I certainly couldn't move a horse with sharpened beaver stumps planted in each end, but if the horse were cut in half, with each half free to turn on a single stump, it would be easy to free the Ute warrior.

I plunged the blade into the horse's back, behind the last rib, and began to cut. At first the cutting was clean and fast, but it quickly turned into a messy job. The inside of the horse was soon a cauldron of blood, mud, and green, half-digested grass oozing from severed intestines. I had to reach in up to my shoulder in order to cut along the bottom side of the dead animal. The warm insides felt good on my cold hands.

As I was cutting the hide along the bottom side, the warrior yelped in pain as I accidentally pushed the knife too far and sliced the man's leg. I tried to be more careful but didn't stop, not even for a moment.

It wasn't but a few minutes until I had cut all the way around and only the backbone was holding the carcass in one piece. I scampered over to the bank and grabbed a fist-sized stone, then returned to the horse. Holding the knife blade firmly against the vertebrae, I pounded the stone against the back of the blade, quickly cutting through the backbone.

Slipping the knife back into my belt and dropping the stone, I grabbed the rib cage and turned the front half of the horse away from the Indian. I did the same with the back half, leaving a black, bloody opening above the Indian. He was unable to get up by himself, and I didn't have strength enough to carry him, so I grabbed both his arms and pulled him through the shallow water toward my little camp where I had cooked the trout earlier in the day.

It was dark now, and both of us were numb from the cold, especially the Indian. It took all my strength to get him out of the water and onto the grassy bank. I would liked to have stretched out on the grass too, relishing the victory, but there was a more pressing problem that required my immediate attention. Without the warmth of a fire, both of us would soon freeze in the cold October wind.

I crawled around in the grass, drying and cleaning my wet, bloody hands and wringing out my sleeves. I couldn't have any water dripping onto my fire makings. After checking the coals in the fire pit to see if they were still warm, I broke off some twigs from the trunk of a nearby cottonwood tree, making sure they were dry and brittle.

After carefully carving a little hole in the middle of the bed of warm coals, I quickly crumpled up the smallest twigs and pushed them to the bottom of the hole. After letting them get hot for the better part of a minute, I started blowing into the hole. The coals around the edge began to glow a soft amber. Then the twigs began to smoke. A few sparks appeared, then a little flame. I blew a little harder, and it wasn't long before all the twigs were burning. Soon I had a blazing fire.

The Ute was still unable to move his legs, so I dragged him over to the fire and propped his back against a tree. His legs didn't appear to be broken or hurt except for a few bruises and one nasty slash where I had accidentally cut him. His inability to use his legs was probably the result of cold and lack of circulation. All he needed was a little time and the healing warmth of a good fire.

He was tired and pale, but he managed a friendly smile for me. I didn't have any more worries about his scalping or torturing me. I wished we understood a common language so we could talk about our recent adventure.

I sat down across the fire from him, and we exchanged smiles for a while until hunger pangs began gnawing at my stomach. The strength I had derived from the three trout earlier in the day had long since been spent.

The next time the warrior looked at me, I pointed at my mouth with one hand and rubbed my stomach with the other, thinking he might have some jerky or dried corn stashed away in his leggings or quiver.

He responded by pointing to his mouth and rubbing his stomach exactly as I had done. He was hungry too, but it was obvious from the expression on his face that I should be the one to get the food. I shrugged my shoulders and gave him the most questioning expression I could muster, hoping he would understand that I didn't have any food, nor did I know where to obtain any. I certainly couldn't catch fish now that it was dark.

He responded with an understanding smile, rubbed his belly again, then pointed out across the pond toward the dead horse. I felt a little silly for not thinking of it myself. Without any further attempts at communication, I waded back across the pond to the dead horse and carved a huge roast out of the uppermost hindquarter. I had never eaten horse meat before, but in the present circumstances, I couldn't be choosy.

I dropped the roast in a clump of clean grass near the fire and began carving off fist-sized chunks of red meat, which we roasted on the pointed ends of green willow sticks.

There was no conversation as we feasted into the night, but even though neither of us knew the other's language, I felt increasingly confident that a lasting friendship had been forged by the events of the day.

The Utes were one of the most powerful tribes in and around the Rocky Mountains. They were one of the first tribes to learn to use horses, and their warriors were reported to be fierce fighters, able to stand their own ground against the Apaches to the south and the Blackfeet to the north.

Probably my new friend was a Ute, as indicated by his braided hair. Perhaps he would let me come with him and be part of his tribe. I could learn their ways and make a new and exciting life for myself, far from the reach of the Missouri sheriffs.

As I looked across the fire at my new friend, I was glad that I had saved him from a miserable death in the beaver pond. There was a new dimension in my life now, a more certain future.

The Indian and I did indeed become good friends, even though at first there was no verbal communication. The fact that we had been thrown together in a life and death struggle in the beaver pond seemed to pull us together into an unspoken bond of trust and mutual commitment. And the bonds grew stronger as we grew accustomed to each other. As we lazed around the campfire the next few days, feasting on roasted horse and waiting for his legs to regain their strength, we communicated as best we could. I learned he was called Neuwafe (new snow) and was a sub-chief in one of the primary Ute tribes.

Even before his legs were strong again, we knew we would be traveling together to join his tribe. He sensed my desperate situation, being alone without supplies with winter approaching. And I sensed his willingness to take me under his wing to live with him and his tribe.

As a boy I had sometimes dreamed of living the wild, carefree life of an Indian. Now it looked like I would get the chance to do it. Maybe I would like it well enough to spend the rest of my life as a Ute warrior, far from the reach of the Missouri law.

Chapter 2

As I began this history, it seemed prudent to begin with my experiences among the Utes, leaving out or quickly glossing over the events in Missouri that forced me to flee to the Rocky Mountains at such a young age. My thinking was that some of what took place in Missouri would be offensive to some readers. I wasn't worried about legal retribution, knowing that my history wouldn't be read or published until after my death.

After thoughtful consideration, however, realizing that my history cannot be fully understood and appreciated without an accounting of what happened in Missouri, I have decided to go back to the beginning and tell it all—at the risk of offending those who conform closely to the standards of social piety. I apologize in advance to anyone I might offend, hoping they will understand why I am impelled to tell the truth, the whole truth. I hope posterity doesn't judge me too harshly.

My older brother, David, and I became orphans when our parents died in a hotel fire in Toronto, Canada, in 1828. I was five years old at the time, and David was ten. We went to live with an aunt and uncle, Henry and Sarah Watkins, who lived on a small farm near Toronto. They were old and not very well, so they left us pretty much alone to raise ourselves. We first heard about the Church in 1835, when I was twelve.

One Sunday we were invited to a neighbor's home to hear Parley P. Pratt preach. He wasn't one of the typical go-to-hell-and-burn-forever preachers we were used to hearing. He didn't make you feel that God was mad at you for every little thing you had ever done wrong.

Elder Pratt was youthful and strong, like a young bull. He had a warm smile and a quick wit. The local preachers hated him. They went wild at the mention of his doctrine that men could become like God. They'd scream, yell, and spit out their protests, hardly able to contain themselves at such bold doctrine. They responded the same way when Elder Pratt mentioned that the Book of Mormon was a new scripture in addition to the Bible, written by ancient prophets who lived on the American continent. These teachings seemed kind of logical to me, but the ministers went wild at the suggestion there could be more scripture in addition to the Bible.

Two of the local preachers attended that first meeting where we heard Elder Pratt speak. David and I were sitting in the front row. We certainly weren't religious boys, or involved in any serious quest for truth. We had already heard about the Mormons' gold bible and their boy prophet, Joe Smith. There was something new and exciting about the Mormons, not the usual hellfire and damnation fare dished out every Sunday by the local preachers. We were in the front row because we were curious. And when the two preachers walked in the door, we knew we could expect an exciting evening.

As soon as Elder Pratt began his sermon, the two preachers began throwing objections and questions at him. At first he tried to handle their questions in a polite, thoughtful manner. Most of the time they didn't give him a chance to finish his answer before throwing something else at him. I started to feel sorry for Elder Pratt because the ministers were ruining his sermon. Seeming to sense they were getting the best of Pratt, the preachers became louder and more hostile in their attacks. I sensed the people around me were annoyed, as I was, that Elder Pratt was unable to tell his story.

All of a sudden, I noticed that Elder Pratt hadn't said anything for some time. At first glance, he appeared to be calmly watching the frenzied protests of the preachers, but as I looked closer from my front row seat, I noticed some little things that made my heart beat faster. He was holding the edge of the podium with his hands. His knuckles were whitening as his muscular hands tightened their grip. I had the feeling that soon the wood was going to splinter from the force.

His nostrils were dilated slightly more than normal to accommodate an increased breathing rate. At close inspection I could see that his knees, although covered by loose-fitting trousers, were not straight, but slightly bent, like a wild animal preparing to spring. His sideburns were dampened by perspiration. He was like a volcano about to erupt, and the entire intensity of his being was focused through his clear brown eyes directly upon the two babbling ministers, too involved in their arguments to notice the change in Elder Pratt.

I didn't know much about the Mormons and their customs, but I wouldn't have been surprised if Elder Pratt had leaped upon the two preachers and crushed them in his powerful arms. I could feel the growing intensity in the room, almost electric. It was overwhelming.

Soon everyone in the room was watching Elder Pratt, aware as I was of the mounting intensity within the Mormon missionary. Everyone, that is, except the two preachers, who continued their empty prattle, unaware of the changes.

I was surprised at what Elder Pratt finally did. Instead of springing upon them as a lion upon bleating goats, he simply told them to shut up, not in a loud or angry tone of voice, but with the quiet firmness of a man who knows he will be obeyed. The ministers looked at him in surprise, halting their babblings, shocked that a so-called minister, though uneducated in the arts of the ministry, would have the nerve and the bad taste to tell them to shut up, and in public.

Before they could say anything in response, Elder Pratt pointed to the door and said, "Out!" in the same firm voice. One of the preachers began to say something in protest to the command, but Elder Pratt caught him in the middle of the first word, repeating the order to leave.

The preachers looked back and forth at each other, then at the other people, in apparent confusion as to how they should respond. Elder Pratt stood firm and quiet, clearly expecting them to obey his command. No one seemed very surprised when the two preachers picked up their coats and headed for the door, resuming their babbling. They were saying something about Pratt being the devil himself.

With nothing more than the intensity of his will, Elder Pratt had overpowered and defeated two of the most influential and powerful men in our community. I looked up at him in admiration, thinking that if that's what Mormonism could do to a man, I wanted to be a Mormon.

During the next two weeks, Elder Pratt baptized and confirmed eleven people, including Uncle Henry, Aunt Sarah, David, and me. Three years later, we moved to Missouri.

Chapter 3

Joining the Church didn't change my life in the way one might expect. It was still difficult for me to pray with any regularity or intensity. The Book of Mormon lulled me to sleep just as the Bible had done. The biggest change wasn't in me but in my friends. Now that I was a Mormon, their parents told them not to play with me anymore, that I was "different" and a bad influence.

I didn't like being shunned. That, combined with my desire to be bold and brave like Elder Pratt, started getting me into an increased number of fights with the other boys at school. I had a chip on my shoulder, and it didn't take long until all the boys knew that if they said anything about the Mormon Church they could expect a fight with me.

The fighting kept me in constant trouble with Miss Finch, our teacher. She was a tall, skinny lady with a mouth like a prune and eyes like a goat. Her hair was always the same, pulled straight back and tied in a hard knot at the back of her head. She whipped me on the rear with a willow whenever I fought and cracked me across the knuckles with a hickory stick whenever I gave a wrong answer to her questions. I didn't have much interest in school, so my answers were usually wrong.

Miss Finch was supported in her work by the parents of the schoolchildren. Some gave her money, but most paid with food and clothing. She lived in the homes of the students, changing to a new home every month. Our turn came up once or twice each year, but after we joined the Mormons, she never stayed with us again, not once. Even though I had never been glad to have her stay with us, it hurt when she stopped coming;

I assumed that she too was shunning us because of our religion. I began to feel that she whipped me more frequently than she did the other students, and with greater intensity, because I was a Mormon. I couldn't fight her like I could the boys, so my resentment grew and festered.

I became a loner. The only person I talked to was my brother, David, who was experiencing similar difficulties. Fortunately for him, he was old enough to get away. He landed a job with the Hudson Bay Company and was sent to the Rocky Mountains to trap furs. If there had been any way I could have gone with him, I would have done it. He promised to come back and get me when I was sixteen.

I didn't know if I could wait that long; three years seemed like forever. I moped around for a week or two feeling sorry for myself, miserable and alone. Then one day the thought occurred to me that, even though I had to wait three years before joining my brother, I didn't have to wait three years to learn how to trap. I found two rusty muskrat traps in the barn, oiled and cleaned them, and began my career as a trapper.

There weren't any valuable furs in the vicinity; they had been trapped out years earlier. But there were plenty of big Canadian river rats. The local creeks became my Madison and Yellowstone Rivers; the huge rats, my beavers. Sometimes when I caught an extra big one, I'd skin it, salt and dry the pelt, and hang it from the rafters in my sleeping compartment in the attic of the cabin.

My rat trapping continued for several years, and I was getting very good at concealing traps in just the right places to catch the wary varmints. One afternoon, after receiving a severe beating with the willow from Miss Finch, I was sitting on the bank of a nearby creek carefully skinning one of the biggest rats I had ever caught. It must have weighed nearly three pounds.

Uncle Henry and Aunt Sarah were getting ready to join the Mormons in Missouri, and I was going with them. I was thinking how glad I would be to get away from Miss Finch, hopefully never to see her again. I remember trying to figure out how often she had whipped me—certainly more than a hundred times.

As I pulled the last of the skin from the rat's head, I noticed for a moment the striking resemblance between the rat's face and the face of my teacher. Holding the skinless carcass up in front of me, I began to give it a piece of my mind.

"Miss Finch, what a pleasant surprise, meeting you down here at the creek. I always suspected there was some rat in you, but such a striking resemblance, I never dreamed . . ." I laughed out loud, then resumed my one-way conversation, saying all the things I had never been able to say to her face.

I don't know how long I talked to that dead rat, but after I had said everything I felt like saying to Miss Finch, I felt spent, but good, like a load had been lifted from my shoulders.

It was getting late. I tucked the pelt under my belt and was about to throw the carcass into the creek, when the thought occurred to me that I might be able to have some more fun with it at school. I knew I could get in a lot of trouble, but we were moving to Missouri soon anyway, and it would be nice to get even with Miss Finch for some of the many whippings she had given me. I decided to be bold like Elder Pratt and do the thing that was on my mind, regardless of the consequences.

I carefully washed the skinned rat in the creek, wrapped it in a piece of oilcloth, and shoved it in my coat, chuckling in anticipation of what was going to happen at school the next day.

It was early spring, still cold during the day, which meant the students and Miss Finch were still eating their lunches at their desks in the classroom, instead of outside. When the students were dismissed for the midmorning recess, I lingered a little longer than usual in the coat room until I was alone. I checked back in the classroom to make sure Miss Finch was still at her desk correcting papers. She was.

Quickly I took her green lunch pail down from the top shelf and opened it. I unwrapped the skinned rat, still wet and slippery, and placed it in the lunch pail, belly up. Actually, it looked quite comfortable, stretched out on an egg sandwich with an apple pillow. I closed the lunch box, returned it to the shelf, and joined the students outside.

When the lunch break finally arrived, I was half wishing I had left the rat at home, but it was too late for second thoughts now as the students and Miss Finch filed into the coat room to get their lunch pails.

Miss Finch's response was better than expected. First she screamed, loud and shrill. Then she sprang out of her chair, violently shoving the lunch pail away from her over the edge of her desk. As the box hit the floor, the skinned rat popped out, sliding down the aisle between two rows of student desks. Kids scattered in every direction.

Miss Finch was backed up against the blackboard, still screaming, both hands pressed against the sides of her face, when the slippery rat came to rest in the middle of the room. Many of the girls were screaming too. Most of the boys had bewildered expressions, still trying to figure out what was happening. I was the only one wearing a bright smile, and the instant Miss Finch looked at me, I realized that was a mistake. I had been discovered.

She didn't even ask me to admit my guilt. After I had deposited the rat in the trash can, she marched me to the front of the room where I automatically bent over and grabbed my ankles, waiting for the expected whipping, which for once I felt was fully deserved.

She whipped me until her arm was too tired to do it any longer. After the first five or six lashes, I didn't mind the thrashing at all. She could have continued for a week and not inflicted enough punishment to compensate for the fear and embarrassment I had brought upon her with the skinned rat.

In the hours and days that followed, as I thought about the rat incident, I realized that in striking out against Miss Finch I had hurt her far more than she had ever hurt me with the many whippings and thrashings.

I realized that I could stand up to her, in my own way, and be victorious. With this new confidence, my fear of her was suddenly gone. And without the fear, my feelings toward her began to change. She was no longer the wicked witch trying to torture her student captives but rather a dedicated old lady trying desperately to teach her students to read, write, and figure—believing that the whippings and thrashings were essential for maintaining classroom discipline.

For the first time in my life I wanted to be a good student, to master the subjects, to get good marks, to please poor Miss Finch. Unfortunately, I never had the chance to show her how I had changed. It was in the spring of 1838 when we moved to Far West, Missouri, to join the Saints.

Chapter 4

Aunt Sarah wouldn't have sent me into Gallatin for supplies had she remembered it was election day. It was August 6, 1838. I was fifteen years old. Gallatin was the county seat for Daviess County, Missouri, and there were reports that the Whig candidate for the Missouri legislature, Colonel William Pennington, was going to prevent Mormons from voting in Daviess County.

Most Missouri Mormons were settled in neighboring Caldwell County near the new city of Far West. As Caldwell County filled up, however, an increasing number of Mormons began settling in Daviess County, where there was still plenty of good government land available at a dollar twenty-five an acre with easy terms.

During 1837, when the Mormons first began settling in Daviess County, Colonel Pennington and his friend Judge Adam Black threatened to burn the cabins of any Mormons refusing to leave the county. Their threats were ignored, and the Mormons continued to move in.

During the spring of 1838, when Pennington could see that there would soon be enough Mormons to control the vote, he experimented with a more peaceful solution to the problem. He began attending Mormon church meetings, slapping his Mormon neighbors on the back, telling them that he had been wrong about them. His sudden change didn't fool anyone, and he soon realized this new approach wouldn't get him the Mormon votes. Pennington's opponent in the election was Judge Warren, a kind old man who had given the Mormons corn when they had been driven from Jackson County four years earlier. The Mormons were going to vote for Judge Warren.

Just before the election, Pennington returned to his old Mormon-hating ways and had been stirring up the Missourians to help him prevent the Mormons from voting in Daviess County. On that fateful August morning, he had gathered sixty or seventy rowdies and Mormon-haters in front of the Gallatin general store, the official voting location, and that is the mess I walked into on that election day morning.

When we had moved down from Canada that spring and arrived at Adam-ondi-Ahman, we discovered that all the land around Far West had been taken. So Uncle Henry had decided to settle in Daviess County. He purchased a hundred and sixty acres on the Grande River about halfway between Adam-ondi-Ahman and Gallatin.

It was a beautiful piece of land, covered with lush green meadows, spotted here and there with dark green patches of timber. The Grande River was quiet and clear as it wound aimlessly through the rich green countryside. It was truly a Garden of Eden. Most of the late spring and summer was spent building our cabin, a barn, and split-rail fences.

On the day before the election, I was cutting wild hay for the mules and cattle when I spotted a bunch of wild hogs lazing in a bog. I hurried back to the cabin for the .40 caliber Hawken rifle and managed to kill two of them before the rest disappeared into the woods. We didn't have enough salt to pack away all the meat, so Aunt Sarah sent me into Gallatin the next morning to get more salt, but not before feeding me a huge breakfast of fried pork, boiled new potatoes, and buttermilk.

As I approached the little town, I could hear the shouting of angry men. I should probably have turned back, but I had to satisfy my curiosity and find out what was happening. Gallatin was a small town, having a total of ten buildings, and, typical for Missouri, three of the buildings were saloons.

The men were gathered in front of the dry goods store. That's where I needed to go. I tied my bay mare in the woods behind the store and crept quietly along the side of the building to a good hiding place behind a pile of freshly cut oak firewood. I had been in Missouri long enough to know I had to be cautious. Just about everyone who wasn't a Mormon was a Mormon-hater, and I had no intentions of being caught by an angry mob.

I had an excellent view of the street and soon spotted Colonel Pennington, smiling and friendly, sauntering among the men, offering free swallows of Missouri corn whiskey from a gallon jug. He was talking about the election and encouraging those who hadn't already done so to go into the store and vote.

There weren't any familiar Mormon faces in the crowd. Most Mormons, including Uncle Henry, hadn't lived in the county long enough to vote. And of the ones eligible, I wasn't sure how many would be brave enough to face Pennington and his crowd. I was glad I wasn't old enough to vote.

A black-coated preacher, after consulting briefly with Pennington, stepped up onto the wooden porch to make a speech. He was tall and thin, his starched white collar stiff and tight around his long neck, appearing to choke off the circulation in his bulging blood vessels. His hair was black, and slicked straight back with thick, heavy grease. His face was wrinkled as a prune and set like stone into an unchanging frown. He was not an old man, perhaps in his forties. He didn't waste any time in stirring up the crowd.

"I hear niggers and Mormons will be voting here today!" He waited for his opening statement to sink in. He waited for the crowd to respond with an angry growl.

Missouri was a slave state at the time, and any mention that black people (slave or free) might vote always made people furious, and this time was no exception. The Mormons, who were mostly from the northeastern part of the country or Canada, didn't believe in slavery. The first Mormons to settle in Missouri in 1832 had brought some free black families with them. There was no room for free black people in a slave state, and the first persecutions against the Mormons began, not for religious reasons, but because the Mormons didn't support slavery.

"Soon as the Mormons control the vote, they'll free our darkies. I don't care to stand in line at the polls behind Mormons and niggers."

The preacher's words lashed out like bolts of lightning, striking anger into the heart of every listener. The crowd drew closer together, expressions of anger and concern on every face. Sensing his power over the crowd, the minister plunged into his sermon.

He said that blacks and Mormons were both cursed by God. The blacks with a dark skin because of Cain killing Abel. The Mormons because they had new scriptures in addition to the Bible. He read the scripture near the end of the New Testament saying that anyone who added to the words of the book would have added to them the curses of the book.

He held his Bible high for all to see, and paused for a few seconds until he had everyone's complete attention.

"Have the Mormons added to the words of this book?"

"Book of Mormon," shouted someone from the crowd.

"They've added the Book of Mormon, the Book of Covenants, and who knows how many other so-called scriptures to the only true words of God."

He shook his Bible furiously at his listeners. I thought the pages might fall out.

"And because they have added to the words of this book," he shouted. He was in a total rage now, his face red, his eyes blazing, and the sweat streaming down his cheeks. The Bible was still high above his head. "God will lay on the Mormons the curses in this book—curses of fire, bloodshed, and destruction."

Slowly he lowered the Bible, pausing a moment to catch his breath while maintaining the full attention of the crowd. As much as I hated what he was saying, I had to admire his ability to control his audience. I was afraid to move for fear someone would see me. I wished I had stayed home.

With his voice suddenly quiet and personal, the preacher pointed to one of the men in the crowd and asked, "Oliver, did you know you are an instrument in the hands of the Lord?" The man looked confused, unsure as to how he should respond.

The preacher pointed at another man. "Jess, did you know you are an instrument in the hands of the Almighty?" This man looked as confused as the other, not sure how he was expected to answer.

Suddenly loud again, the preacher proclaimed, "You are all instruments in the hands of God when you help fulfill Bible prophecy, when you help bring upon the Mormons the curses in this book." He again shook his Bible with such intensity that I thought this time for sure the pages would fall out.

"Oliver," he pointed to the same man he had singled out earlier. "When you beat a Mormon elder with a club, you are fulfilling Bible prophesy!"

He pointed to the other man. "Jess, when you throw a torch to a Mormon home, you are fulfilling Bible prophecy."

"Is ravishing Mormon women a Bible curse?" shouted someone from the crowd. The preacher hesitated, not sure if he wanted to take responsibility for giving license for that. He finally avoided a direct endorsement, saying, "That curse is mentioned more than once in the Good Book." The crowd responded with a loud cheer. The preacher then changed the subject.

"How many Mormons are going to vote in Gallatin today?"

"None. Over my dead body," shouted one of the men, followed by a loud cheer from the rest. The preacher stepped down from the porch, a smug look on his face. He had succeeded in creating the desired effect on his audience.

As soon as the preacher stepped down from the porch, he was replaced by another man, who introduced himself as Dick Boggs. He was a squat, heavyset man. He removed his sweat-stained hat, exposing the bald top of his head, as smooth and white as a frog's belly.

After wiping the sweat away with a dirty yellow handkerchief, he replaced the hat and squinted through his small black eyes at the crowd. His eyes were too close together, and the red of his puffy lips was barely visible through his thick brown beard. His clothing consisted of full-length red homespun underwear, gray trousers with wide brown suspenders, and cowhide boots. His clothing was soiled and greasy. His broken teeth were milky brown from constant tobacco chewing.

His message was plain and straightforward. He was concerned about his property—his land and slaves.

"Once the Mormons control the vote, they'll do as they want. I don't want 'm tax'n my property to build no temple. And I've got too much invested in slaves to have do-gooders set 'm free. I never seen a Mormon with a slave. They're abolitionists, every one of 'm, and as soon as they control the vote, they'll set the darkies free."

Boggs did not have the preaching skill of the minister and he didn't speak with the same finesse and control, but he talked about things the men in the crowd understood—property, land, slaves, taxes. Even though he didn't have the preacher's skill, his influence over the crowd seemed even stronger. They understood Boggs's concerns, and apparently felt the same way.

"I want to ask you men a question," he continued. "If we chase the Mormons off today, do you really think they will stay away, that they won't be back to vote next election?" He paused for a moment to give the crowd a chance to think about his question.

"They'll be back all right, like flies to a dead hog. You can shoo 'm away for a time, but they'll be back, in bigger numbers, until they fill the whole country. Then they'll be shoo'n us away.

"It ain't enough to chase 'm away. They need to be taught a lesson, a strong lesson, so they won't want to come back. They need some humility, some manners. They ain't scared now."

There was a unanimous nod of agreement from the crowd. Everyone waited to hear what Boggs would suggest as a solution to the Mormon problem. He had the full attention of every man and was in no hurry to give away his secret. He reached into his hip pocket for a thick brown stick of tobacco. He shoved it into the corner of his mouth, clamped down with his molars, and twisted off a chunk. After returning the stick to his pocket, he began, "Now I know somethin' about teachin' manners and respect." His words were mumbled in his efforts to speak and handle the tobacco at the same time. "I'll show you what I mean," he said, and then shouted to a black man standing over by the horses, "Ike, come here!"

The black man stepped forward, moving carefully through the white men. The slave was one of the biggest men I had ever seen, over six and a half feet tall and weighing more than 250 pounds. His only clothing was a pair of worn trousers cut off at the knees. His feet and back were bare. His shoulders were broad and well-muscled. His legs were like trees. The lack of fat indicated he was accustomed to long days of hard work. In contrast to his powerful body, however, he had the face of a child. His eyes focused uneasily on the ground in front of him, as he realized everyone was looking at him.

"This is Ike," said Boggs. "He belongs to me, and he's got the kind of manners and respect the Mormons ought to have."

"Do you have manners?" Boggs demanded of the black man.

"Yassah," responded Ike without taking his eyes off the ground.

"Show these gentlemen you got respect," continued Boggs. "Kiss my boots."

Without hesitation, the big black man dropped to his knees and kissed the cowhide boots of his master. He accomplished the humiliating task with such unthinking quickness, it was obvious that he had been asked to do it before, perhaps many times. I wondered what kind of man this Ike really was, to allow himself to be humiliated so easily in front of so many people. I was only fifteen, but I felt fairly confident that if Boggs ordered me to kiss his boots, he'd find one of my skinny fists buried in that fat belly of his.

"Will you do anything I say?" demanded Boggs of the black, loud enough for everyone to hear.

"Yassah," responded Ike, his eyes still on the ground.

Then Boggs spoke to the crowd. "I've got four more bucks like this one—as obedient as oxen, every one of them—and almost as dumb." Everyone laughed.

"Those of you who've been around a while know I've got the best behaved bucks in the county, but I'll bet you don't know how I get 'm to be that way."

Boggs had Ike turn around so everyone could see his back. "Does that back look like a whipping post?"

The smooth, black skin fit tightly over the big muscles. There were very few scars, and it was apparent the slave had not been the victim of frequent whippings.

"I won't say I never whip my niggers," continued Boggs. "Every boy needs to be knocked around once in a while, but there's a better way to teach manners and respect."

There were a few faces in the crowd showing grins of recognition, knowing what Boggs was talking about. Most of the men, however, appeared curious to find out Boggs's secret for teaching manners to his slaves. The crowd drew in closer, waiting to hear the explanation.

Realizing that he had everyone's full attention, Boggs reached into his pocket and pulled out a medium-sized pocketknife. He opened the small blade with the rounded tip, and ran the blade easily along the top of his forearm, shaving away his black, curly hair. Then he raised the razor-sharp blade high in the air for all to see.

"Only takes five minutes to cut a buck, makes 'm tame as oxen. And all the others too, like Ike here. He knows what'll happen if he gets out of line."

Suddenly I felt sick, like I was about to lose my breakfast of fried pork and buttermilk, realizing Boggs was talking about castration. Having been raised on a farm, I was certainly familiar with the operation, a common thing for cattle, sheep, and horses. But to do it to a man—I had never thought of that before. I was shocked, sick, then angry. I was only fifteen years old, and not much interested in politics, but in five minutes, I became a sure-fire abolitionist.

I no longer felt any contempt for the big black. I probably would have behaved the same way with a threat like that hanging over my head. I wished I had enough money to buy Ike and set him free.

"Can't understand why more folks don't cut an ornery buck once in a while. Keeps the rest tame as kittens.

"By the way," he continued, "if any of you men have a boy that needs cut'n, and you don't know how to do it yourselves, bring 'm over to my place and I'll do it for ya. But bring 'm in a wagon cause they won't be able to walk or ride a mule for a few days. I charge a dollar.

"But lemmie tell ya someth'n." Boggs was suddenly loud and angry. "I'd be more than happy to teach a lesson in manners and respect to any Mormon you can catch, a lesson no Mormon will ever forget."

He twisted the knife in the air as if he were performing the operation. "And I won't charge no dollar, neither."

I forgot about abolitionism, realizing that if my hiding place were discovered I might become Boggs's first Mormon victim.

The crowd cheered as Boggs stepped down and Colonel Pennington took his place. He had given up the jug, which was passing freely among the men. He began to shout about how the Mormons were horse thieves, plunderers, and claim jumpers, but I was no longer curious to hear what was going on. I was trying to decide whether or not to make a run for my horse. I realized it was only a matter of time until someone would discover me, and the thought of being captured by the mob made me nearly sick to my stomach.

I decided to make a run for the horse. But no sooner had I sprung to my feet than I was grabbed from behind by a pair of strong arms. Instinctively I kicked back with all my strength, smashing the back edge of my heel into a shin bone. My captor shrieked in pain, but his grip only tightened. Before I could try anything else, three or four men were on top of me—big rough hands grabbing my arms and legs, tearing at my clothing, pulling my hair. The harder I struggled to get away, the tighter the mob held onto me.

Gradually I ceased my useless exertions. I was stretched out horizontally in midair, strong hands holding tightly to my arms and legs, pulling in every direction. I looked up into angry bearded faces silhouetted against the blue Missouri sky. My nostrils filled with the smell of human sweat, whiskey, and dust. My ears thundered with the shouting and cursing of the angry men, and the wild throbbing of my heart.

Realizing I was powerless against the mob, I began to pray like I had never prayed before. I prayed so hard that tears slid out of the corners of my tightly closed eyes. I repented of all the things I had ever done wrong, including putting the skinned rat in Miss Finch's lunch pail. I promised to do anything the Lord wanted if only he would help me out of this desperate situation.

While I was praying, I suddenly noticed a familiar voice over the noise of the mob. At first far away, but suddenly very close, I recognized the gruff voice of Dick Boggs ordering men to stand aside so he could get to me.

I opened my eyes and there he was standing beside me, knife in hand, grinning broadly, exposing broken, brown teeth tangled in his filthy beard. He had a relaxed, matter-of-fact appearance, as if he were going to peel a potato or slice a ham.

With all the strength I could muster, I tried desperately to jerk one of my legs or arms free. My efforts were useless against the strong hands of the mob.

Realizing there was absolutely nothing I could do to save myself, a feeling of overwhelming panic filled my entire being and wrapped around me like a heavy black blanket, choking, paralyzing me, and making me sick to my stomach.

The world was in slow motion. So much had happened in just seconds. Boggs still had not touched me. The sickness in my stomach pushed harder and harder against my throat. I could taste my half-digested breakfast and tried desperately to hold it down.

Suddenly there was a pinpoint of light against the blackness of my mind, a slight ray of hope, the beginning of an idea, something I could do to improve my desperate situation. Without any further thought, I relaxed and let my breakfast come forth in a brown burst, like a fire hose, aimed directly at Dick Boggs's broad chest. It splattered in all directions upon the yelling, swearing mobbers suddenly scrambling to get out of the way.

In the confusion, my leg closest to Boggs was let free. Before anyone could regain the hold, I drew back my knee and got a full-strength thrust, driving the heel of my boot deep into Boggs's soft belly. Breathless, he bent forward, his startled eyes bulging like those of a toad stepped on by a draft horse. A second blow caught him square in the cheekbone and sent him sprawling backwards into the mob.

I was getting ready to launch a third blow, when I was suddenly dropped to the ground. The mobbers had let go of me and began hurrying toward the general store. My first thought was one of unbelief that my sickness could have driven them away so easily. Then a voice from the mob shouted the true reason for their departure.

"The Mormons are coming to vote!"

I scrambled to my feet to see eight Mormon elders beginning to dismount from their horses across the street. The mobbers were aligning themselves on my side of the street in front of the general store, the official voting place.

The mob had suddenly forgotten me. I realized that what to me had been a life and death struggle had been only child's play to the mob, a way to kill time until the important business of the day—the business of preventing the Mormons from voting.

Dick Boggs was sitting on the ground in front of me half-stunned from the kick I had delivered to his cheekbone. I was just turning to run for my horse when I noticed Brother John Butler walking toward me. He was our neighbor and had come with the Mormons to vote.

I no longer felt any threat from Boggs, knowing John Butler was around. Brother Butler was reported to be the strongest Mormon in Daviess County. He had even beat the Prophet Joseph at stick pulling. He was a quiet man, never saying much in church meetings, but when it came to raising a cabin or digging a well, John Butler could do more than any two men.

He put his hand on my shoulder and asked me what had happened. But before I could answer, our attention was diverted to the street, where the rest of the Mormons were heading toward the general store to cast their votes.

The first to reach the steps was Brother Sam Brown, who asked one of the mob to move aside so he could enter the building to vote. Poor Brother Brown was answered with a blow to the side of the head. As he dropped to his knees, the man who had struck him, and three or four more, closed in upon him, cursing him as they continued to beat him.

The rest of the Mormons hesitated, realizing they were badly outnumbered, knowing the mob was trying to draw them into a fight. Brother Butler was the first to act. Removing his hand from my shoulder, he grabbed an oak heart from the pile of firewood where I had been hiding before the mob found me.

Brother Butler didn't charge into the mob like an angry man seeking vengeance for an injured brother. Instead, he just walked quietly among the Missourians, almost apologetically, swishing his stick swiftly and lightly at nearby heads, as if he were swatting flies. It didn't appear that he was swinging the stick hard enough, but the Missourians fell like dead men. Three, four, five, down they went. Good Brother Butler was single-handedly destroying the mob, almost before they realized what was happening.

Delighted to see the mob getting their just reward, and thankful I was now on the winning side, I leaped to the woodpile and tossed sticks to several nearby Mormons who joined Brother Butler in his assault on the mob. Then I stationed myself in front of the woodpile, determined to prevent the mobbers from getting their own oak sticks in an effort to equalize the Mormon advantage.

I had barely established my defensive position beside the woodpile, oak club in hand, when I was challenged—not by one of the faceless members of the mob but by Dick Boggs, the man I had kicked senseless a few moments earlier.

"I'm going to slit your belly wide open," he hissed between broken brown teeth. He seemed unaware of the battle between the eight Mormons and the Missouri mob. His attention was focused completely on me, the object of his revenge, and nothing else mattered.

"Stand back, if you don't want your head smashed," I warned, tightening my grip on the oak club. I could feel the woodpile at my back; there was no turning and running. I was cornered and would have to fight.

Crouched like an animal about to spring, Boggs narrowed the gap between us, one step at a time. The knife was in his right fist, waving rhythmically back and forth, like the tail of a cat preparing to spring on a mouse.

The moment he stepped within range, I lunged forward, swinging the club with all my strength, hoping that by making the first move I could catch him by surprise. I wasn't so lucky. Anticipating my swing, his left hand caught the club in midair before it could do any damage. His grip was like steel, and I could not pull the weapon free. I tried to back away but was already against the woodpile with nowhere to go.

Knowing he had the advantage, the corners of his mouth curved upward into a wicked grin. His little black eyes sparkled with pleasure as he thrust the knife toward my stomach. I saw the knife narrow the gap between life and death, and then suddenly stop as if in front of an invisible shield. I looked at the knife in disbelief, not understanding why it stopped—not until I saw the big black hand clamped tightly on Boggs's forearm, just above the knife. I looked up into the face of Ike, the big slave whom Boggs had humiliated a few minutes earlier.

"No massah," begged Ike.

Boggs's grin vanished from his mouth as he turned upon the slave, cursing violently. In his other hand, Boggs held the oak stick he had wrestled from me minutes earlier. He began beating the slave over the head and shoulders. Ike defended himself as best he could with his free forearm but refused to let go of the hand holding the knife. Boggs was beside himself with rage.

I grabbed another stick from the woodpile, took several quick steps toward Boggs's unprotected back, and swatted him on the side of the head as if I were beating Aunt Sarah's rug. Without the slightest whimper, he dropped to his knees, then rolled forward upon his face in the August dust, where he remained perfectly still.

The street was quiet now. The mob had departed, dragging their wounded and unconscious with them, unable to contend with the club-swinging Mormons. Two by two the Mormons were entering the store to cast their votes while their comrades stood guard on the porch. It was still too early to relish the victory—the defeated mobbers were expected to return at any moment with firearms. One of the Mormons was crossing the street to fetch the horses so they could make a hasty getaway as soon as the last man had voted.

I turned to run for my horse and nearly ran into big Ike. He was standing over Boggs's limp body and looking into the woods, not sure if he should stay with his master or run away. Boggs's pocketknife was in his hand. In grabbing his master's arm, Ike had crossed an uncrossable line. He knew the punishment that awaited him.

If I had been in Missouri long enough to understand the seriousness of helping a slave run away, I probably would have thanked Ike for helping me and continued on my way alone. As it was, realizing he was in big trouble for helping me, I shouted as I ran past, "Come on, Ike, let's get out of here!"

When I reached the horse, Ike was at my side. I mounted first, he swung up behind, and we galloped northward into the Missouri woods.

Chapter 5

The Daviess County citizens didn't take kindly to the beating they received at the hands of the Mormon voters on that August 6 election day. Eight Mormon elders, armed with nothing more than oak sticks, had sent nearly a hundred Missouri mobbers scampering for cover. Before the Mormons could finish voting, however, the Missourians returned, this time armed with muskets and pistols. The Mormons wisely retreated. By that time, the big slave, Ike, and I were headed north riding double on my bay mare.

Unable to catch the Mormon voters, the mob headed into the nearby countryside looting and burning homes, beating any Mormon they could catch. Like Ike and me, most of the Mormons around Gallatin spent the night hiding in the woods, huddled under trees for protection from the thundershowers that lingered through the night.

The next morning, while the mobbers were sleeping off their drunkenness, the Mormons began leaving. Those fortunate enough to have been missed by the mob tossed what they could into their wagons and headed north toward Adam-ondi-Ahman (called Di-Ahman), or south toward Far West. Those who had lost their belongings to looting and burning tagged along on foot.

Ike and I watched some of the exodus from our secluded camp on a thickly wooded hillside above the road about halfway between Gallatin and Di-Ahman. After leaving Gallatin we had traveled along the roads for a while, but with two of us on its back, the horse soon became tired. Guessing that the mobbers might be traveling throughout the countryside, we abandoned the horse and the roads and continued our journey through the woods and thickets along animal trails. We hiked through the afternoon and into the evening, heading north.

There was little conversation between Ike and me. We were strangers thrown together in a street fight. As we hiked along the wooded trails, I wondered why the powerful black man had prevented Boggs from knifing me. Once when we stopped for a drink at a cool spring, I asked him why he had saved my life—me, a stranger.

He looked at me thoughtfully and began to speak, but stopped. No words would come. Finally he shrugged his shoulders to say he didn't know why he had done it. He bent over to get another drink at the spring.

Ike had violated one of the cardinal rules of slavery in physically preventing his master from knifing me. He had multiplied the seriousness of his crime by running away, and now I was an accomplice by traveling with him and aiding his escape.

At first we had no particular reason for heading north, other than the general feeling that escaped slaves always went north. I had no intention of taking him home and getting Uncle Henry and Aunt Sarah involved in the crime. Besides, I realized that my home would probably be one of the first places they would search for us. I hoped that Boggs and his friends would be so involved in the conflict with the Mormons that they would forget about Ike and me.

At any rate, I had no intention of getting caught. I knew how much I was hated because of my religion. Add to that the fact that I had helped a slave run away. I didn't expect to receive any mercy if the old citizens ever got ahold of me again. I figured the best thing for both of us would be to get out of Missouri as soon as possible, then take Ike to Canada and get him a job as a hired man on a farm. Then I could decide whether or not I wanted to come back.

Once, late in the afternoon, we stopped in our tracks as we heard the distant howl of a hound. If we had seen Dick Boggs himself standing in the middle of the road, it couldn't have been more frightening. We both knew that once the hounds got on our trail there would be no getting away. No matter how far or how fast we ran, there would be no escaping the nose of a good hound. The first howl we heard was directly behind us, but as we continued to listen, it moved farther to the east. Relieved, we continued on our journey.

Ike generally led the way, with me tagging along behind. I was half walking, half running in my efforts to keep up with his long, steady stride. When I first saw Ike back in Gallatin, he had appeared very docile and unsure of himself. He showed an apparent lack of confidence among the white mobbers—constantly looking down at his feet, his willingness to kiss his master's boots. Big and strong like an ox, but timid as a child.

Now he was different. His movements were quick, bold, and sure. His head was high, his eyes alert to catch any unusual movement in the woods around us. His nostrils quivered at each new smell or change of the wind. He was alert and responsive to the things around him, like a hungry lion seeking prey.

Ike seemed tireless. We stopped to rest occasionally, but only when I began to lag behind. Sometimes we'd stop at a cool spring, or stream, to quench our thirst. Other times we'd just fall upon our bellies in a huckleberry patch and stuff our mouths with the purple sweetness while our weary legs rested.

About sunset, as the thunderstorms began rolling in over the western hills, we crawled under a huge old cedar tree on a thickly wooded hill. After scratching out beds among the pine needles, we remained warm and dry during the all-night drizzle.

At first I couldn't sleep, trying to figure out the details of our journey. When I tried to discuss the situation with Ike, he would say, "Canada," and point north. I couldn't get anything more out of him. He was ignorant of geography, the locations of towns, the flow of rivers, state boundaries, and roads. Any attempt to discuss these details in an effort to plan our journey seemed to confuse him. He had been sheltered on a plantation all his life, had not traveled about except once or twice when he had been sold, and simply was unable to grasp the things I wanted to talk about. He wasn't dumb. He was ignorant.

I finally concluded that I would have to figure things out for myself and hope I made the right decisions. The easiest way to get to Canada would be to float down the Missouri River to St. Louis, then get work as a deckhand on a riverboat heading up the Mississippi. But to take an escaped slave down the river to St. Louis would be pure stupidity and certain disaster. The next alternative would be to head east across upper Missouri to the Mississippi River, then north on a riverboat, but the idea of trying to avoid the Missouri farms and settlements for almost two hundred miles seemed very risky too. The third and best alternative seemed to head almost straight north, possibly all the way to the sparsely settled

Iowa Territory, then gradually work eastward to the Mississippi River. This seemed like the safest alternative, if we could survive in the wilderness.

We were not prepared for a long journey. I had the clothes on my back and a small pocketknife. Ike had only a pair of cut-off trousers and no shirt or boots. When I finally dropped off to sleep, I had decided that we must return to Uncle Henry's for supplies.

We hadn't been following the roads, so I wasn't exactly sure where we were, but I guessed we were north and east of Uncle Henry's, hopefully not more than five or six miles away.

When I awakened, the sun was just beginning to shine over the eastern hills. I propped myself up on one elbow, brushing away the pine needles. I looked up to see if Ike was awake. He was gone.

I scrambled out from under the tree and stood up. My legs were stiff from the long march, and my leg muscles screamed in protest at the sudden movement. I called for Ike, but there was no answer. I sat back on a fallen log. My stomach was growling with an intense hunger. I wondered what I should do. I knew that if I returned to life with Uncle Henry and Aunt Sarah, Dick Boggs would find me for sure and get his revenge for the beating I had given him and for helping his slave escape. I couldn't go home. Before Ike left, Canada seemed like the logical place to go, but now that Ike was gone, I didn't know if I wanted to go to Canada alone. The thought occurred to me that possibly I could go to the Rocky Mountains and find my brother, who was working for the Hudson Bay Company.

As I was contemplating the alternative, I was startled by the sudden cracking of a tree limb behind me. Without thinking, I lunged for a club on the ground in front of me, assuming one or more members of the mob were upon me. Then I whirled to face my attackers.

There were no attackers. It was only Ike, grinning brightly at my wild response to his approach. His arms were piled high with light green roasting ears. He hadn't deserted me after all, but had ventured forth in the early dawn to raid a nearby cornfield.

He dropped the corn on the ground, then began gathering dry willow branches for a smokeless fire. Neither of us had any flint for striking a spark, but Ike soon demonstrated his skill with a bow and drill after borrowing one of my boot laces for the bow. In a few minutes we were carefully piling ears of corn around a hot little fire.

The corn was tender and sweet, not too ripe, and the moist kernels popped in my mouth as I chewed them from the cobs. As we began our morning feast, we noticed the first of the Mormon refugees heading along the road to Di-Ahman. Five or six groups passed within the hour, and I watched carefully for any sign of Uncle Henry and Aunt Sarah but did not see them.

After Ike and I had gorged ourselves on the fresh corn, we put out the fire and resumed our journey, but not before I had tucked the remaining five or six ears of uneaten corn into my shirt so we would have a handy trail snack later in the day. Our plan was to head east, avoiding roads and farms as much as possible, until we reached the Grande River, then follow the river downstream until we came to Uncle Henry's farm.

Shortly after noon we reached the edge of the woods, just across a hayfield from Uncle Henry's cabin. At first I thought everything was normal. I was relieved to see that neither the cabin nor the barn were burned. But then I noticed that there were no chickens in the barnyard, the cow was not in the pasture, and neither were the mules. The wagon was gone, and there was no smoke coming from the chimney. I concluded they had left to join the other Mormon families in Di-Ahman.

We remained in the woods for a few more minutes watching the barnyard, the lane, and the far woods for any signs of human life, friend or foe, then moved cautiously across the meadow to the cabin. Uncle Henry had left in a hurry, leaving various items behind, mostly furniture. I climbed the ladder to my sleeping quarters in the loft, which appeared untouched since the previous morning. I threw down my wool coat and two blankets, and shoved my fish hooks and line into my pocket. When I came down the ladder, Ike showed me some flour and salt he had found on a shelf near the door. I had hoped that Uncle Henry might have left behind the .40 caliber Hawken rifle, or perhaps a knife, but he hadn't.

The only thing of value remaining in the barn was an extra harness for one of the mules. While Ike was removing a strap from the harness, which he planned to fashion into a belt, I noticed Uncle Henry's old bear trap half-buried in the straw beneath the harness. I picked up the mean-looking trap, not wanting to leave behind an item of such obvious value. However, realizing the added weight would slow me down, and not seeing any direct benefit of having the trap, I dropped it on the ground beside the harness.

We spread out the two blankets on the floor of the barn and began to divide up the items we had collected. The lighter items, like the jacket and ears of corn, went into my blanket. The heavier items, including the flour and a side of bacon we found in the smokehouse, went onto Ike's blanket. Just as we finished rolling up the blankets, Ike crawled over to where the harness was hanging and picked up the old bear trap.

"If you want to carry it, you can have it," I told him. He tossed it near his blanket. We slung our gear over our shoulders and headed back across the meadow toward the woods and the Grande River. Though we didn't have a rifle, and Ike was still barefoot, we were still much better prepared now for our trek through the wilds of northern Missouri and the Iowa Territory.

Chapter 6

It was early the following afternoon that we first heard the hounds. We had stopped to rest in a grove of young maple trees. We were sitting on a fallen, half-rotten log, chewing on cold roasted ears left over from breakfast.

Ike heard the sound first and sprang to his feet. Once I stopped chewing, I could hear it too—the distant howling and yelping of not just one hound but several. From the intensity of the barking it appeared the dogs were on our trail. In silence we waited another minute or so, hoping they were following something else besides us, and the dogs would move in a different direction. Our hopes were not realized. The sounds from the dogs remained on our trail and continued to get closer. I began to feel sick to my stomach as the adrenaline surged into my veins. I realized my mistake in taking Ike back to Uncle Henry's place for supplies. I was sure that's where Dick Boggs and his hounds picked up our trail.

Our only alternative was to run and hope to lose the dogs in a stream or find some horses. We had left the Grande River early that morning and were headed straight north. Because we were in unfamiliar territory, we could only guess as to which direction we ought to go.

I tossed my blanketed bundle of food into the bushes, knowing the extra weight would only slow me down. I expected Ike to do the same. He kept the bear trap while throwing his blanket and food into the bushes. The trap was heavy, but I didn't protest, thinking the chain and pin would make a pretty handy weapon against the dogs if they caught up with us.

Ike led the way, loping easily up the trail, the steel bear trap grasped tightly in his right fist. I followed, trying to relax my muscles for what I knew would be a long run, unless the dogs were closer than I had figured.

After going north for a short distance, Ike veered off to the west where the woods were thicker and the running more difficult. At first I questioned the wisdom of the new direction, knowing we could travel more easily in open country. But then I remembered that Boggs and his men would probably be riding horses as they followed the dogs. The thick woods would force Boggs and his men to leave their horses behind and follow us on foot. I grinned at the thought of Boggs, fat and out of shape, trying to catch us on foot. I was only a skinny kid, but my muscles were tough, and I could run long distances. The big Ike looked like a well-conditioned athlete in his prime. We wouldn't have any trouble keeping ahead of Boggs, but his hounds were a different story. It was only a matter of time until the dogs caught up with us. I gathered from the howling that there were at least four or five hounds in the pack.

Ike seemed tireless as he trotted ahead of me through the woods, his big muscles in perfect rhythm. Occasionally he would bend or twist his body to miss a limb or a bush without slowing his long steady stride. I was determined to stay close on his heels. The howling and yelping of the hounds grew louder and closer.

I don't know how many miles we covered, but we finally stopped on a narrow deer trail in a dense part of the forest where the trees were mostly pine. It was apparent from the howling of the dogs that they would soon be upon us.

After taking a few seconds to catch our breath, Ike dropped the bear trap and started up the trail in the direction of the dogs, indicating for me to stay where I was. He picked up a stout limb from the ground beside the trail, then stationed himself among some thick bushes about thirty feet up the trail. I quickly caught on to his game. With me in the middle of the trail to attract the attention of the attacking dogs, he was going to ambush them with his club as they ran past him. I quickly located a club of my own just in case any of the dogs got past Ike.

No sooner had I picked up my club than the first hound scrambled out of the brush about twenty yards behind Ike's hiding place. It was a big, red, raw-boned hound, both ears torn from earlier fights with wolves and cats. I could hear the other hounds, but they were not yet in sight.

As soon as the red hound saw me standing on the trail facing him, he stopped. He was about ten feet short of Ike's hiding place. He sat back on his haunches and let out the long, drawn-out howl of a hound who had treed his prey. I shook my stick and yelled at him. He accepted my challenge and lunged toward me.

Ike's timing was perfect. His descending club caught the hound squarely on the shoulders, driving the animal to the ground. A swift second blow finished the job.

No sooner had Ike removed the limp body from the trail than three more hounds scrambled out of the underbrush as the first hound had done a few moments earlier. Ike, with raised club, was ready for them. Again, I yelled and shook my stick, challenging them to come after me.

These dogs weren't as bold as their fallen leader. They seemed to notice that the big red hound was missing, that something was wrong. They began trotting around with their noses to the ground, as if they hadn't seen me, as if they were waiting for the big red dog to show up and lead them into battle.

The thought occurred to me that if the dogs wouldn't come after me when I threatened them with a club, perhaps they would be braver if I turned and ran from them. It worked. As soon as my back was turned, they galloped after me. Again Ike's timing was perfect as he clubbed down the lead dog. The others scattered into the woods after Ike, howling and barking to let their masters know where we were, but careful to stay out of reach of Ike's club. I had no idea how far back Boggs and his men were, but I knew they were getting closer and closer while we fought the dogs.

"Set da trap," ordered Ike, as he continued to swat at the dogs with his club. "Cover it up, in da trail."

Using the weight of my body and the heels of my boots, I pressed down the steel clamps until I was able to pull open the jaws and set the center pan. Carefully I stepped back. Then, in the center of the trail between two trees, I covered the trap with pine needles and leaves.

I had barely finished covering the trap when Ike started running toward me, the hounds nipping at his heels. I waited until Ike was almost upon me, pointing emphatically at the location of the concealed trap. I didn't want to take any chances that Ike would misjudge the location of the steel jaws and step on them. Just before he reached the trap, I turned and scooted down the trail ahead of him.

Ike leaped over the pile of leaves and pine needles, as did the first hound. But the second one, a blue tick bitch, felt the clank of cold steel on both front feet. After the trap clanked shut, Ike turned and headed back.

The hound that had been on his heels scampered into the brush. By the time Ike had finished off the blue tick bitch and recovered his trap, the remaining dog was headed back up the trail, tail between its legs, to find its masters, who by this time probably weren't very far.

Ike and I resumed our journey at a fast walk, too exhausted from the battle with the dogs to continue running. The nagging question in both of our minds was whether or not Boggs and his men would continue following us, protecting the last dog from us by keeping it on a leash.

The trees began to thin out, and the terrain became more hilly, with an increasing number of open meadows. If Boggs and his men had horses in this country, they could run us down in a hurry. We climbed the back side of a rocky hill just before the late afternoon sun touched the western hills. While it was still light enough to see, we looked back to find out if we were still being followed.

Our worst fears were realized. About a mile away, we could see the hound, now on leash, leading five or six burly men in our direction. Each of the men carried a rifle.

Running again, we headed back down the hill, across a meadow, then up a dry gully joining two of the biggest hills we had yet seen. It was tough running uphill, and even Ike slowed down as his huge legs began to tire. He still carried the heavy bear trap, and I thought that he would soon toss it aside.

He had a better plan. As we came to a point where the gully passed between two big rocks with no way to step to either side of the trail, Ike dropped to his knees, bending down the clamps of the traps with his iron fists. While he held the clamps down, I opened the jaws and set the pan. He placed the trap in the center of the trail between the two rocks and we covered it with sand and leaves. We continued our climb until we crossed over the saddle where the two hills came together. We circled around the back side of one of the hills until we entered a grove of trees. Staying in the thickest part of the forest, we continued our journey past the end of the hill until we came to a point where we could look back on the location of our bear trap. Exhausted, we crawled under some bushes to rest and watch Boggs and his men work their way up the gully.

The steep incline slowed them considerably. It was apparent the long hike through the woods had exhausted them. It appeared that Boggs was in the lead, holding the leash of the hound, which was pulling eagerly ahead as it followed our trail.

As they approached the point where the trail passed between the two big rocks—the place where the trap was set—Ike and I rose to our feet to get a better view. The sun was already down, but there was sufficient light for us to tell when the first man with the dog reached the trap. The other men were strung out single file down the gully.

We were too far away to see exactly what happened, but when we heard the yelping of the injured dog, we knew we had caught the last hound. There was no way they could follow our trail now, especially with night approaching. They would have to get more dogs, and that would take at least a day. Ike and I slapped each other on the back.

After a few minutes, the weary Boggs and his men turned and headed back down the trail, one of them carrying the injured dog on his shoulders. What a relief to see them headed back, knowing we were safe again, at least until the next day.

It would have been nice to curl up under a tree for the night and rest our tired legs, but we had to figure out a way to cover our trail. There was no doubt in my mind that Boggs would get more dogs and return to hunt us down. Ike agreed with me and had a plan that seemed reasonable.

We walked over to a huge pine tree with lots of thick branches near the top, branches that would provide plenty of excellent camouflage if someone were hiding in the top of the tree. The lowest branch was at least twelve feet above the ground, so anyone attempting to climb the tree would need a rope.

After walking around the tree several times and rubbing the trunk with our hands so there would be plenty of scent for the dogs, we headed back the way we had come. I grinned at the thought that Boggs and his men would surround the big tree and order us to come down. When we failed to do so, they would probably fire their rifles into the upper branches and finally climb the tree to make sure we were not there.

I removed my boots to avoid leaving clear tracks, which would give away our backtracking. With our bare feet, we carefully avoided stepping on our earlier footprints, which were headed toward the tree, and stepped only on leaves, grass, and rocks in an effort not to leave any new tracks.

By the time we reached the place in the gully where we had trapped the dog, it was almost dark. To our amazement, the bear trap was lying in the grass below the rocks. I supposed they were too tired to carry it back with them and figured on picking it up when they returned with horses the next day. They wouldn't find it, though, because Ike wasn't about to leave such a trusty friend behind.

We backtracked along our original trail for about another mile as darkness came upon us. Then we headed straight south in an effort to reach the Grande River, where we could float downstream, our trail impossible for any dog to follow. We were certain that when Boggs and his men returned, they would go directly to the place where the last dog had been trapped and follow our trail from there to the big pine tree. By the time they figured out that they were backtracking, we would be far down the river and out of reach.

We reached the river just before dawn. Using green willow branches for lashings, we tied two cottonwood logs together, climbed aboard, and pushed into the center of the current. As soon as it was light, we hid our raft in some tall swamp grass, where we spent a lazy day sleeping and fishing, using the line and hooks I had picked up at Uncle Henry's cabin.

As soon as it was dark again, we pushed out into the main current and continued our journey, safe for a time from Boggs and his men.

Chapter 7

After floating down the Grande River for a number of miles, Ike and I became more and more concerned about the increasing number of cabins. In a slave state like Missouri, news of a slave escape travels fast, and there was no doubt in either of our minds that a lot of people would be on the lookout for us. The Grande River was taking us south toward the Missouri River, toward the more populous areas of the state. The river had served a useful function in carrying us away from Boggs and his hounds, but it would lead us to almost certain capture if we continued downstream.

Just before dawn of the second day, we approached the mouth of a smaller stream coming in from the west, which I guessed to be Shoal Creek. If we followed it upstream, it would lead us past Haun's Mill into the heart of Caldwell County, Mormon country, and eventually to Far West.

We pushed our log raft into the mouth of Shoal Creek, where we abandoned it and began to wade upstream, Ike carrying the steel bear trap in his right fist. At the first sign of morning light, we stopped at a place where the stream swirled around a huge boulder to cut out a deep hole that appeared to be an excellent fishing spot. Ike turned over a half-rotten log, and we quickly gathered a plentiful supply of worms and grubs to use as fish bait. We tied our lines to stout green willow poles, then stabbed our hooks back and forth through the fat worms.

The deep hole was kind to us, and in less than half an hour, we had a nice mess of trout and catfish, which we carried to a secluded, sandy spot among some thick willow bushes. We built a small, smokeless fire with dry willow twigs and spent a lazy day munching on roasted fish and sleeping on the warm sand.

After all the running and the narrow escape from Boggs and his men, it felt good to be safe and comfortable, with nothing to do but sleep and eat. Ike didn't say much but seemed to be enjoying our rest too. He didn't seem to be in a hurry to get back on the trail to Canada. In fact, in his childlike way, he seemed perfectly content to do whatever I wanted to do. He seemed happiest when I was leading out and making the decisions. I felt rather flattered that a grown man, even if he was a slave, would look to me for leadership. He valued and trusted my opinions. I had never felt that way around any adult before. I was determined to take good care of Ike and make sure he succeeded in his escape to freedom.

I liked lazing around the willows with nothing to do but eat and sleep. It gave me time to think about our situation. I knew Boggs would be furious that we had escaped from him and his dogs. He wouldn't give up the hunt. Whether or not he would get much help from others depended on the Mormon situation. If things were settling down after the election-day battle in Gallatin, then people would be more inclined to go on a slave hunt. On the other hand, if the fight in Gallatin had aggravated relations between the Mormons and the original citizens, if they were preparing for a battle with the Mormons—possibly a final showdown—there would be little interest in finding an escaped slave.

I decided to do two things. First, I figured that since we were pretty safe in the thickly wooded creek bottoms, we ought to stay in hiding for a while, at least until Boggs and his men had given up searching for us. There were plenty of hiding places where men couldn't see us and, as long as we traveled in water, we knew the dogs couldn't follow our trail. And there were plenty of fish to eat.

Second, I decided I had to sneak out, locate a nearby Mormon farm, and find out what was happening between the Mormons and the mob. If things were quiet, we would need to watch more carefully for slave hunters. If things were explosive, perhaps we could slip away while the original citizens focused all their attention on fighting Mormons. I had to find out what was happening. I had to do it alone too. Ike would be too easily recognized. Nobody would think anything if they saw a skinny kid like me walking down the road, but if they saw Ike, they might ask him where his master was, or what he was doing in the area, particularly if they had heard about the escape. Curiosity would be high since there was usually a reward for anyone who helped find an escaped slave.

As soon as the sun went down, I crawled out of the river bottoms and headed north, keeping as much in the woods as possible, in search of a Mormon who could bring me up to date on the conflict between the Mormons and the old citizens. I didn't know if Ike and I were in Caldwell County yet. If we were still in Livingston County, there were pretty good odds that anybody I ran into would be an old citizen rather than a Mormon. The problem was how to tell the difference before it was too late. I certainly didn't want to become the prisoner of some Mormon-hater.

I hadn't gone any more than a mile when I heard the tapping of a distant hammer. It wasn't the booming sound of a hammer pounding nails into wood, but the clicking sound of a blacksmith shoeing a horse. I moved carefully in the direction of the sound, thinking I would find a small farm.

I came to a wagon path winding through the meadows and trees, which I followed in the direction of the tapping hammer. I hadn't gone far when I spotted a wagon parked beside the path. There was an old black horse tied to the rear of the wagon. A man was hunched under one of its hind legs nailing down a loose shoe. The smoke from a nearby campfire indicated that he was camped here for the night. There were three goats grazing in the meadow, two nannies and a billy. I couldn't see any other people or dogs.

Staying close to the bushes, I crept closer, looking for any sign that might indicate whether the man was friend or foe, Mormon or local citizen.

He walked over to the fire, picked up a stick, and pushed a black Dutch oven out of the gray-white coals. After dusting away the ashes, he carefully removed the lid and dropped it in the grass. Even from my hiding place I could see that the pan was full to the brim with steaming golden-brown camp biscuits. My mouth began to water. The last time I had tasted anything like that was at Aunt Sarah's table, and that seemed like years ago. He left the uncovered biscuits to cool and returned to finish shoeing the horse.

No sooner had he picked up the horse's foot than I noticed some movement beyond the fire. The billy goat was headed for the biscuits. The man had his back to the fire and couldn't see the goat coming. I wanted to shout a warning to the man but didn't dare. The two nannies, seeing purpose in the billy's walk, began to follow. Since fleeing Gallatin, my diet had consisted almost entirely of corn, fish, and a few wild huckleberries, and the smell of those fresh biscuits was like something from heaven. I simply could not sit back and watch those goats destroy such a treat.

I picked up a stone the size of a hen's egg, and threw it in the direction of the goats, then crouched down lower behind my bush to avoid detection. The stone struck the ground just in front of the billy. He stopped and looked toward his master, thinking that's where the rock had come from. The man was still hunched under the hind leg of the horse, unaware of the danger threatening the biscuits. After watching the man for a few seconds, and determining that the rock must have been accidental, the goat took another step toward the biscuits.

I threw another rock, hoping I might be lucky enough to strike the goat in the middle of his hard head. The stone missed the billy but struck the lid to the Dutch oven in the nearby grass.

The clank of the stone on steel caught the attention of the man, who looked in the direction of the sound just in time to see the billy closing in upon the biscuits.

The man dropped the horse's foot and shouted, "Gadianton, you devil!" and began running toward the fire to save the biscuits. The goat, seeing his mischief discovered, ran back into the meadow, the two nannies not far behind, but not before reaching into the pan and grabbing one of the golden-brown biscuits.

As the man picked up the pan and started walking over to the wagon, I left my hiding place and headed toward the camp, confident the man was indeed a Mormon. Who else but a Mormon would think to name a goat after Gadianton, probably the worst villain in the Book of Mormon and founder of the Gadianton robbers? It seemed to me like a pretty good name for a goat, especially a biscuit-stealing billy.

When he saw me coming, the man stopped and looked me over carefully. He had a confused look on his face, as though he didn't know whether to greet me or run to his wagon and get his musket. I knew he was a Mormon, but he didn't know if I was friend or enemy. As I came nearer and he could see that I wasn't carrying a weapon, and that I was just a boy, he looked less worried.

I told him my name was Dan Storm and explained that I had been watching him from the bushes, not sure if he was a Mormon or a

Missourian until he called the goat Gadianton. I said I figured anyone who would call his goat by that name would have to be a Mormon. I told him that I had been throwing rocks at Gadianton to keep him away from the biscuits, that it was one of my rocks that had hit the lid to attract the man's attention. He laughed at my explanation and invited me to have supper with him. The man said his name was Lester Smith and that he was on his way to Far West.

I accepted his invitation for supper. Together we walked to the back of the wagon, where he put the biscuits down next to a box of groceries. While he was getting things ready, I told him I had been separated from my Uncle Henry and Aunt Sarah when they were driven from their home near Gallatin, that I had been hiding in the woods ever since and was anxious to hear the latest news concerning the conflict between the Mormons and Missourians. I decided it would be best not to say anything about Ike.

I watched with interest as he fixed the sandwiches. After breaking the biscuits in half, he spread thick, soft butter on each half. Then he unwrapped a bundle of oilcloth that contained wet chunks of boiled beef. After putting a huge chunk of beef on each sandwich, he sliced a thick piece of yellow onion to cover the meat. As he was sprinkling the onion slices and meat with salt, I reached out to get mine, not wanting to wait any longer. He pushed my hand back, indicating he wasn't finished. He lifted a big jar out of the box and scooped out a huge spoonful of sugary honey, which he spread on top of the onion slices. I had never had a honey, onion, and beef sandwich before, but it looked good, and it tasted great.

As I began to wolf down the sandwich, Lester handed me a tin cup full of fresh apple juice. While we were eating, Lester brought me up to date on the conflict between the Mormons and the Missourians.

He said that after the Mormon voters whipped the mob in Gallatin, an open invitation was sent to Missourians everywhere to come and help the citizens defend themselves against the Mormons. According to the last report, there were over ten thousand men gathered in the Gallatin area making preparations to attack the Mormons.

Lester Smith said he had come from Kirtland, Ohio, just a few months earlier. His wife had died of pneumonia about a year ago. Upon arriving in Missouri, he had decided to settle at DeWitt, a little Mormon settlement farther down the Grande River. He had just made a down payment on a piece of land and was about to start building a cabin when the mobs started looting and burning. He had decided to pack his things and head to Far West.

"I ain't scared, not at all," he said. "If I thought there was just going to be more of this looting and burning by local ruffians, I'd have stayed and fought." He lifted up a blanket to show me a .50 caliber Hawken rifle, just like Uncle Henry's.

"But the situation is getting a lot bigger than the neighborhood mobbing. Thousands of Missourians are gathering near Gallatin. Wagonloads of guns and ammunition are being shipped up from Richmond. The mobs are being organized into companies by Generals Clark and Wilson of the state militia with promises of government pay for their services in helping settle the Mormon question . . .

"They are preparing for war, boy," he continued, looking me straight in the eye, his voice shaking with the importance of his words. "They are preparing to wipe us Mormons off the face of the map, and Governor Boggs won't lift a finger to stop them.

"When they attack Far West to take Joseph and the Apostles, Betsy, here," he patted the butt of the rifle again, "and me plan to be there to make some of them wish they had never come against the Mormons. There's sure to be a big battle at Far West, and I aim to be right in the middle of it."

It was dark now. He walked over to the smoldering fire. I felt I ought to be returning to Ike, who was probably starting to worry about what had happened to me, but Lester wanted to keep talking.

"The kids is all growed up, and with the wife gone now, there ain't much left for me but to grow old and feeble." He sounded sad. "Nobody to look out for, nobody to talk to on rainy nights, except them goats, and they can't talk back."

He stopped talking for a minute, then continued. "Yep, I'm look'n forward to a shootout with the mob. Won't be no loneliness in that, and we'll whip 'm too. We're the big rock Daniel talked about in the second chapter, rolling down from the mountain, crushing the kingdoms of men, and filling the whole earth. Them old citizens ain't seen nothing of us Mormons yet. The kingdom is going to fill the whole earth, starting right here in Missouri."

I had heard about the Daniel prophecy before. Earlier in the spring, before we had arrived from Canada, President Sidney Rigdon had preached a sermon on the Daniel prophecy, comparing the Mormons to the stone that was going to fill the earth. The Missouri settlers got wind of the speech, printed it in a little booklet, and passed it around as proof that the Mormons were conspiring to take over the whole state, and eventually the whole world.

Lester Smith invited me to go with him to Far West, to become a defender of Zion, a Christian soldier, and shoot holes in the thick hides of the old citizens. He made it sound like a great adventure, but after my close call with the Gallatin mob and my narrow escape from Boggs and his dogs, I was unable to catch his enthusiasm for getting into a shootout with the Missourians.

I thanked Lester for the biscuits and beef and told him I was heading back to my hiding place in the woods. I told him I might go to Far West on my own. If so, I would look him up. He tossed two more biscuits to me as I started to leave. I thanked him again as I tucked the biscuits under my coat, thinking how much Ike was going to enjoy them.

Chapter 8

Early on the morning of October 30, 1838, Ike and I walked out of the brush bordering Shoal Creek and entered Far West. I had been there once before, early in the summer, when the town had been alive with the excitement of new buildings going up and new families moving in.

Now it was different. The town had nearly doubled in size in the past week, and the streets were crowded with wagons, livestock, and people—not new settlers as had been the case earlier, but refugees, families who had been driven from their homes by the Missouri mob.

Ever since the election day in early August when the Mormon elders had whipped the mob at Gallatin, the mob had been increasing in size and number. Now there were bands of armed men in Daviess, Caldwell, and Ray Counties, galloping about the countryside—burning, looting, beating, molesting, and taking prisoners. Even as Ike and I entered Far West, over a thousand Missourians were camped within sight of the town, across the fields, waiting for reinforcements to help them attack Far West. Earlier in the month they had attacked Di-Ahman in Daviess County and DeWitt in Carroll County, scattering Saints in all directions. Some were leaving the state, and others were coming to Far West.

On October 9, the Mormons had sent a plea to Governor Lilburn Boggs (a cousin to Dick Boggs, I think), asking him to help establish peace in the area, but his response was to do nothing, to let the Mormons and the old citizens "fight it out." When the Church leaders could see that the Mormons would receive no help from the government, they encouraged members to gather at Far West to defend themselves.

To make matters worse, some of the Mormons, under the direction of Sampson Avard, had formed a secret organization called the Danites. Their purpose was to protect the Mormons from the mob violence. However, because they never knew in advance when and where the mob would attack, they usually arrived at the scene of a skirmish too late to help.

With time, the Danites abandoned their defensive efforts and turned aggressors—seeking revenge on known mobbers, looting and burning property belonging to the old citizens. The Danites became known as the Mormon mob. The Missourians were furious when they realized that their homes and businesses could be looted and burned too. As the Mormons had done earlier, the old citizens protested to Governor Boggs, demanding that he do something. Whereas Boggs had ignored the Mormon request for help, he quickly responded to the plea from the old citizens by issuing the famous extermination order. In a letter to General John Clark of the state militia, dated October 27, 1838, he said, "The Mormons must be treated as enemies and must be exterminated or driven from the state, if necessary, for the public good. Their outrages are beyond all description." Clark was ordered to carry out the governor's orders immediately.

While all of this trouble was brewing between the Mormons and the old citizens, Ike and I were camping in the thick brush along Shoal Creek, gradually working our way toward Far West. Nearly every day we had observed bands of galloping riders going in every direction. Unless they were close enough for us to hear speech, it was hard to tell if the riders were Mormons or Missourians. We kept out of sight of everyone.

To minimize the chances of our being discovered, we moved our camp every few days. We always moved farther upstream, closer to Far West and farther away from the land settled by the old citizens.

We were sometimes tempted to leave the river bottoms and head north for Canada, thinking the old citizens were so wrapped up in their conflict with the Mormons that they wouldn't be on the lookout for us. We would probably have done it if we hadn't lost nearly all of our supplies when escaping Dick Boggs and his dogs.

In addition to the clothes on our backs, we had a jackknife, some fish hooks and line, and the big bear trap. Ike still didn't have any shoes.

As we neared Far West, I decided that I would go into town and try to get some food, two blankets, and a pair of boots for Ike. If I succeeded, we would head north, traveling at night and hiding during the day.

I wondered if perhaps Uncle Henry and Aunt Sarah were in Far West.

They would surely give me the things we needed. However, if they saw me, I was pretty sure they would not approve of my running off to Canada with an escaped slave. They still thought of me as a little boy. I had done a lot of growing up since that August election day when I had run off with Ike. It was a big responsibility taking care of an escaped slave who didn't know about anything but growing cotton and corn. I was determined to see Ike north to permanent freedom, and neither Uncle Henry or anybody else was going to stop me.

The original plan was for me to go into Far West for supplies while Ike remained hidden in the creek bottom, but when we saw the camp of the state militia—over a thousand men scattered among the grain and cornfields—it seemed best that we stay together. With that many old citizens in the neighborhood, and more coming, plans could change in a hurry. Maybe Far West was the safest place to be anyway.

On the evening of October 29, as soon as it was dark, we left the safety of the river bottom and headed for Far West. We avoided roads and made a big circle around the camp of the mob. We crawled through cornfields and walked near the shaded edge of forests as much as possible. When we finally reached the outskirts of town, we hid in some tall grass next to a cornfield to await the morning light. I figured that if we tried to go into town during the middle of the night, a sentry might mistake us for old citizens and shoot at us.

It was too cold to sleep as we waited for dawn. I wondered what the chances were that Ike and I could make it to Canada, where he could be free. I wondered how happy Ike would be in a civilized society, making all his own decisions. There was so much he didn't know. Not only could he not read or write, but he couldn't even count. He didn't know his last name. Maybe he didn't even have one. I was sure if I obtained him a pair of boots with laces, he wouldn't know the right way to tie them. I wondered if he would really be happy in a world of bankers, merchants, lawyers, and preachers—a world where he wouldn't fit, where he couldn't understand what was going on around him. Of course, he could eventually learn the ways of civilization, but how long would it take and how would he survive in the meantime? It would probably be easier and more comfortable for him to remain a slave.

On the other hand, he seemed perfectly at home in our wilderness environment, where the traditions of civilization didn't count for much. He could sleep like a baby on the cold, wet ground while I was wide awake shivering, yet he would be the first to hear the approaching hoofbeats. He could climb to the upper branches of the tallest tree in seconds, quietly and effortlessly, to get a better look at nearby riders. Even though he was a big man, his powerful muscles enabled him to move about with the grace of a cat, quickened by confidence and strength, whether in the trees or on the ground.

If the wind changed, bringing a new smell our way, his nostrils would quiver with excitement and curiosity. If we ran out of food and the fish were not biting, he always managed to find something to eat—the sweet inner bark of a cottonwood tree, roasted cattail roots, a squirrel's winter supply of pine nuts and acorns. There was always something to eat—often not to my liking, but Ike never complained.

Ike was an ignorant misfit when measured by the standards of civilization, but in the forest he was the noble savage with keen senses and superhuman strength—the master, not the slave.

It occurred to me that perhaps I was making a mistake in wanting to take Ike back to white civilization, even to Canada, where there was no slavery. Perhaps he would be more at home, and happier, in the Rocky Mountains, in the wilderness where he could be himself, free from the awkward demands of civilization.

I had never thought of that before, but as we rested in the tall grass outside Far West waiting for the morning light, it suddenly seemed so clear to me that Ike simply did not belong in a society of merchants, lawyers, bankers, and preachers. Even with his freedom, he could never be more than a servant in such a society.

On the other hand, it was easy to see him galloping on a half-wild horse across the endless prairie, shooting arrows at stampeding buffalo. It was easy to see him wrestling the strongest braves at an Indian camp, taking them on one by one and winning every time. It was easy to see him dressed in buckskin, leading a packhorse through a high mountain pass where no white or black man had ever been before. It was easy to see him in a land where strength, stamina, and athletic ability were more important than book learning; where keen senses were of greater value than careful table manners; where a man protected himself with his hands rather than his mouth.

As the stars began to fade in the gray of first dawn, I asked Ike if he had ever thought of going to the Rocky Mountains.

He didn't know anything about the Rocky Mountains. When I asked him if he wanted to go there to become a mountain man and live among the Indians, he just shrugged his shoulders, indicating that it would be all right with him. I'm sure that I would have received the same response if I had suggested that we go to China or back to Africa. Ike had no conception of what lay beyond the borders of Missouri.

I was just sixteen and hadn't seen much of the world either, but I had gone to school and could read books and newspapers. I had a more complete picture of what the world was like than Ike did. I had never been farther west than Missouri, but occasionally I had received letters from my brother who was with the Hudson Bay Company in western Canada. I had read a number of articles about William Ashley, Jedediah Smith, and Jim Bridger, and figured I knew more about the Rocky Mountains than most people. The thought of going out there with Ike, building a cabin, and living off the land was exciting.

As we stretched out in the tall grass, waiting for the morning light, I began to tell Ike everything I knew about the Rocky Mountains—the trappers, the buffalo, the Indians. I wanted him to share my enthusiasm. I told him I didn't think the Indians were as dangerous as the Missouri mobs.

Chapter 9

As we entered the streets of Far West on the morning of October 30, 1838, we quickly forgot about the Rocky Mountains. News of Governor Boggs's extermination order had reached the town during the night, and thousands of sober-faced Mormons were busy making preparations for war. The days of scattered mob violence were over. With the order from Governor Boggs, the state militia now had official permission to wipe out the Mormons or drive them from the state. Violence against the Mormons was now perfectly legal. War had been declared, and the first major battle, possibly the last, was about to begin at Far West.

It was in every mobber's best interest to join the state militia so he could be paid by the state for killing Mormons. There were already almost two thousand troops camped across the cornfields within sight of town, and hundreds more were expected during the day.

Ike and I were swept up in the tide of war preparations. Nobody bothered to ask us what our business was. We were simply given assignments and expected to carry them out. We helped turn over wagons to form barricades where the roads entered the town. We helped prepare the sandbag fortress by shoveling dirt into flour sacks.

Ike wasn't a Mormon, but he worked with as much determination as any of the Mormon men. He had a lot of pride in being stronger than other men. Singlehandedly, he tipped over two of the barricade wagons. The Mormon men were amazed at his strength. I was glad he was my friend. As a team, Ike and I filled more sandbags than any other team. I held the bags while Ike shoveled. He was fast and tireless, never complaining.

During a brief rest, while we were waiting for more bags to arrive, I reminded Ike that this was not his battle, that he was not a Mormon. I told him he ought to sneak out during the night and return to the creek bottom.

Without much thought, he responded in his usual way with very few words. He asked, "I's free?"

"Yes," I responded.

"I stay."

Nothing more was said. The escaped slave was going to stay and fight with the Mormons. He was neither educated nor civilized, but somewhere deep in his heart there was a spark of idealism and plenty of courage. In fact, he seemed more committed to the upcoming battle than I was. I kept thinking how badly outnumbered we were. There were thousands of armed Missourians and more arriving every hour. There were only about five hundred armed Mormons to defend the town. Our chances didn't look good. I was too young to die, and I had no intention of being taken prisoner. I had vivid memories of the mob at Gallatin, Dick Boggs, and his knife. No, I would not be their prisoner again, not if I could help it.

As we were finishing the fortifications, a lone rider galloped in from the east on a foaming, puffing horse. The rider was taken directly to Joseph Smith, but his news spread throughout the city. The small Mormon settlement at Haun's Mill had been attacked by over two hundred Missouri militiamen. The Mormon men and boys who gathered in the blacksmith shop to defend the community were shot down like fish in a barrel.

An old man named McBride, who had been a hero in the Revolutionary War, was hacked to death with a corn cutter. A nine-year-old boy, Sardius Smith, was found hiding under the bellows in the blacksmith shop. A mobber held his rifle to the boy's head and pulled the trigger, saying, "Nits will make lice, and if he had lived, he would have become a Mormon."

The rider said the women and children scattered into the woods during the battle but returned as soon as the mob departed. He said that at the time he left to come for help, the women were busy throwing the dead menfolk into an open well to prevent further desecration of the bodies. The women and children needed wagons and riders to bring them safely to Far West. Three wagons and about fifty armed riders were assembled in a few minutes and headed east toward Haun's Mill.

My former reluctance to fight the Missourians was gone now. I wanted to fight back. I too wanted revenge for Haun's Mill.

Ike and I went to the town square where rifles and ammunition were being dispensed from a wagon that had been captured from the mob a few weeks earlier. It had been loaded with guns and ammunition for the mob at Gallatin. Each of us was given a Hawken rifle with plenty of powder, wads, and balls.

Colonel Hinkle, who seemed to be in charge of the Mormon defenses, assigned us a place behind one of the overturned wagons. By standing on the wagon, one could see the militia camp across the fields. They were preparing for battle the same as we were. It appeared that their numbers had increased substantially during the day.

Occasionally two or three of the mobbers would ride toward Far West, stopping two or three hundred yards of town. They would shake their rifles in our direction, fire a shot or two, then return to their camp.

Our rifles were brand new and in excellent condition. I had been hunting with rifles for almost ten years and considered myself an excellent shot. I had knocked down a lot of squirrels at distances farther than fifty yards. Those mobbers who had ridden within a few hundred yards of town looked like fairly easy targets to me.

After loading my rifle, I helped Ike load his, showing him how to pour in the powder and shove the wad and ball into place. As a slave, he had never been permitted to handle firearms. I figured that since I was the better shot, Ike would do the reloading while I did the shooting. We would make a good team.

I was about to unload Ike's rifle so he could practice his loading again when I heard the distant crack of a rifle. I looked over the wagon. About two hundred yards away in a cornfield, three mounted mobbers were shouting obscenities in our direction.

Rather than unload Ike's rifle, I figured I might as well break it in by firing at the mobbers. After indicating to Ike what I was going to do, I raised a wet finger to test the wind. There was a slight breeze from my right. Resting the rifle barrel on the wagon, I aimed a little to the right and above the head of the nearest rider. I pulled the trigger.

I had judged the wind correctly, but not the distance. My ball dropped the horse instead of the rider, who climbed up behind one of his comrades before galloping to a safer distance.

A cheer went up from the Far West fortification. It was as if we had just won our first battle and the enemy was retreating. Someone shouted, "One down, two thousand to go." I handed the rifle to Ike for reloading, feeling proud about the excellent shot I had made.

My glory was short-lived, however. A few minutes later, Colonel Hinkle rode up behind me, shouting so all could hear, that if I fired again, without being commanded to do so, he would personally wrap the rifle around my neck. Apparently an order had been given for no one to fire until ordered to do so. I hadn't heard it. Now I knew why no one else had shot at the other mobbers who had approached the camp during the day. I felt kind of sheepish, but at the same time I felt more confident about my aim and figured I would drop more than my share of riders once the battle began.

During the late afternoon, there was a noticeable increase in activity in the enemy camp—more horses galloping about, groups of armed men moving here and there, and a lot more dust. It appeared they were getting ready for the assault on Far West, their two thousand against our five hundred.

I suppose we were as ready as we would ever be. All the streets entering the town were barricaded with overturned wagons. Armed men were stationed behind all the barricades, with the greater number on our side of town facing the enemy camp. Some of the men seemed eager for the battle to begin, but most were rather somber, realizing we were badly outnumbered and didn't have a very good chance of winning the battle. Most of the women and children were gathered in buildings near the center of the town. Several times during the day I had seen Brother Joseph, mounted on his horse, checking the defenses or trying to offer words of comfort to worried people.

The sun was still well above the western horizon when three riders were spotted heading toward Far West from the enemy camp. They carried a white flag tied to a long stick. They pulled the horses to a stop several hundred yards away, about the place where I had shot the horse out from under its rider a few hours earlier. They waved the flag back and forth. They wanted someone from Far West to come out and talk with them.

I figured the truce flag was probably a trick, and the men around me agreed. Why would the mob want a truce when they had us so badly outnumbered? They were probably trying to lure Brother Joseph out in the open where they could shoot him. We hoped Joseph wasn't foolish enough to ride out and talk with them. The Missouri mob could not be trusted, not even under a flag of truce.

We were relieved when Colonel Hinkle, not Joseph, galloped out to meet the men with the white flag. Without dismounting from their horses, the four men talked for what seemed a long time. Finally, Hinkle turned and galloped back to town.

News of his meeting spread quickly through the ranks. General Samuel Lucas of the state militia wanted to negotiate a peace to prevent an unnecessary slaughter. That was good news. On the other hand, General Lucas insisted that the peace be negotiated directly with Brother Joseph and other Church leaders. That was bad news. Perhaps the mob would take advantage of the truce situation by capturing or killing Joseph. I'm sure Joseph was aware of the risk, but he decided to go anyway. I suppose his concern for the innocent people in Far West prompted him to take such a dangerous chance. As long as there was any hope for peace, he had to go for it.

When Joseph rode out to meet General Lucas, he was accompanied by Colonel Hinkle, Sidney Rigdon, Lyman Wight, Parley Pratt, and George Robinson. I had mixed feelings about a negotiated peace. While it was a relief to know the battle might not happen, it was also a disappointment. I had been eager to start shooting, to see how many mobbers I could knock off their horses. I knew I was an excellent shot, and I had been looking forward to getting revenge for some of the many injustices the mob had heaped on the Mormons. If peace was negotiated, my chance for revenge would be gone. I knew these thoughts were wrong, that I should have been totally delighted with the prospects of peace.

The peace didn't come as expected, however. No sooner had Joseph ridden his horse up to General Lucas than he was pulled to the ground by Lucas's men and taken prisoner along with his companions—except for Colonel Hinkle, who was free to ride back to Far West. The white flag had merely been a ploy to capture Joseph. And it appeared that Colonel Hinkle was involved in the scheme.

With Joseph suddenly a prisoner in the enemy camp, a feeling of total helplessness and desperation went through the town. Everyone was talking; nobody knew what to do. Total confusion everywhere.

I learned later that Colonel Hinkle had made a deal with General Lucas during the first meeting when Hinkle had ridden out alone. Lucas had agreed to hold back the attack and subsequent slaughter if Hinkle would agree to four demands. First, to turn over Joseph and other leaders as the prisoners of the state militia. Second, to have the Mormons sign over their farms to the state as payment for the expenses incurred by the militia in handling the Mormons. Third, to get the Mormons to leave the state under the protection of the militia, and fourth, to surrender the Mormon arms to the militia.

Hinkle had lied to Joseph as a ploy to get him out in the open where General Lucas could take him prisoner. Apparently Hinkle felt he had to betray the prophet in order to maintain peace, or maybe to save his own neck. I don't know which.

Chapter 10

There was no battle the next morning as over two thousand state militiamen rode into Far West under the command of General Lucas. With Joseph and other Mormon leaders now in chains, there was no organized resistance to the mob. It appeared that the conditions of the agreement between General Lucas and Colonel Hinkle were going to be met, even though nobody in the Mormon camp would take any further orders from Hinkle.

As the militia entered the town, I realized that my decision to come to Far West had cost Ike his freedom. Now it was certain that he would be returned to his legal owner, Dick Boggs. Our hopes of becoming mountain men, roaming free and wild in the Rocky Mountains, were suddenly ended. He would return to Boggs's farm to grow corn and cotton.

I told the big slave I was sorry. I had truly intended to lead him to freedom but had failed. He just looked at me and shrugged his shoulders as if he hadn't really expected to be successful in his escape anyway. It was as if he really didn't care, as though he could take anything in stride. In the end it really didn't matter what happened along the way—pleasure or pain, happiness or sadness, freedom or slavery.

I moved away, feeling angry about what years of slavery could do to a man. I figured that I wanted Ike's freedom more than he wanted it for himself. I had gone to all this trouble to help him escape, and now it appeared that he may have been just as content to remain a slave. How could I have been so stubborn?

I looked at Ike. He was tinkering with his rifle, which would now be turned over to the militia.

"Ike," I shouted, "Do you want to be free?"

He looked up in surprise but didn't say anything. I stepped closer.

"Do you want to be a man, instead of a slave?" I demanded, looking him straight in the eye.

Still he did not say a word, though he looked straight into my eyes. I don't know how long we stood there in silence, looking into each other's eyes, neither of us speaking. But after a few moments I suddenly noticed a crystal clear drop of water break from the corner of his right eye and streak down his cheek past the corner of his mouth. His powerful hand reached up to wipe the tear away. For the first time since I had known him, I saw his hand tremble. Still he didn't say anything.

I didn't know what forces were at work in the huge slave, pulling at his heartstrings, pushing tears from his eyes, causing that powerful hand to quiver. If only he could tell me how he felt! I put my hand on his muscular arm and asked, "Ike, do you understand what it means to be free?"

After looking back at me for a long moment, his jaw began to drop, just a little, and his lips parted, letting out three quiet, confident words: "I be free." That was all; he didn't say anything else.

"Do you still want to go to the Rocky Mountains with me?" I asked. He answered with a nod.

I looked about to make sure we were by ourselves, that no one was listening, and then said, "When the grass is green and the ice is gone from the Missouri River, I will come for you. If I am alive and able to walk, I will come. We will go to the Rocky Mountains. We will be free men, living off the land, with the Indians, in the Rocky Mountains. I will come for you. Don't forget."

"When the grass is green, and the ice gone," responded Ike, "I be ready." For the first time that day, Ike had a bright smile on his face, his white teeth flashing with the confidence of a man who knew where he was headed. He put his powerful arm about my shoulders and gave me a hard squeeze, his way of expressing his friendship, something he couldn't do with words.

A few minutes later, two militiamen tied Ike's hands behind his arms and led him away. To my surprise, they didn't show any interest in taking me too.

Ike didn't offer any resistance to his captors, and not a word passed between us as he departed, but I knew the same words were going through our minds: "When the grass is green, and the ice is gone from the river."

After the armed mobbers bound Ike's hands and led him away, I found myself temporarily alone. Remembering that the first item of business for the mob was to collect the Mormon arms, I quickly gathered up the rifles, powder, and lead that had been issued to Ike and me, and Ike's bear trap, and carried them between two buildings. After scratching out a shallow trench with my hands, I buried the weapons and the bear trap.

Just as I walked back into the street, an approaching militiaman ordered me to join the group of Mormon men who were being herded like sheep up the street. We were marched to the north end of the town square to join hundreds of disarmed Mormon men surrounded by armed guards.

The men who owned property in Caldwell and Daviess Counties were being singled out and lined up in front of tables in the middle of the square, where they were being forced to sign away the titles to their lands. General Lucas had what appeared to be a whole platoon of lawyers preparing the necessary documents at tables that had been carried from the church.

Some of the men had to be forced at gunpoint to sign away their lands, while others didn't hesitate in the least, knowing the resistance would be useless. While this business was taking place in the town square, the majority of the mob (well over a thousand men) was turned loose to loot the town, unleashing months of pent-up hate and anger on the defenseless Mormon community.

I couldn't see very much from where I was being held prisoner, but the sounds coming from the nearby neighborhoods told the ugly story. An occasional rifle shot, the crying of children, the splintering of wood as doors gave way to smashing rifle butts, the occasional scream of a woman who was being assaulted by one or more of the mobbers.

One of the guards told us that Mormonism was about to end because Joseph and Hyrum were going to be executed before a firing squad. He said General Lucas had already given the order in writing to General Doniphan, and the execution would soon take place, probably right here in the town square.

As predicted by the guard, a wagonload of prisoners, including Joseph and Hyrum, soon rumbled into the square. But there was no firing squad. The mob had leadership problems. General Doniphan had refused to obey General Lucas's order to execute Joseph. Doniphan was a lawyer who believed in due process of law, and he was determined to take the prisoner to Richmond, where due process would determine the fate of the Mormon prophet.

Joseph and the other prisoners were taken at gunpoint to their homes to get coats and clothing they would need for the trip to Richmond. They were hardly given time to say good-bye to their crying wives and children before being loaded back into the wagons. As the wagons rumbled across the square and onto the road leading toward Richmond, and eventually Liberty Jail, General Lucas shouted for everyone in the square to hear, "Mormons, take a good look at your Joe Smith. You'll never see him alive again."

The day before, as we prepared for a shootout with the mob, the idea of negotiating peace sounded desirable. Most everybody, including me, was relieved when Colonel Hinkle rode out under a white flag to discuss peace with General Lucas. Even after Joseph was betrayed and taken prisoner, there was still a feeling of relief, knowing that at least we would not see the slaughter of a lot of innocent people.

This morning the mood had changed. All the men around me regretted having surrendered without a fight. Hinkle was a traitor, and there were reports that he had left town because some of his fellow Mormons were after him. The men expressed the feeling that at least there was dignity and honor in doing battle. And even though they had been badly outnumbered, perhaps they could have held their ground against the mob. We had all been well armed, the city was seemingly well fortified, and hopefully the Lord would have been on our side.

Now it was too late to defend ourselves. The mob had taken our guns, our property, our leaders, the virtue of some of our women, and any hope we had for a future as a people. To me that seemed like a pretty high price to pay just to avoid a battle and save a few lives. Many of the men about me felt as I did, but it was too late to do anything about it now. We were at the total mercy of the mob and General Lucas.

I moved to the edge of the area where the men were being held and sat down on the ground. I wanted to be by myself to think. I began to feel what it was like to be a slave, to be totally under the control of selfish and cruel people. I began to understand why Ike wanted so badly to be free but was reluctant to hope for freedom. Whereas my fellow Mormons and I had been under the heavy hand of the Missourians for only a few hours, Ike had been a slave his entire life. I was renewed in my determination to flee with Ike to the Rocky Mountains, where both of us could enjoy total freedom.

I wondered where the Mormons would go now that they had to leave Missouri. I wondered if they would be able to stay together with Joseph and Hyrum gone. I wondered if Joseph and Hyrum would really be killed as General Lucas promised. I wondered why the Mormons were hated so much by the people around them. First they had been driven from upstate New York, then from Jackson County, and the past winter from Kirtland, Ohio. Now they were being forced to leave Missouri under official proclamation from the governor.

I had been with the main body of Mormons less than six months. I had battled with the mobs in Gallatin on election day. I had seen the widows and orphans from the Haun's Mill massacre, and now the Church leaders being carried off as prisoners. I was witnessing the fall of Far West. How much more could the Mormons take? Why did a people with a message of peace and Christianity invoke so much hatred from their neighbors? Why did the Lord allow the Mormons to be so cruelly persecuted?

I had a lot of questions, but not very many answers. I supposed that a boy just turning sixteen years old was too young to understand such things. Maybe after a few years in the Rocky Mountains I would become wise enough to find answers to these nagging questions.

As I sat there on the ground, deep in meditation, my back toward the town square, facing a long narrow side street leading away from the square, I noticed a sudden movement at the end of the side street. A young woman was running toward me. She held out the hem of her light blue dress in her hands so the dress wouldn't slow her down. Her slim legs and bare feet moved with the grace of a deer. Her long, auburn hair billowed behind her in the cool morning air. I guessed she was about my age, fifteen or sixteen. She was a strong runner, beautiful to watch.

The reason for her running was soon apparent. A puffing, heavy-footed mobber stumbled into the street, not far behind the fleeing girl. As he turned toward her and extended his heavy stride, it was evident that he did not have the speed to catch her.

Just when it appeared that the girl would leave her pursuer far behind, another mobber lunged into the street in front of the girl, blocking her path, forcing her to stop. I was on my feet now, wanting to help the girl, but looked directly into the barrel of a cocked rifle. The other prisoners wanted to help too, but the guards made it clear that anyone attempting to help the girl would be shot.

I looked past the guard to the girl who was now standing in the center of the street between the two mobbers who were closing in on her. They were half crouched, ready to head off the girl if she tried to get past them. As they closed in on her, it was as if they were trying to herd a wild calf or horse into a corral. If the girl started to move toward an opening, one of the mobbers would immediately spring in the direction of her movement, blocking her escape.

There was a high board fence on one side of the girl and a church on the other side. I thought she might have a chance to scramble over the fence before they could get their hands on her. Then she would have had a good start on them, and once out of sight could find a hiding place in someone's home.

Just when I thought the girl would make her final escape attempt, a third mobber appeared in the street not far behind the first one. There was something strangely familiar about his red beard, fat belly, and confident stride. It was Dick Boggs, Ike's cruel master, the man who had tried to cut me with his knife on election day in Gallatin. He was joining his two companions in an attempt to capture and assault a helpless Mormon girl.

As Boggs moved along the fence blocking what appeared to be the girl's best chance to escape, she suddenly darted toward the church and disappeared through a doorway. One of the mobbers ran around the back door, while the other one and Boggs followed on the heels of the terrified girl, closing the door behind them.

I could hear the crashing of benches or chairs and what seemed to be a muffled scream. Then all was silent.

I wanted to kill Boggs when he walked out of the church grinning broadly. If my rifle had been in my hand, I would have had no difficulty pulling the trigger. My heart was full of hate and revenge. It wasn't just this incident with the girl. It was a culmination of all the acts of mob violence during the last six months, the election day in Gallatin, the burning and looting, the Haun's Mill massacre, the betrayal of Joseph. I didn't know the extent of Boggs's involvement in the Mormon persecutions other than the election day violence in Gallatin and this incident with the girl, but I did know he was capable of doing the worst of anything that had happened, including the worst atrocities at Haun's Mill. It was people like Boggs that brought all this misery upon the Mormons.

As Boggs walked away from the church, seemingly satisfied with what he had done to the girl, I vowed to get revenge. I swore that I would punish Boggs for what he and people like him had done to the Mormons. I knew it was wrong to take the law into my own hands, and that revenge belonged to God, but I didn't care. I was determined to make sure that Dick Boggs paid dearly for what he had done and what he was, and I would do it before I departed with Ike for the Rocky Mountains.

Chapter 11

As the winter of 1838–39 approached, things looked pretty bleak for the Mormons. Joseph, Hyrum, and other Church leaders were in jail at Liberty, Missouri. We had given up our arms and signed away our Missouri lands without payment or compensation of any kind. Most of the crops had been destroyed or confiscated, and there was little food to get the families through the winter. To make matters worse, we had been ordered by the governor to leave the state before spring, a tough trip over hundreds of miles of rough roads. It was a difficult journey even in summer, but the Mormons had to do it in the middle of winter. Many families simply did not have resources to make such a journey—no food, no wagons, no draft animals, no money.

Probably the most difficult thing for the Mormons to bear was the uncertainty of their future. The biggest question was whether they should stay together in a main body or scatter to the four winds, meeting in small congregations here and there like other churches did, attracting very little attention from neighbors. It seemed whenever the Saints gathered in large groups, there was always controversy with non-Mormon neighbors. It had happened in New York, Ohio, and Missouri—and it would probably happen again if the Mormons stuck together.

Just when many people began to think that it would be best to scatter in all directions, Brigham Young, the presiding Apostle, took the reins and began making plans for an organized exodus to Illinois. He said the Mormons were going to stick together. He promised that if they did, the Lord would lead them to a place where they would be free from the persecutions of their enemies.

My plans didn't include joining the Mormon exodus to Illinois. When the grass turned green in the spring, I would be heading in the opposite direction, toward the Rocky Mountains with Ike.

As soon as the mobs left Far West, I uncovered the two Hawken rifles and the bear trap and carried them to a brush hut that Ike and I had built a few weeks earlier in a secluded thicket in the densely wooded river bottoms along Shoal Creek. I figured my things would be safer in the brush hut than in Far West, where there might be frequent searches by returning mobbers.

We had built the hut by lashing together three poles to form a tripod, then piling on brush and bark, leaving a doorway in one side and a ventilation hole in the top. The inside remained dry, even in the worst rainstorms. When I built a fire in the little fire pit, the hut remained warm and comfortable during the coldest nights. Ike and I had gathered a plentiful supply of dried corn, still on the cobs, which was stored at the back of the hut. That, along with fish from the nearby stream, would keep me fed during the winter months while I made preparations for the trip to the Rocky Mountains.

After carefully cleaning the rifles and wrapping them in oilcloth, I began my list of things Ike and I would need in our outfit when we departed for the Rocky Mountains. Items on the list included powder, ball mold and lead, skinning knives, extra clothing, needles and thread, flint and steel, an axe, fish hooks and line, salt and flour, beaver traps, blankets, and trinkets for trading with the Indians. As the list began to get long, I realized that we would need at least one packhorse to carry everything.

I didn't have any money but hoped that by helping the Mormons in Far West prepare for their trip east, I could trade my services for some of the things I needed.

The next morning, just as I was leaving the hut on my way to Far West, I was startled by the sound of some large limbs cracking in the nearby thicket. It was unlikely that a deer or elk would make so much noise. It was long past the time when they were rubbing the velvet from their horns. I hoped it wasn't a bear who might be inclined to tear my hut apart to get the corn. But even worse, I hoped it wasn't people who might discover my secret hiding place.

Again I heard branches breaking, and as I listened more closely, I could hear the splash of feet in shallow water. Whatever it was, it was coming toward me.

I picked up a heavy club and pushed against the soft branches of a young cedar tree. I waited for what seemed a long time, my heart beating wildly in anticipation of the approaching visitor. When the sound indicated that the visitor was very near, I regretted not having taken one of the rifles from the oilcloth.

I couldn't have been more surprised, or relieved, when a beautiful brown and white cow stepped from behind a nearby bush. Her mouth was full of grass and she was dragging a long, wet rope.

When she saw me, she didn't look surprised at all. She merely raised her nose and greeted me with a soft, guttural moo. Her milk bag looked hard and swollen, and milk was dripping from the two front teats. Apparently she hadn't been milked in several days. I had been around cows enough to know how uncomfortable she was.

Speaking to her in a reassuring manner, I picked up the end of the rope and tied her snugly to a tree. She offered no resistance. I didn't have any container for the milk, but wanting to give her immediate relief, I milked it onto the ground, with the exception of an occasional squirt aimed at my mouth. I had always loved the taste of sweet, warm milk, direct from the cow.

The cow seemed grateful for the milking and chewed contentedly on her cud as I led her into a meadow where I staked her out in the grass near a small spring. I marveled at my good luck at having found a cow. I named her Sally. Some of the milk I could sell for money, and the rest I could trade for outfitting items. When it came time to leave in the spring, I could sell the cow for enough money to buy a good packhorse, with possibly enough left over to buy fare on a riverboat heading up the muddy Missouri River. My future was looking bright.

Chapter 12

After moving into the brush hut on Shoal Creek and finding the brown and white cow, I fell into a regular daily routine that lasted throughout the winter of 1838–39. Every morning after milking Sally and staking her out to graze, I headed into Far West carrying four gallons of fresh milk, bottled in stone cider jugs left behind by the mob.

There was a ready market for the milk because the mobs had killed or stolen most of the cows belonging to Mormon families. Some of the milk I sold for money; some I traded for items to become part of my outfit for the Rocky Mountains. I got a lot of trade items that I thought would find favor with Indians—mirrors, pieces of bright cloth, beads, kerchiefs, combs. I also traded for many of the items Ike and I would need for survival. After several months, thanks to Sally's regular milk supply, I traded for or purchased most of the items Ike and I needed for our outfit.

In my daily visits to Far West I had to be careful to avoid Dick Boggs, who was now a regular visitor. Even though he lived in Daviess County, he had now been made a deputy sheriff in Caldwell County with the specific assignment to hurry up the Mormons in their exodus from Missouri.

Thanks to the organizational abilities of Brigham Young, who had assumed leadership responsibilities while Joseph spent the winter in Liberty Jail, most of the Mormons migrated to Illinois during the winter. But as the early spring winds began to thaw out the partially frozen ground in late February, there were still hundreds of families not yet ready to join the migration to Illinois.

These families lingered behind for various reasons—some waiting for a sick person to get well, some waiting for a mother to have her baby, some hoping to sell some property before leaving, and some simply too stubborn to leave, wanting to show Lilburn Boggs that they didn't care a hoot about his extermination order.

Dick Boggs's assignment was to put the fear of hell into the lingering Mormons and get them moving out of Missouri. He was the right man for the job. I don't know how his plantation fared with him down at Far West harassing the Mormons, but his hatred for the Mormons was so intense that he didn't seem to mind being away from his plantation.

Whenever Boggs came to town, I tried to keep out of sight, not knowing what he might do if he recognized me as the boy who helped his big slave, Ike, escape. I knew he would try to kill me for sure if he knew of my plans to help Ike escape again in the spring and go with me to the Rocky Mountains.

Boggs drove a light four-wheeled buggy, drawn by a tall, spirited gelding. It was the kind of horse that was always dancing about and would step on people who happened to get in its path. Boggs made a conscious effort to get a Mormon in the path of the horse as frequently as possible. The horse seemed to understand and share Boggs's hatred for the Far West pedestrians. Whenever Boggs saw a Mormon ahead of him in the street, he would pull the horse's head just enough to point in the direction of the Mormon. The animal soon learned that this slight change in direction was a signal to run down the person or persons in its path. Without any more coaxing from Boggs, the animal would lay back its ears and quicken its pace toward the intended victim.

I had been raised in the farm country of eastern Canada and had noticed how horses used in handling cattle sometimes developed aggressive attitudes toward cattle—laying their ears back, biting, pushing. Boggs's horse had been trained to express its aggression toward people, and Boggs loved it.

Whenever I saw Boggs driving through town, I remembered the election day in Gallatin and how he had tried to castrate me with his pocketknife. I remembered his cruel treatment of his slave, Ike. I remembered the Mormon girl in the light blue dress, the one Boggs and his friends had assaulted in the church, and I renewed my determination to get revenge, to make Boggs pay for his evil doings. I saw him frequently through the winter, and gradually a plan began to form in my mind, a plan that involved Ike's big bear trap, but I never managed to find the right opportunity to carry out the plan. I knew I had to be careful. I didn't want to risk going to jail and ruining the chances that Ike and I could go to the Rocky Mountains.

It was in March, just when the grass was starting to turn green, that Sally stopped giving milk. I hadn't noticed the increasing size of her belly, and it wasn't until her milk dried up that I realized she was carrying a calf, which she would probably deliver in the next thirty days. I had been planning to sell her in April, but now that the milk was gone, I decided to start looking for a buyer right away. I couldn't risk bringing anyone to my secret hut, which was now half full of items for our trek to the Rocky Mountains, so one sunny morning I led Sally to town.

One of my first stops was at the home of one of the more prosperous Mormons who had been buying milk from me during the winter months. He lived on the main street of Far West, across from the surveyor's office. When I mentioned to him on one occasion that I planned to sell the cow in the spring, he asked to see her when I was ready to sell.

I tied Sally up to the front gate and entered the home. My friend was discussing business with companions in his study, and I was asked to wait in the parlor for a few minutes.

As I stood there by the window, looking down upon the mostly deserted main street of Far West, Dick Boggs suddenly appeared at the far end of the street, riding in his four-wheeled buggy, pulled by the spirited gelding. I watched intently as the buggy headed toward me, wondering if I would be successful in getting revenge on such a wicked fellow.

Suddenly I noticed that Sally was right in the path of the approaching horse and buggy, but it was too late to move her. I couldn't let Boggs recognize me. I had no idea why anyone would want to hurt a helpless old cow tied up to a garden gate, but knowing Boggs and how he loved to run over people with that wicked horse of his, I knew my cow wasn't safe.

When the horse saw the cow in its path, it laid back its ears and increased its speed toward the helpless victim. Boggs allowed more slack in the reins, sat back, and grinned. Surely he wasn't dumb enough to think he could just run over a cow and not suffer any consequences—a broken wheel, or perhaps even a capsized buggy.

Just when it appeared that Boggs was going to drive his willing horse right over the top of poor Sally, he pulled the horse's head to the side and stopped in front of the surveyor's office across the street. Good old Sally didn't give Boggs or his horse any satisfaction in their attempt to frighten her. She was still chewing her morning cud, paying no attention whatsoever to Boggs and his horse.

Apparently Boggs had some business at the surveyor's office. He jumped down from the buggy and was about to tie the dancing horse to the hitching post when he discovered that the tie rope was missing from the harness. From inside the house, I couldn't hear what Boggs was saying, but from the angry look on his face and the emphatic movement of his lips, I knew he was cursing his bad luck at not having a tie rope to hold the nervous animal. He obviously didn't want to use one of his long reins as a tie, knowing how easily a rein can break if the animal is startled.

Tying the horse temporarily with one of the reins, he went to the buggy in hopes of finding a tie rope in a box under the seat. He couldn't find one, and began looking about for a suitable substitute. I was finding immense satisfaction in Boggs's frustrations and was grinning ear to ear at his bad luck—until his gaze came to rest on Sally and he began walking toward her.

It was obvious to me that Boggs was going to steal Sally's lead rope. My first thought was to prevent him from taking the rope, but my good sense told me to stay where I was. I knew Sally would be easy to catch, even without a rope, and if my friend didn't buy her, he would give me a rope so I could lead her to the house of the next potential buyer. It was better to give Boggs the rope than to face a conflict with him.

When Boggs was about five feet from Sally, he stopped with his hands on his hips and looked her over very carefully. She ignored him, still chewing her morning cud. I began to worry that perhaps he would steal her too, along with the rope.

Without warning, Boggs reached into his coat, pulled out a long revolver, pointed it coldly at Sally's side, and pulled the trigger. There was a puff of white smoke, a loud explosion, and Sally dropped to her knees, a mortal wound in her side. I stared in disbelief as she rolled over in the dusty street and died. I would have run into the street and leapt upon Boggs had not my friend and two of his companions prevented me from doing so.

I watched from the window as Boggs opened his pocketknife and began cutting along the back of my dead cow. He removed a strip of hide about two inches wide and almost eight feet long. Before he was finished,

I realized that he was fashioning a cowhide tie rope for his horse. I could hardly believe what had happened. Boggs had killed a gentle old cow and her unborn calf for nothing more than a strip of skin.

Boggs tied up his horse with the strip of Sally's hide and entered the surveyor's office. After telling me to stay out of sight because of my problems with Boggs in the past, my friend and one of his companions went into the street to dress out the dead cow and salvage as much meat as possible. I stood in the shadows of the house, disgusted with myself for having wavered in my resolution to make Boggs pay for his wicked deeds. If I had acted earlier, perhaps Sally would still be alive.

The men were still working on the cow when Boggs came out of the office. He didn't give them any more than a quick glance as he untied the horse and shouted back to the surveyor, "I'll be back for those papers about dark."

A few minutes later, working out the final details of my plan for revenge on Dick Boggs, I loped back to my hut. The adrenaline was already flowing in my veins, knowing I would be attempting to execute my plan that very night.

The sun was just touching the western hills when I returned to my friend's house. I was carrying the heavy old bear trap and about ten feet of new one-inch rope. I crawled under some bushes where no one could see me, waiting for the coming of darkness and Boggs's carriage.

Just when I was beginning to worry that it would soon be too dark to see what I was doing, Boggs's carriage stopped beside the hitching post in front of the surveyor's office. After securing the horse with the cowhide tie rope, Boggs disappeared into the office. There was no time to waste. After making sure there were no observers, I crawled out from under the bush and headed for the carriage, the bear trap in one hand and the rope in the other.

My plan was very simple. There was an iron step right behind the left front wheel where Boggs placed his foot when getting into the carriage. I set the trap and buried it in the dust just below the iron step and a little bit away from the carriage. I tied one end of the rope to the trap chain, and the other end to one of the spokes near the inside of the left back wheel. I figured that after Boggs untied the horse he would step into my bear trap as he approached the iron step. The clank of the steel trap and Boggs's screams of pain would certainly startle the spirited horse and start it running up the street, jerking Boggs's feet from under him and dragging him along behind. I tied the rope to the spokes so Boggs would be dragged along by a series of jerks rather than by a steady pull. I was sure the jerking motion would make the experience more miserable for Boggs while having an unsettling effect on the horse to ensure its continued running.

As I was kicking the last of the dust over the trap, chain, and rope, I heard the unmistakable clomp of hobnailed boots on the wooden floor of the surveyor's office. I darted into the alley just as Boggs stepped onto the porch, the surveyor close behind. I watched him untie the nervous horse.

Without another word to the surveyor, Boggs walked to the back of the wheel, and to my astonishment, stepped right over the open jaws of the bear trap onto the iron step and into the carriage. My plan had failed.

A thousand thoughts raced through my mind in that desperate instant. Not only had I missed my chance at revenge, but I had lost my bear trap. I wondered what kind of cruel punishments Boggs would inflict upon Mormons when he discovered what a Mormon had tried to do to him.

Boggs made a few parting comments to the surveyor, and was about to lead his horse up the street when a sudden idea entered my mind. There was not time to consider the consequences.

I stepped out of the alley into the dim light coming from the surveyor's window.

"Are you the mobber who killed my cow?" I demanded of Boggs.

His first reaction was to reach for the pistol under his coat, the same pistol he had used to shoot my cow. But when he saw that I was only a boy, and apparently unarmed, he left his pistol in its place.

Instead of answering my question, he responded with a question of his own. "Aren't you the kid who tried to steal my nig . . ."

Without finishing his question, he sprang from the buggy to grab me before I could disappear into the darkness. Instinctively, I sprang back to get out of his reach, but my reaction was unnecessary. As soon as his first boot touched the dust, there was the unmistakable clank of cold steel followed by a startled scream.

As predicted, the horse bolted up the street, giving the deserving Boggs a ride he would never forget. The screaming Boggs disappeared into the darkness. I looked at the surveyor, and he at me. I turned and darted into the alley before he had time to think.

Chapter 13

On April 1, 1839, Ike and I were camped on a hillside several miles south of Liberty, Missouri, overlooking the Missouri River. Most people called it the Big Muddy. It is the longest river in North America, reaching from St. Louis clear to the Rocky Mountains.

Below us, two steam-powered riverboats were secured to log pilings, taking on supplies and passengers bound for the upper Missouri and the Rocky Mountains. Ike and I had arrived during the night, hoping somehow to get passage on one of the boats. We had all the supplies we would need for survival in the mountains—rifles, knives, flour, beans, salt, trinkets for trading with the Indians, and a mule to carry everything—but we didn't have any money.

I had planned to buy passage with money received from the sale of my cow, but Dick Boggs had ruined that plan by shooting Sally.

Boggs had paid dearly for his cruel deed, losing his foot and nearly his life after being dragged down the road in my bear trap. By the time the carriage was brought to a halt by two mounted riders, Boggs's foot was so badly mangled that the doctor had to cut it off.

Even while Boggs was squirming on the operating table, gulping down corn whiskey to ease the pain from the doctor's sawing, I was jogging north toward the Daviess County line and the Boggs plantation to get Ike.

The surveyor had seen me lure Boggs into the trap. I knew I had no time to lose. There was no doubt in my mind that within a few days every lawman in Missouri would be looking for me.

Just after first light, I reached Boggs's plantation and spotted Ike heading into the fields with a mule and plow. An hour later, we were headed south, riding double on the mule. If we were lucky, Ike wouldn't be missed until evening.

We headed straight for my hidden camp on Shoal Creek, where I had stashed the supplies we would need for our expedition to the Rocky Mountains. We arrived in late afternoon and because I had not slept at all the previous night, I promptly collapsed on the floor of the brush hut and fell into a deep sleep.

It was dark when Ike awakened me. He had loaded our supplies onto the mule while I was sleeping. After a brief supper of dried catfish and creek water, we resumed our journey south to the Big Muddy.

Since we didn't have money for passage, I figured our only chance of getting aboard a riverboat would be to hire on as deckhands—and that would be risky for a fugitive and an escaped slave.

Leaving Ike behind with the mule and supplies, I walked down to the dock to check out the deckhand opportunities. Both boats were sternwheelers. One was called the *General Washington*, the other the *Yellowstone Queen*. Both were scheduled to head upstream the next morning.

As I approached the *General Washington*, I spotted a weathered old man sitting at a wooden table next to the oak planks leading to the deck. He had an air of authority about him, as though he were handling an important assignment. I walked up to him and asked if he needed any deckhands.

Instead of answering, he looked me up and down, very slowly, as if he hadn't heard my question. I was about to repeat the question when he raised a hand for me to be silent.

"Too little for a deckhand. Not strong enough. Just a boy." I was about to protest this rejection when he continued. "But we might be interested in put'n you on as a cabin boy. Go see Captain Harris." He pointed up the oak planks to the deck of the ship.

As I was about to walk up the plank to the deck of the *General Washington*, two black men, carrying a huge crate, appeared at the other end of the plank. I moved aside to let them pass.

While waiting for them to leave the plank, I saw a chance to get some information that might be helpful in getting Ike aboard as a deckhand, so I asked the old man, "Do you hire many black deckhands?"

"We don't hire any nigger deckhands. This is a slave state," was his instant reply.

"But what about . . ." I nodded toward the two black men carrying the crate down the plank.

"We don't hire 'm, we rent 'm, from their owners. They're slaves. If a nigger walked down here ask'n to be hired, we'd have 'm in chains in a hurry, figur'n he was a runaway. Sometimes they bring good rewards."

As I stepped onto the deck of the *General Washington*, I was grateful for this latest bit of information about black deckhands. I was grateful I hadn't brought Ike with me to hire on as a deckhand. Had I done so, perhaps he would already be in chains. Somehow I had to find another way to get Ike on one of the boats, but first I would try to land the position as cabin boy.

From the deck, the *General Washington* looked much larger than from shore. The boiler looked bigger, the spars taller, and the wheelhouse more impressive.

I located Captain Harris standing near the big paddle wheel at the deck of the boat. He was a big man, almost as tall as Ike, but much heavier. His hair was black and greasy, his face marked with pox scars and shaded with a three-day beard. His eyes were fierce and penetrating.

"Captain Harris," I called to get his attention. He turned and looked at me. There was a cane in his left hand to help compensate for an injury to his left leg.

"I understand you are looking for a cabin boy."

"That's right," he responded, looking me over from head to foot. "You think being a cabin boy is a soft job, a lot of fun and games?" he continued.

"I'm not afraid to work, sir," I responded.

"Will you empty and clean the chamber pots of the cabin passengers?"

"If that's part of the job, sir."

"Does your ma and pa know you're here? I don't want any sheriff stopping this tub to look for a runaway kid."

"My parents are dead, sir. I'm an orphan."

"I see," he said, rubbing his whiskered chin and looking me over a second time, more closely.

"Can I have the job, sir?"

"Oh, one more thing," he said slowly.

Suddenly his cane struck out viciously at my head, a wide sweeping blow. I didn't have time to duck, and barely got my arm up in time to protect my head. The impact was sufficiently powerful to send me sprawling across the deck, leaving a stinging red welt on my arm and shoulder.

"Why did you do that?" I shouted, without the "sir." Surprised and angry, I was tempted to draw the knife from my belt and throw it at his big belly.

He began to chuckle, then said, "The job's yours, if you still want it. Be back at dark; we leave at first light. Harvey at the table will tell you what to do." He turned and hobbled away.

I climbed to my feet, not sure if I wanted to be cabin boy on the *General Washington*. I walked across the deck and down the ramp to Harvey's table.

"Why'd he hit me?" I demanded.

Harvey was all smiles this time. "You did good, kid. You passed the test."

"What test?"

"The crybaby test. The cap'n can't stand cabin boys who cry when things get tough. He hit you to see if you would cry. You didn't, so you got the job. Congratulations. See you tonight."

He looked back down at a book where he was doing some figuring, and I headed up the hill to tell Ike how I planned to get him aboard the other boat, the *Yellowstone Queen*.

I figured that since Missouri was a slave state, any free black applying for a job that would carry him out of the state would be suspected of trying to escape his master. My plan was to present Ike as a slave to the captain of the *Yellowstone Queen* and get the captain to rent Ike's services for the journey, as he had rented the services of the other slaves on his vessel. According to the sailor Harvey, rented slaves made the best deckhands, being accustomed to hard work and frequent orders.

Leaving the mule and supplies in the woods, Ike and I approached the *Yellowstone Queen* from upstream. I didn't want to be seen by people on the *General Washington*, where I had been hired on as a cabin boy.

Before seeking out the captain of the *Yellowstone Queen*, I made inquiries of several of the men on shore to learn some details about renting slaves to riverboat captains. I learned that the average rent on trips to the upper Missouri and back was one dollar a day. The estimated length of the trip was a hundred and twenty days. The slave got to keep the dollar earned on Sundays while the rest of the money went to the master. Generally half the fee was paid to the slave owner in advance of the trip, with the balance due upon return. If the slave did not return, the captain was obligated to pay the owner the fair market value of the slave.

I was pleased to notice that a good portion of the *Yellowstone Queen*'s cargo was still on the wharf, waiting to be loaded. Hopefully the captain would need Ike's services badly enough so as not to inquire very thoroughly into our circumstances.

As we approached the boat to talk to the captain, walking among crates and bundles, Ike had an idea of his own to help our cause. Hardly breaking stride, he hoisted a one-hundred-pound sack of oats onto his left shoulder. Then, using his head to balance the bag, he placed another one-hundred-pound bag on his right shoulder. Ike's huge muscles rippled with ease and grace under his glossy, black skin as he walked beside me carrying the two hundred pounds of oats onto the deck of the *Yellowstone Queen*.

Ike dropped the oats at the feet of Captain Robinette, a short, wiry man with a bald head and a thick, black beard. Deciding to keep my story as close to the truth as possible in case the captain decided to check up on us, I told him that Ike belonged to my uncle, Dick Boggs, who had recently been injured in an accident with a runaway horse. I explained that because of the expenses related to his injuries, Uncle Dick had decided to rent some of his best fieldhands for cash income. As I began to add more details about the extent of Uncle Dick's injuries, the captain interrupted me.

"I'll pay seventy-five cents a day with a thirty-dollar advance, not a penny more." It was apparent the captain was satisfied with my story and wanted to get on with the business of putting Ike to work loading the cargo. I didn't dare look at Ike, but I knew he was as delighted as I was at the way things were developing.

I didn't want to raise any suspicions by seeming too eager to accept the terms, so I said, "Uncle Dick thought Ike would bring more than that. I don't want my uncle mad at me. I'd better check with the captain of the *General Washington*. Maybe he'll pay more." I turned to Ike as if we were going to leave.

Almost too quickly, the captain responded. "Wait a minute. I really need help getting this cargo loaded. Do you think your uncle would be satisfied with a dollar a day and a fifty-dollar advance?"

I turned to the captain, smiled broadly, and offered him my hand. "It's a deal," I said.

Ike was immediately put to work loading the *Yellowstone Queen*. I collected the advance money, signing for Uncle Dick, and returned to the woods to get Ike's things. I divided our supplies into two bundles, one for me and one for Ike, and sold the mule to a man for thirty dollars. When I delivered Ike's bundle to him aboard the *Yellowstone Queen*, I gave him two twenty-dollar gold pieces, half our money and probably more than Ike had ever seen at one time in his entire life. I told him to sew the coins into his trouser pockets. We would need the money for horses when we arrived at Fort Benton, where the boats turned around and headed back home.

After saying good-bye to Ike, I returned to the woods for my bundle of supplies, then boarded the *General Washington* as the new cabin boy.

Chapter 14

The next morning men were hurrying everywhere in last-minute preparations. It was a race to see which riverboat would shove off first, the *General Washington* or the *Yellowstone Queen*. The last of the cargo was being loaded—sacks of flour, sugar, and oats; iron; barrels of whiskey; and to my surprise, wooden cages full of cats. House cats, all colors and sizes. I later learned that the army posts along the Missouri were being overrun with field mice and rats that ate the government grain faster than the soldiers and horses. Cats were being shipped up the Big Muddy by the thousands to eliminate the plague of rodents.

Billows of gray wood smoke were pouring from the smokestacks on each side of the huge boiler. Captain Harris was shouting orders in every direction.

Harvey, the first mate, was at his table on the dock busily checking and double-checking passenger and cargo lists. When I asked him what I was supposed to be doing, he didn't even look up, but just told me to keep out of the way until the boat was underway, then to come and see him.

I returned to the deck. I had never seen so much hurrying, sweating, and cursing in my life. Even the passengers were busy—arguing about how long the voyage was going to take, bidding farewell instructions to loved ones, or just pacing the deck, taking frequent glances at pocket watches.

The only calm individual in sight was the pilot up in the wheelhouse. He was calmly studying his river maps. His pilot's cap was back and to one side on his bushy head of red hair. His long sideburns, bright blue eyes, and cocky manner indicated that he was probably an Irishman.

Most boys my age wanted to be river pilots. The pilot was king of the river. The boats couldn't go anywhere without him. He didn't have the problems and details to worry about as did the ship owners and captains. He didn't have to work, just steer the riverboats safely to their destinations. He had the freedom to do as he pleased when the boat was in port, and he was paid handsomely for his skills.

I approached the stairway to the wheelhouse.

"Hello, lad. You the new cabin boy?" asked the cheery pilot.

"Yeah, mind if I come up?"

"Not at all." Most pilots enjoyed the envy of boys and took every opportunity to glamorize their profession.

"What's your name, boy?"

"Dan Storm, sir. And yours?"

"Benny Potts they call me, and I'm getting ready to steer this tub up the Big Muddy for the fourth year in a row. Know much about riverboats, lad?"

"This is my first trip," I said.

"You've got a lot to learn. Yes-sir-ree, a lot to learn." He pointed his finger at me. "Don't ever turn your back on Captain Harris, and never let him catch you crying."

"I've already learned that lesson," I said. I showed him the welt the captain's cane had left on my arm.

He drew a corncob pipe out of his pocket and lit it with a big wooden match, which he struck on the sole of his boot. He looked thoughtfully over the toiling, hurrying people below.

"See them roustabouts?" He was referring to the deckhands. "Every one of them is carrying at least one concealed knife. The mates all have pistols tucked in their trousers and ain't afraid to use 'm.

"The best roustabouts," he continued, "are the nigger slaves. They don't mind being bossed around, and they are used to working hard. Don't mess with one of them slaves, or you'll be in big trouble."

"What do you mean?" I asked.

"The captain's just renting the niggers from their owners." I didn't tell him that I already knew about that part of the business.

"If one of them gets hurt the captain not only has to pay the vet bill, but he must compensate the owner for any permanent injury, and if the buck dies, the captain has to pay the full price that the slave would sell for if he were alive. Some of them big fellers is worth a thousand dollars. If you and one of them were to fall overboard, and the captain had only one rope, you can bet he wouldn't throw it to you!

"The next best workers is the krauts," he continued.

"The what?" I asked.

"The Germans. They don't know enough English to talk back, so they just work all the time.

"The Missouri farm boys don't work out nearly as well as slaves and Germans. They are usually the ones that left the farm because they didn't like the work. They come to the riverboats to see the country, not to work."

He took out his pipe, looked at it. "And, of course, the worst roustabouts of all is us Irish. Do you know why?"

I shook my head.

"It takes a lot of bossing around to get one of these tubs up three thousand miles of treacherous river to Fort Benton. Us Irish don't like being bossed. I was the orneriest roustabout you ever saw."

"You used to be a roustabout?"

"Yep, and I never made it all the way even once without getting fired or my wages docked. As I said, us Irish don't like being bossed around."

"How did you ever get to be a pilot?" I asked.

"Just a lucky chance, lad. We had started back from Fort Benton eight years ago on the *Lord Byron*, when an Indian shot an arrow right through our pilot's neck, poor fellow. Before anyone realized what had happened, painted Injuns were swarming up and down both banks, sprinkling us with bullets and arrows. And without a pilot, the boat was out of control, heading for those mean rapids just this side of Benton.

"Well, I climbs into the pilot house and guided her through before the captain even knew the pilot was shot. When he found out what had happened he made me the pilot—not because he liked me or anything. By the time I had guided the tub through the rapids, I had more piloting experience than anybody else.

"The Indians were bad all over that year; a number of pilots caught arrows. There was a shortage the next year, so I got on permanent."

The passengers were coming aboard now—mostly trappers, miners, and soldiers. A few had women with them.

"See that fat lady in the purple dress?" remarked Benny. I nodded. "If she slips overboard, you don't need to worry about her drowning."

"Is she a good swimmer?" I asked.

He took a good, close look at the lady in the purple dress, and said, "I've never seen one fall into the drink, so I guess I don't really know. Everybody that works the river says they do float. Maybe some night when she's on her way to the can, we'll sneak up behind her and toss her over the rail. Then we'll know for sure." He laughed and winked at me.

"Better get below, lad; we're about to shove off."

He turned from me and shouted into a pipe that headed down through the deck, "Henry, got a full head of steam yet?"

When I reached the main deck, the captain was shouting and cursing louder than ever. Anyone who didn't have something to do was looking at the *Yellowstone Queen*, already pulling away from the dock and moving up the Missouri River under a full head of steam.

The captain shouted over the rail to Harvey, "We're shoving off in sixty seconds, and anyone who isn't on board will have to wait until next year."

"Ready, Mr. Potts?" shouted the captain to the pilot. "Remember there's an extra hundred dollars for you if you can beat the *Yellowstone Queen* to Benton."

"Aye, aye, sir," responded Benny in a calm but loud voice. While several roustabouts prepared to untie the boat from the pilings, others got ready with long poles to push it out into midstream. As the ropes loosened from the pilings, Benny pulled hard on a cord that released a loud, shrill whistle announcing to the world that the *General Washington* had begun its three-thousand-mile journey up the longest river in North America.

Chapter 15

The May sun was bright and warm as the *General Washington* began its course up the Missouri River. Ahead of us we could see the big paddle wheel of the *Yellowstone Queen*, churning through the brown water. We would be in fierce competition with that boat for the next sixty days. Nearly everyone who had anything to do with the operation of the boat had a bonus coming if we were first to reach Fort Benton.

The incentives had nothing to do with pride of friendly competition. It was a simple matter of economics—the first boat to reach Fort Benton received the highest prices for its goods and gained a reputation, as word spread, of being the fastest boat, resulting in more passengers and cargo in the future.

The passengers and roustabouts who had been so busy during the launching were soon lounging about the deck enjoying the spring sunshine. Nobody had given me anything to do, so I approached a water barrel just below the wheelhouse with the intention of quenching my growing thirst.

I removed the lid and scooped out a dipper full of clear, cool liquid. Just as I was about to drink, a rude voice declared, "You're in a lot of trouble, boy, if you drink that water."

I turned around to face several sneering roustabouts. I looked back at the water. It appeared clear, and suitable for drinking.

"Barrel water's for cabin passengers and officers," explained one of the men. "Cabin boys drink like the rest of us hands, out of the Big Muddy." He pointed to a bucket near the railing, indicating that I needed to dip my drink out of the muddy river. There was a long rope attached to the bucket handle.

I picked up the bucket and was about to toss it overboard, when one of the roustabouts warned, "If the current jerks the rope out of your hand and you lose the bucket, the capt'n will throw you overboard for sure. That's what he did to the last cabin boy. Better tie the other end of the rope to your wrist, just to be sure the bucket doesn't jerk away from you."

It sounded like good advice. I certainly didn't want to get in trouble with the captain by losing the bucket. On the other hand, I was suspicious of the roustabouts. Why would they want to keep me out of trouble? I wondered if they knew something I didn't know. Anyway, I was thirsty, so I tied the free end of the rope to my wrist.

Just as I was about to drop the bucket overboard into the water, I was surprised by a loud voice from the wheelhouse. "Don't drop that bucket!" shouted Benny Potts, the pilot. "Take that rope off your wrist and come up here."

Still not sure what was happening, but trusting Benny more than the roustabouts, I untied the rope and climbed the ladder to the wheelhouse.

"Dan, do you know why those hands told you to tie the rope to your wrist?"

Shaking my head, I felt I was on the receiving end of a prank, still unable to guess what that prank might be.

Benny got right to the point. "You wouldn't have tied that rope to your wrist if you had any idea how much drag there is on a full bucket of water when we're moving along at fifteen knots—enough force to jerk you overboard for sure."

So that was it. The roustabouts were trying to get me jerked into the Missouri River.

"When you want water," continued Benny, "drop the bucket overboard, tip it just enough to let the water start coming in, then jerk it up. Never tie the rope to your wrist. If the bucket happens to go under and get away from you, you'll be in trouble, for sure, but you won't be drowned. We had one cabin boy a few years back who lost five or six buckets drawing water for the cook. Good thing he didn't have a rope tied to his wrist."

I thanked Benny for watching out for me and returned to the deck to get my drink of water.

I couldn't help but wonder about my future in this new world among the frontier river people, where men played games with people's lives and laughed about it. I knew if I was going to survive on my own, I would continually have to be on the alert for trouble. I wondered how Ike was getting along on the *Yellowstone Queen.*

The next few weeks were relatively uneventful. The river was full and smooth, easy to navigate, and we were not yet into hostile Indian country. Occasionally we'd stop to cut wood for the boiler or take on more passengers or cargo.

My cabin boy duties were easier and less time consuming than I had anticipated. My main responsibilities were cleaning cabins and delivering trays of food.

The cabin passengers were fed regularly, three times a day. The leftovers went to the roustabouts and the cabin boy. In addition to the leftovers, we had all the cornbread and molasses we wanted.

Since I was the one who picked up the meal trays, I usually got first crack at the remains, but living on leftovers was a frustrating experience. When something good, like cherry pie, was served, there was never more than just enough remaining to tease one's taste buds. On the other hand, if the cook came up with something nobody liked, like the morning he whipped up a sauerkraut omelette, the roustabouts wouldn't touch it either.

Some of the passengers, while enjoying after-dinner smoking, would empty cigar and pipe ashes on their food plates. At first none of the hands would touch a plate with ashes on it, but after a few weeks of cornbread and molasses three times a day, more and more of the men began flicking away ashes to get at the unwanted food underneath. I missed Aunt Sarah's cooking more and more and wondered if I would ever enjoy good civilized cooking again.

There was a bar on the boat, and many of the passengers developed a routine of drinking all night and sleeping all day. When the boat was traveling, it was noisy and smelly. There was loud squeaking and clanking from the engine, and everything smelled of burning engine oil and wood smoke. Captain Harris was in a pretty good mood as long as the boat was moving and we were ahead of the *Yellowstone Queen.* We passed it during the second week and were still ahead at the halfway point.

I spent as much time as possible in the wheelhouse with Benny. He taught me how to read the river—the deep and shallow points, the swiftness of the currents, and how to spot submerged snags. During the spring runoff, many dead trees washed downstream. If a tree had been in the water a while, its butt end might sink to the bottom, while the upper, pointed end would be suspended near the surface, pointed downstream—just waiting to spear a hole in the bottom of an approaching riverboat. Benny taught me how to locate these snags by reading the ripples on the surface.

Benny told me about the Indians that wandered the banks of the Big Muddy—the Arikaras, Pawnees, and Minatarees on the lower river, and the Crows, Assinibons, Sioux, and Blackfeet on the upper river.

He told me of the fateful voyage of the *St. Peters* in 1837, just two years earlier. One of the crewmen came down with smallpox. At the first stop, a Mandan chief stole an infected blanket. Within two weeks, the Mandan tribe, once numbering seventeen hundred people, was reduced to about thirty Indians. The disease spread to other tribes, not only from Indian to Indian but also by the *St. Peters*, which continued its journey upriver.

In an attempt to prevent the epidemic at a new trading location, the captain ordered thirty Assiniboine women vaccinated with the virus. Unfortunately, the experiment failed and the women died; the disease spread to other tribes, including the Blackfeet. Benny said it was estimated that on that one voyage the *St. Peters* killed over eighteen thousand Indians.

"If you want to scare an Injun right out of his scalp," said Benny, "just paint red spots on your face, wrap up in a blanket like you was freez'n, and start yellin' 'pox, pox, pox.' "

Every few days, we'd stop and take on firewood for the boiler furnaces. The captain paid about five dollars a cord for the wood from homesteaders along the lower river. On the upper river, starting in Sioux country, we had to cut our own, mostly cottonwood piled up along the bank by the high water in the spring. As close as I could figure, going upstream, we got about five miles out of a cord of wood.

There was a lot of runoff water from the upper forks of the Missouri this year, so we didn't have much trouble with sand bars. Even though riverboats such as the *Yellowstone Queen* and the *General Washington* could float unobstructed in less than thirty-six inches of water, there were often numerous sand bars obstructing the trip to Fort Benton.

If a ship couldn't force her way over a sand bar, she resorted to "grasshoppering." The spars were lowered into the water and pushed into the sand at a forty-five-degree angle in an upstream direction. Then cables attached to the bottom ends of the spars would be winched back to the boat. As the spar ends were pulled toward the boat, the bow would be forced up and over the sand bar. The spars would then be set ahead to a new location. The process was called grasshoppering because the spars and boat worked together resembling a big grasshopper.

Chapter 16

After we had been on the river about forty days, we reached the first rapids. The water was higher than normal, a combination of heavy winter snowfall and hot summer weather. The increased water flow was gushing through the rapids with such force and velocity that it seemed impossible for any boat to make it through.

Benny said the sensible thing to do would be to wait a week or two until the high water subsided. But with the *Yellowstone Queen* close behind, Captain Harris had no intention of waiting.

After several unsuccessful attempts at grasshoppering through the rapids, the captain decided to unload the cargo and passengers, hoping that when it was empty, the *General Washington* could outrun the rapids.

Because of numerous boulders in the shallow water, it was impossible to get close enough to shore to unload the cargo directly. It was necessary to load the yawls and haul the goods to shore a little at a time.

As the first yawl reached shore, the rapids became a secondary concern. Four or five mounted Indians appeared on a knoll above the spot where we hoped to unload the cargo. I was in the wheelhouse with Benny at the time. He said they were Blackfeet.

The roustabouts in the yawl started rowing back to the ship. This infuriated Captain Harris. He waved them back to shore, ordering them to drive off the "thieving Injuns." One of the men in the yawl raised his rifle and fired at the Indians.

His aim was good, but not deadly. One of the Indians got off his horse and, holding his side with one hand, began yelling and shaking his other fist. Soon thirty more Indians rode into view. They dismounted and disappeared into the rocks and brush and commenced firing on the yawl and the ship.

I was about to head down to the hold to find a safe hiding place among the boxes and bales, but Benny ordered me to stay in the wheelhouse. He said it was the safest place on the boat. He reminded me that it was paneled all the way around with bullet-proof boiler plate. I ducked a little lower behind the protective shield. Occasionally an arrow would sail down from the sky and thunk harmlessly into the wooded deck. We were too far away for any accuracy with arrows.

Every man with a gun was soon firing back at the Indians. The only casualty in the battle at this point was that first Indian. A lot of ammunition was being wasted on both sides. Most of the men seemed to be enjoying the battle. After forty days of monotonous river travel, there was finally some excitement.

"Reinforcements!" shouted someone, as the *Yellowstone Queen* churned into view, about a half mile downstream. Everyone cheered, except the captain. I guess most of the men liked to pretend the Indian danger was worse than it really was. When back in St. Louis, they'd probably tell their families and friends how the reinforcements saved us just in time.

At the sight of the *Yellowstone Queen*, the Indians started scampering toward their ponies. I was a little disappointed with my first Indian battle—no scalps taken, no feats of daring bravery. I didn't even get a good look at a warring Indian.

The *Yellowstone Queen* paid no heed to the Indians but headed directly for the rapids under a full head of steam, seizing upon the opportunity to pass us and be the first to arrive in Fort Benton. Captain Harris responded quickly, ordering the firebox filled to overflowing.

The boilers on riverboats have safety release valves to prevent them from exploding when the pressure becomes too great. Nevertheless, boiler explosions are frequent. Several occur every year on the Big Muddy, mostly near the upper reaches of the river where maximum speed is needed to assault rapids or produce that last burst of speed in order to be the first in port.

It was impossible to know exactly how much pressure a boiler could stand. There were some boilers that seemed to be able to hold any amount of pressure without breaking a seam, and most captains thought they had that kind of boiler.

Several weeks earlier, we had cut some pitch-filled pine for just such an emergency. The furnace was now filled with the pitchwood, and our steam was almost to maximum pressure.

"Full steam ahead!" ordered the captain.

We cruised into the main current about a hundred feet ahead of the *Yellowstone Queen*. I could see the captain shaking his fist and cursing us from the wheelhouse. He had been trying to beat us into the rapids, and now he had to slow down to avoid a collision.

Captain Harris called for more fire. The heat from the furnace was so intense now that the men who were throwing in the pitchwood had to douse themselves with water between trips from the woodpile to the furnace door to shove in another log.

Roustabouts were stationed at each spar, ready to plant them firmly into the river bottom if and when we lost our forward motion.

The *Yellowstone Queen* followed closely, violating an unwritten agreement on the river that the second boat should wait for the first to get through before entering the rapids. I suppose the captain was so furious that the *General Washington* had cut in front of him that he threw caution and good sense aside. He had just arrived on the scene and wasn't as aware as we were of the difficulty in getting over these swift waters.

The increased power from our pitchwood made a difference. Inching ahead to the top of the rapids, we felt we were going to make it, while the *Yellowstone Queen* was falling behind.

The women who had hidden in the cabins during the Indian attack were now out on deck, reveling in the excitement of conquering the rapids. Everyone was cheering, shouting, laughing back at the *Yellowstone Queen*.

"More fire!" called Captain Harris, confident now that we would be the first to reach Fort Benton, that victory and huge profits would be his.

Suddenly a burst of steam shot across the deck, blowing one roustabout overboard. Then the entire boiler came apart in one massive explosion. People and debris were literally flying in every direction. The only thing that saved Benny and me from complete annihilation was the steel plating around the wheelhouse. As a result of the blast, however, the wheelhouse came apart at the base, and, following the initial explosion, we had to scramble for safety. It was every man for himself.

The *General Washington* had now turned sideways, displaying a gaping hole where the boiler had been. Her bottom was already rubbing on the rocky bottom, so she couldn't sink any deeper, not until we reached the still, deep water at the bottom of the rapids. The rushing river began to carry us backwards, downstream, with increasing speed. The current was sweeping us down upon the *Yellowstone Queen*. It appeared that a collision was unavoidable, and people from both boats began jumping into the water. The biggest fear was that the collision would cause water to wash over the deck and against the boiler of the *Yellowstone Queen*, triggering a more powerful explosion than ours had been. A shrill whistle filled the air as someone hung on the *Yellowstone Queen*'s whistle cord in an effort to relieve some of the pressure from the boiler.

I saw a barrel bobbing along about twenty yards out, so I slipped out of my boots, dove into the icy water, and swam to the barrel. From this position of relative safety, I looked back upon the pending collision. I figured if there was no explosion, I would swim back to the *Yellowstone Queen*.

The fat lady, who had been wearing the purple dress the first day, jumped from the hurricane deck. She didn't make a very large splash, and contrary to Benny's predictions, she didn't float like a cork. She didn't even surface after the initial plunge but was soon forgotten as the two boats came together. The collision wasn't as dramatic as might be expected. There was merely a mild thump as they made contact, a subdued creaking and splintering of timber until all was still and quiet, except for the rushing of water.

The *General Washington*, after washing sideways into the bow of the *Yellowstone Queen* began to offer more resistance to the rushing current. The result was a tipping motion, the upstream side going up, the downstream side going down, which pulled the bow of the *Yellowstone Queen* down with it, allowing the melted snow water of the Missouri River to rush over her decks and up on the over-heated boiler. The explosion made shambles of both boats.

The rushing torrent was cluttered with people, bodies, floating debris, and cargo. I decided to cling tightly to my barrel until we reached calmer water, then swim to shore.

Above the roar of the rushing water, I could hear the desperate shouting of men and the frantic screaming of women.

As one of the first to reach the bottom of the rapids, I looked toward shore to find a spot where I could swim to. I was suddenly sick to my stomach. The Sioux had returned and were waiting patiently for the desperate white men and women to crawl ashore like half-drowned rats.

Chapter 17

Though the river was moving slowly now, I hung tightly to the barrel, keeping it in the middle of the stream. Some of the Indians had crossed the river; they controlled both banks.

Some of the people who didn't have anything to hold onto and were exhausted from swimming headed into shore, hoping for mercy from the Indians they had been firing upon an hour earlier.

When the first three swimmers were almost to shore, the nearest Indians opened fire with their bows and arrows, killing all three of them. Two of the braves waded out and scalped the bodies. The rest of the swimmers headed back to the middle of the stream, looking for pieces of debris to hold onto.

The Indians rode their horses up and down both banks, shooting at bobbing heads and retrieving items of floating cargo.

The water was quiet now, and I could hear the shouts of others. One man was ordering everyone to bunch together. I guess he figured there was strength in a united defense. I don't know how he planned to defend us against the Indians. There were no guns, just a few knives.

Another man was shouting for everyone to spread out as much as possible. There were only about thirty Indians, but more than a hundred of us. His idea was that the Indian's couldn't keep track of all of us, and some would be able to escape, instead of everyone being killed like fish in a barrel.

There was some comfort in the idea that everyone was together, but I didn't like the idea that I was part of one great big target. I yearned to find a hole where I could crawl out of sight, where no one would ever find me. I started kicking and paddling my barrel downstream in an effort to get ahead of the main group.

Just as I was leaving the calm water into the rapids below, a group of eight or ten men scrambled ashore onto a huge pile of dead cottonwood logs that had been washed there during the spring runoff. The swimmers began throwing rocks and swinging clubs to protect themselves from the Indians as they began to arrange some logs into a fortress.

As two Indians galloped by the log fortress, a huge black man stood erect at the top of the pile of dead trees, his muscles bulging in the afternoon sun as he flung an entire tree upon the mounted riders. As the Indians and horses went down in a tangle of branches and flailing hooves, the black man's companions piled upon the Indians, killing them with their own weapons. The black man picked up another tree in preparation for the next Indian who dared to come too close. I was too far away to distinguish facial features, but I knew the black man was Ike. Seeing his strength and confidence in fighting the Indians made me want to join him, but it was too late. The rapids were carrying me downstream. I wondered if I would ever see Ike again, and if he could survive the hostile wilderness. I thought that perhaps I should have left him in slavery, where he could have remained healthy and safe. After taking one last look at Ike, I turned to face the approaching rapids.

Some of the Indians rode downstream, staying abreast of the floating people. Every so often they would drag a body from the water, scalp it, strip off any valuables, and then leave it to rot in the summer sun.

Even though I had been paddling hard to get ahead of the main group, my teeth were now chattering from being in the icy water so long. I longed to swim ashore and roll in the warm, white sand but decided I'd rather freeze to death than get scalped. My bones ached with the cold, and there was a sharp pain in my forehead.

At a narrow place in the river, an Indian put a bullet through my barrel. I didn't do anything but continue drifting. I was beyond feeling any more fear. The thought of the bullet striking me was not upsetting at all. At least my painful struggle would end.

The river widened again, taking me away from the Indian who fired at me. I became aware that my senses were being revived by some kind of potent odor. I realized that the barrel I had been clinging to was full of whiskey. The Indian's bullet had made an opening for the golden liquid to ooze out.

I remembered Uncle Henry coming into the cabin after doing chores on a cold morning. He would take a sip from his stone jug, saying there was nothing like a little sip to take the chill out of a man's bones. After we joined the Mormons, where whiskey drinking was discouraged but not prohibited—that came many years later—Uncle Henry used the jug less often, but still, on those very cold winter mornings, he continued taking a sip now and then to keep the chill out of his bones.

If anybody ever needed warming up, I did. I turned the barrel until I found the bullet hole, put my blue lips against the hole, and started sucking. After the initial sting went away, I was able to gulp down quite a lot. Gradually a warm dullness filled my body. The Indians had good reason to call it firewater. I didn't feel cold anymore.

It seemed like an eternity before the sun finally set and darkness covered the land like a protective blanket. Even though my mind and body were deadened beyond feeling by the cold and the drink, I knew I must get out of the water soon or I would die.

Because the Indians couldn't see me now, if I could find a place to hide, now would be the time to go ashore. I tried to kick my legs to push toward shore, but they were so deadened that I couldn't tell if they were kicking or just floating motionless in the water.

After a while, I became aware that I was tipping to the side, as if something was picking up my feet. I held tighter to the barrel, unable to figure out for a few seconds what was happening.

Suddenly I realized that I was washing ashore in shallow water at the upper end of a small island. The sandy bottom had caused the tipping motion by pushing my legs out behind me.

Using all the strength I could muster, I crawled out onto the still warm sand, taking the barrel with me. I didn't have any particular reason for hanging onto it. It was just that I had been clinging to it for so long that it just didn't occur to me to let go.

I don't know how long I lay in the sand, but the feeling gradually returned to my body. I was shivering again, the sand was cold now, and I longed for the warmth of the sun. I looked to the eastern sky; it was now gray. Soon it would be light, and with the light would come the searching eyes of the Indians.

In the middle of the island, well above the water line, was a huge pile of driftwood, white-gray cottonwood logs, like a huge pile of dinosaur bones in the gray dawn. I had no intention of getting back into the water, so I crawled into the tangle of trees—over, under, and around the logs, until I was in total darkness again. I felt my way into somewhat of an opening, a den, where I figured there would be room to stretch out and relax. It had a sandy floor.

Suddenly there was a movement. I heard it. Instinctively, I sprang to my feet, smashing my head and neck on the log above.

"White or Injun?" whispered a threatening voice.

"White," was my immediate response, noticing a hint of familiarity in the voice.

"From the boat wreck?"

"Yeah," I answered, trying to recall the voice.

It was quiet for a moment, then I remembered.

"Benny," I shouted. "Benny Potts, the pilot. How did you get here?"

"The same way you did. Are you Dan, the kid who used to come into the wheelhouse?"

I told him I was, and he reached out, touched me, took my arm, and shook it with a warm greeting.

"Is anybody else still alive?" he asked.

"Don't know. You're the first one I've seen or heard since dark."

We talked about the collision, the scalpings, the cold water, and our prospects of escape until the morning sunshine began to filter light and warmth down through the tangle of logs. We had no idea if there were any Indians around, and neither one of us wanted to go outside for a look. We decided to wait until dark, make a raft out of dead logs, then shove off in the night. By the next morning, we would be many miles from here, and hopefully out of danger.

Chapter 18

Our hiding place gradually warmed up with the morning sun. After a few hours, I was warm again for the first time since the wreck.

Both of us were hungry and sleepy, but since there was nothing to eat, we stretched out to sleep. The next thing I remembered was Benny shaking me.

"Injuns out there!" he whispered.

As I came to my senses, I could hear the splashing of horses' hooves in shallow water and men's voices in a language I couldn't understand. They were Indians, all right.

"Did you cover your trail across the sand before crawling in here?" asked Benny, his voice still in a whisper.

It had never occurred to me to cover my trail. In dragging myself across the sand, I'd probably left a trail an Indian could spot a mile away. I felt so stupid. It was bad enough, setting myself up for capture, but I had also uncovered Benny's hiding place in the process. I wished I had drowned and never found this place.

"That's all right," comforted Benny, sensing my regrets. He picked up a stout, three-foot club.

"Guess we better be get'n ready for 'm."

The Indians didn't come right in after us as we thought they would. We could hear a lot of what sounded like laughing, boasting, arguing, and more hooves plashing through the water. More Indians were coming. It sounded like the entire party of thirty or so braves were at the entrance to our log fortress.

I couldn't figure out why Benny and I would draw such a large crowd when undoubtedly there were other white men hiding here and there up and down the river. Benny couldn't figure it out either.

Then I knew. The whiskey barrel, of course. The Indians were drinking the firewater. They'd get their scalps later. Boy, was I thankful I'd dragged that barrel ashore.

We hoped that if the Indians got drunk enough, we could sneak out during the night, lash a couple of logs together, and be on our way.

Suddenly Benny was silent. After a moment he whispered, "Listen."

For a minute I couldn't hear anything except the lapping of the nearby river against the sandy shore, and the occasional shriek of a drunken Indian. Then I heard the sound that had disturbed Benny, the unmistakable rubbing of naked skin against the rough surface of cottonwood logs. One or more of the Indians was coming after us.

Each of us picked up a stout club. Then Benny moved quietly in the direction of the sounds, stationing himself beside the opening where the Indians would most likely enter our den. The midday sun gave us just enough light to see what we were doing.

Apparently the Indians found it too difficult to crawl among the logs with bows or rifles, because the first brave to crawl into view was armed with only a knife.

He had time to yell once before Benny batted him senseless with a club. All was quiet for a few minutes. Then we could hear the retreat of other bodies. We had won the first round.

Benny handed me the Indian's knife. Except for moccasins and a loincloth, the brave was naked. His lifeless body was smeared abundantly with red, black, and white paint.

All was quiet for a long time—too quiet. Benny was the first to smell smoke. The Indians were setting our log jam on fire.

It took a few minutes for the significance of the smoke to set in. Our log fortress would make a campfire that would light up the evening sky for miles. If we didn't want to be roasted, we could give ourselves up to the Indians for torture and scalping. The situation was desperate. There didn't seem to be anything we could do to avoid capture. I almost laughed at the unusual turn of events. The night before, I had nearly died of cold. Now I was facing death by fire.

We became silent as the smell of the smoke became stronger. There wasn't much brush mixed with the logs, so I guessed it would take a while for the blaze to really get going, but once the big logs caught fire, the heat would force the Indians to take their whiskey barrel to the other side of the island.

I began to wonder what it would be like burning to death. I had heard that burning was a lot worse than freezing. I thought back on the time I had burned my hand on a hot horseshoe, or what it was like working under a blazing summer sun. I remembered the fever I had with smallpox.

I was eight at the time I had the smallpox. I thought my skin was going to burst into flames. I remembered how good it felt when my mother put her cool hand on my forehead. She had been dead for four years now. Maybe I would see her today, after I was dead too, if there really was life after death. I figured there was an afterlife, like the scriptures said, but today it appeared I would find out for sure.

I thought back again on the heat of the smallpox fever. It was still cool in our den under the logs . . .

Smallpox. Benny had talked about it on the river, how many thousands of Indians had died of the disease two summers ago. All the Indians on the river knew about smallpox, and all were terrified of it . . .

I picked up the knife that had belonged to the dead Indian. Holding the point firmly against my arm, I twisted the butt in a circular motion, pressing the point harder and harder against my skin. When I pulled the knife away, there was a red dot on my arm.

I did the same thing on my cheek. Benny wasn't paying any attention to what I was doing.

"Benny," I called. "I think I'm coming down with the pox. Look at my cheek."

"Looks like a pimple," he said after looking at my cheek for a moment. He turned away, not interested in my problem, and not caring why I would be interested in a little red spot at a time like this.

I quickly made another red dot on my other cheek. It was painful, but that didn't matter. I made about a dozen more red dots with the knife before I asked Benny to look at me again.

He responded exactly as I hoped he would.

"Hell, you really do have the pox! But wait a minute . . ."

He was wondering how the spots could have appeared so quickly, without any fever or symptoms. I held the knife point against my arm and made another red spot, then asked, "Do you think them Injuns will dare scalp me if they think I have the pox?"

There wasn't any time to waste. Benny grabbed the knife and began making more pox marks on me, on the backs of my hands, on my neck and chest, and on my feet. It hurt, but he made sure that every piece of exposed skin had red spots.

The Indians hadn't expected us to come out so soon. They didn't even see us until Benny started yelling.

"Pox, pox, pox," he shouted, as he stood up among the logs, holding me in his arms. "Help me, the boy has the pox. Please help."

Every Indian knew what pox meant without having to discuss the matter. Each recognized the red dots and the shivering. And each one knew the dreaded smallpox could kill more Indians in a few weeks than famines, grizzly bears, and white man's bullets could kill in years.

Within seconds the Indians were scrambling for their horses. They were in such a hurry to get away, they even left their firewater behind. Most didn't even bother to look back as they plunged into the water.

Three days later, Benny and I were picked up by a steamer called the *Rocky Mountain Belle*, headed for Fort Benton. Benny would rather have been picked up by a boat heading downstream, but not me. I was anxious to find out if Ike was still alive, and if he was, to resume our journey to the Rocky Mountains.

Chapter 19

"When I came to the Rocky Mountains, by damn, there were no lawmen to tell us what to do, no tax men to charge us for doing it, and no preachers or high-falutin' women to tell a man that his pleasure wasn't right.

"In those days, a man knew why he was in the mountains: to wade up a creek and think that no man—no white man—had ever been there before. We gave names to the creeks, valleys, ridges, and peaks. Everything was new, fresh, and innocent as God made it. A man felt like Adam in the Garden of Eden—all the world newborn, ready to be looked at, touched, smelled.

"When spring seeped into the mountains, and the streams were jammed with beaver, I wouldn't have traded places with God himself."

I was listening to George Franklin Chesterfield III, more commonly known as Beaver George. We were riding along a grassy hillside overlooking the Madison River. I had joined up with George in Fort Benton. We were both headed for the Snake River country, George to trap beaver, and me to find Ike.

When I arrived in Fort Benton and began asking about Ike's whereabouts, I learned that he had left a few days earlier with a group of prospectors headed for Snake River country. I suppose Ike figured I had been killed in the boiler explosion down the river and didn't see any need to wait for me.

"Every summer," continued Beaver George, "we'd all gather for a rendezvous at Pierre's Hole on the Green River, or in Cache Valley.

Sometimes over a hundred trappers would show up, and lots of Injuns too. Ashley and his men would bring trade goods and supplies all the way from St. Louis so they could rob us blind tradin' us out of our furs. In '30 I brought in just over three hundred pelts, worth eighteen hundred dollars. Could have bought me a hundred-acre farm in Missouri. But after three weeks of tradin', gamblin', drinkin', and fightin', all I had to show for my year's work was enough powder, balls, and traps to get through another season.

"Ashley would buy 100 percent corn whiskey for a dollar a gallon. Then he'd water each gallon down with three gallons of creek water, flavor it up with tea, tobacco, ginger, red peppers, and molasses. He'd sell it to us for a dollar a quart. He never seemed to run out.

"As the rendezvous progressed, he just kept adding water to make sure he didn't run out. Nobody cared, though. We were eatin' fat cow and havin' shinin' times."

Beaver George pulled up his big bay horse and looked back at me. He had a strong, athletic build but was a little too fat in the middle. While the top of his head was bald, the sides and back bristled with curly black hair. He had a short, black beard, rosy cheeks, and a quick smile.

He wore an elk skin shirt, grease-stained in front, with fringe of varying lengths on the sleeves and around the bottom. As he turned to look at me, there was a faraway look in his eyes.

"But those times are gone. The beaver are mostly trapped out, except in a few hard-to-reach places, like where we're headed now. The dandies in the cities don't like beaver hats anymore; they've switched to silk, so beaver ain't worth much anyhow. The old hosses that warn't scalped have switched to huntin' buffler or guidin' wagons, if they haven't left the country altogether.

"The mountains are now crowded with a lot of people who hadn't ought to be there—gold diggers, soldier boys, sod busters, and cowboys. Used to be a feller could trap all spring and never run into anybody, 'cept maybe a few Injuns. Now when I head into the mountains, seems like I run into somebody every week or two—a feller no longer has room to breathe. But nothin' I can do about it; that's the way the stick floats."

He pulled his horse's head around and started moving again. Our little black packhorse followed behind, loaded with a crosscut saw, twelve eight-pound beaver traps, and one bear trap. George said the bear trap worked just as good on Injuns as it did on bears.

I had spent all the money that was sewed into the lining of my trousers to buy a horse, a saddle, and a rifle—a .50 caliber Hawken muzzle loader with a ram rod, ball screw, bullet mold, wadding, powder, and lead.

For food supplies we had salt, coffee, and tobacco for smoking the peace pipe. When I suggested we take along some flour, sugar, beans, and bacon, George said he didn't see any sense loading ourselves down with a lot of stuff we didn't need.

"I don't travel with pig eaters, anyway," he said. "Pig meat makes a man soft and fat, whereas buffler keeps a man lean and strong. Plenty of buffler where we're going. Elk and deer too. Won't be any problem keepin' our bellies full."

Just before we left Fort Benton, George took me to the tepee village near the fort and traded away my shirt, trousers, and boots for a buckskin shirt, leggings, and moccasins. When he saw that I hesitated to get into the new clothing because they smelled so strongly of smoke, he explained that the smoky smell was evidence that the merchandise was good. The reason for the smoky smell was that the leather had been cut from the upper part of an old tepee cover. This leather had been softened from its long exposure to buffeting winds and waterproofed by the smoke of many cookfires. It didn't stretch or sag, either.

It didn't take long until I was used to the smoky smell of my clothes. I was proud of the new outfit. I looked just like an authentic mountain man.

In addition to the clothing, Beaver George had one of the squaws sew me up a leather pouch to be worn on my belt. George called it my possibles bag. Inside was a flint and steel for starting fires, some jerked buffalo meat, a small horn flask of beaver scent, salt, trinkets for trading, and tobacco for smoking the peace pipe.

"With that bag and your rifle, you can go into the hills and stay a year or more, eat'n fat cow," he said.

Chapter 20

We left Fort Benton around the first of July. Because we were traveling light, I had hopes of quickly overtaking Ike and the prospectors. But George had other plans. He was not in any kind of hurry.

First, there was concern over the horses. For months they had been grazing themselves fat in the lush green pastures around Fort Benton. Their feet, as well as their muscles, had grown soft from the easy life.

Even though there was a blacksmith in Fort Benton, Beaver George refused to have the horses shod. He said that an unshod horse with properly hardened hooves could go anywhere a shod horse could go. On the other hand, he said the protected hooves of a shod horse never get tough enough.

"If you throw a shoe when you're trying to outdistance some hostile Injuns," he said, "or if you're crossing a rocky divide and lose a shoe, you've got a lame horse in a hurry."

Because of our horses' soft feet, we started out traveling only a few miles a day. George spent considerable time carving the hooves down the desired shape and size with his knife. Occasionally we'd scatter coals from the fire over the ground and lead the horses back and forth through the hot coals. This made the soft, moist hooves dry and hard.

At night we'd picket our horses on dry, rocky hillsides. But if a horse's hooves started to crack from being too dry, we'd picket that particular animal in a marshy area for a few nights. After about two weeks the hooves were properly conditioned and the animals didn't show any signs of tenderness, even on the rockiest of trails.

Once the horses were ready, Beaver George turned his attentions to me. Said he didn't want to be partners with a greenhorn. First it was the old Hawken rifle. He made me practice shooting and reloading from every possible position—standing, sitting, kneeling, lying down, standing in a rushing stream, or mounted on a horse. He showed me how to use a forked stick as a rest to steady the barrel when shooting long range.

George made sure I knew how to build fires without matches, first with the flint and steel method, then by bow drill. He said white men usually built big fires that advertised their whereabouts to everyone within ten miles, friend or foe. He showed me how to maintain a small, efficient Indian fire by arranging the firewood like spokes of a wagon wheel, the fire in the center. When the fire got low, one merely pushed some of the sticks closer toward the middle. Willow and cottonwood were the best fuel when one didn't want a lot of smoke to give away his location.

At night, one of us slept on each side of the fire. We took turns keeping it burning because we didn't have any blankets. When I complained about this, saying that we would sleep much better if we had brought blankets along, George said that was the very reason he had not brought blankets.

He said I had to learn to sleep like a mountain man, an ear on the ground and one eye open. He explained that even the friendliest of Indians would run off with your horses if you gave them half a chance, and they would usually try for the horses when you were asleep. Unfriendly Indians might want a little hair too.

One night as we were sitting by the fire I noticed an empty knife sheath sewed into the lower portion of George's right legging. I asked him about it and he explained that Indians sometimes carried concealed knives on the sides of their leggings. He guessed that the first few to do this probably had an advantage when they were taken captive by enemies, but the practice had become so common that now captors always searched leggings for a hidden knife.

"So that's why you don't carry a knife in your leggings anymore," I said, thinking I understood why the sheath was empty.

"No," he said. "That's why I have the empty sheath."

"What do you mean?" I didn't understand what he was talking about.

"When people notice that empty sheath, as you did, they think there is no knife in my leggings, and they don't think to look any further."

He reached to the inside of his other legging, and through a small break in the leather stitching, retrieved a double-edged knife with an elk horn handle. The blade was about six inches long.

"Let this be a lesson to you, kid," he warned. "When you have the drop on an enemy, always figure he's armed until you've searched every inch of him."

George had many clever tricks up his sleeve that I began to learn as he taught me to trap.

The furs wouldn't be in their prime until fall so we didn't trap much, but we did do just enough so I could catch on.

The trapping routine was as follows. We would ride along a sidehill above a small stream, watching for the stretches of still water that indicated the presence of a beaver dam. We would tie our horses maybe a hundred feet downstream from the dam, set the trap, then wade up the middle of the stream to the dam, letting the running water carry our scent away from the beavers. George would set the trap in the shallow water near the dam and secure it to a stick, which he pushed into the mud. Then he would pour smelly black liquid from the horn flask onto the end of the stick. He called the stuff castoreum, which he had extracted from the scrotums of male beavers he had trapped. When he finished with the trap and castoreum, we retraced our tracks back downstream to the horses.

When smelling the castoreum, a beaver would swim over to investigate. He would stand on his hind legs in the shallow water to sniff the end of the stick. Then almost invariably he would step into the trap.

Once trapped, the beaver would swim for deeper water. The heavy trap would pull the beaver down and drown it. George said that if a beaver was trapped on dry ground it would sometimes chew its leg off in order to get free.

Chapter 21

It was late August when we approached the headwaters of the Missouri River. We had been following a tributary stream called the Wisdom River that divided into many smaller streams in a large valley. In front of us we could see the snowcapped peaks of the Bitter Root Mountains, the continental divide. Beyond the peaks lay the Snake River country, where I hoped to find Ike.

Beaver George and I were riding up a little valley with scattered ponderosa pines on either side and willows, alder, and aspen in the bottom, where the small stream wound its way from beaver pond to beaver pond. It was a winding valley, and we couldn't see very far ahead. It was early afternoon; the deep blue of the Rocky Mountain sky made a sharp contrast to the scattered puffy white clouds. The sun was warm but not uncomfortable, thanks to a fresh breeze coming gently down from the mountains ahead of us.

Suddenly George pulled his horse in and, with a wave of his hand, motioned for me to do the same. He rose in his stirrups to get a better look up the trail. After about a minute, he quietly dismounted and again motioned for me to do the same.

"Buffler up ahead," he whispered as we tied the horses to aspen trees. "Smell 'm?"

I hadn't smelled anything, and as I sniffed with renewed interest, all I could detect was a little pine, dry grass, and horse sweat. But I supposed George knew what he was talking about as we crept up the sidehill to where a heavier growth of pine trees provided good cover. We had left everything behind except our rifles.

I followed George along the hill for about half an hour. Every few steps he'd stop and scan the valley ahead. He seemed confident there were buffalo in the area, that it was just a matter of time until we discovered them. I still hadn't smelled anything.

Finally he waved me to come up beside him. As I did so, he pointed to a flat grassy area at the head of a beaver pond. It was surrounded by a thick willow brush. Suddenly a buffalo walked quietly out of the willows at the upper end of the meadow. It was followed by a calf. As the cow began to graze, five more cows and two young bulls emerged from the brush. Four of the cows had calves.

Carefully we moved behind some serviceberry bushes as the animals began to graze. The breeze was blowing down the valley, so there was no danger they would smell us.

My mouth began to water as I thought about fresh hump roast sizzling over our evening fire. We were only about a hundred yards away, so I knew there would be no trouble dropping at least one of the animals. I had already killed two buffalo and an elk with my .50 caliber Hawken rifle and was becoming very confident in my ability to acquire meat. I didn't figure there was much more George could teach me about hunting.

As I raised my rifle to my shoulder to take aim, he reached out and pushed the barrel aside without taking his eyes off the buffalo.

"What's the matter?" I whispered.

"How many do you think we can get?" he asked, without turning his head.

"Maybe two," I responded. "If we both shoot at the same time, and neither one of us misses.

"Any more?" he asked.

"Don't see how. As soon as we shoot, the rest will charge into the willows and we'll probably never see them again."

"If you'll sit still a few minutes, and let me do the shooting, I'll show you how to get five or six."

Impossible, I thought, but I lowered the rifle to my lap. He explained that the chain of command in small herds of buffalo this time of year was very distinct. There was a boss cow, a second in command, a third, and so on. He said buffalo liked to follow a leader, and if the hunter knew the order of leadership—the pecking order—and could shoot down the leaders fast enough, a herd could be kept in confusion until a large number had been shot down.

I wasn't sure I understood what he was talking about. I could sort of follow the reasoning, but I still didn't believe the animals would do anything but run for cover once the shooting began.

George watched the herd for a long time. Apparently he was observing which buffalo moved out of the way of others as they grazed in the meadow. George was taking so long in his observations that I was beginning to worry that maybe there wouldn't be any buffalo meat roasting over the fire. I was afraid the buffalo would scatter into the brush at any moment and we wouldn't even be able to get a shot off.

Finally George nodded that he was ready. He whispered that the cow to the left, the one facing us, was the big boss. The one lying down near the smaller of the two bulls was number two. Number three was grazing near where they had come out of the brush, and so on. He said that when he began firing, I was to do the reloading as quickly as possible, as he alternated firing his rifle and mine.

He picked up his Hawken and was about to take aim, when all of the buffalo suddenly broke into a run toward the lower end of the meadow. The number one cow was in front. George took a bead on her and fired. Nothing happened for a moment, but soon her front legs buckled and down she went. The rest of the herd stopped with her; they were in the middle of the meadow. The second cow, the new leader, had barely emerged from the herd and was heading toward the far side of the meadow when George fired again. The second cow went down. The herd was milling about in utter confusion.

George's shot at the third cow was a little off the mark. The second shot brought her down. By that time, the herd was at the edge of the meadow. George was able to drop one of the bulls before the rest disappeared into the willows.

"I wonder what spooked them," said George, more to himself than to me, as he picked up his rifle and headed down the hill.

George marched down the hill, across the stream, and up through the meadow, directly to the dead bull. Taking his butcher knife out of his pocket, he knelt down and quickly removed the testicles. He took a huge, tearing bite out of one, while offering the other to me. Staring in amazement, I declined his offer.

"Nothing like fresh balls to give a man strength," he said, as he took another bite.

I'd heard stories of how Indians and mountain men ate various parts of animals raw—brains, intestines, liver, heart, and testicles—but I'd never taken such talk seriously. Now I did.

We removed our buckskin shirts so they wouldn't get bloody and set to work skinning the buffalo, removing the tongues and a huge hump roast for our supper. We planned on drying the tongues and taking them with us. Smoked tongues were worth fifteen cents a pound in Fort Benton. The hides were worth about eight dollars each.

I returned to the horses while George continued skinning. By the time I returned, he had finished two of the animals and was well into the third.

I unsaddled the horses, turned them out to graze, and built a blazing fire. Using a large flat stone as a hammer, I pounded a forked stick into the ground on each side of the fire, then began roasting the hump roast on a green willow spit.

While the roast was cooking, I cut a large pile of willow sticks. We needed lots of pegs to stake out the hides while we fleshed them, and we needed to build racks for drying meat and tongues. I was just finishing when George dragged the last hide into camp.

"We'll have to get another horse if we don't want to cache the hides," he said, as he dropped to the ground near the fire.

Pulling his skinning knife from his belt, he sliced off a fist-sized hunk of meat from the partially cooked roast and shoved an entire piece in his mouth, grunting with satisfaction as he did so. I sat down across the fire from him and carved off a chunk for myself, sprinkled it with a little salt from my possibles bag, and started eating. It was rich, juicy, and delicious.

We sat around the fire for a long time, gorging ourselves, not saying much, just enjoying the feast.

I had just about decided to go over to the stream for a drink when I was startled by a strange voice at the edge of the willows.

"Thanks for shoot'n and skinn'n our buffler for us," said a high-pitched, breathy voice. "Mighty kind of ya, yes-sir-ee."

I looked up into the barrel of a .60 caliber Sharps buffalo gun. Behind the gun stood the foulest looking man I had ever seen. He was an older man with gray hair and a white beard, or what should have been white. Around and below the mouth, it was brown with slobbered tobacco juice. In addition, it was greasy—cluttered with bits of tobacco, food, and who knows what else. It was a revolting site. I was surprised I hadn't smelled him coming.

He was of medium height and rather thick around the middle. His eyes were big and protruding, like those of a frog. They looked as if they would pop out if someone gave him a hard bear hug. His eyes and his lips looked wet and sticky. His wrinkled wool pants were caked with dry mud and old blood. His buckskin shirt was black with old grease.

Next to him stood a younger man, similarly dressed, and just as filthy. His hair was brown and matted like a wet pile of manure. Tangled strings of hair hung past his shoulders to the middle of his back. His eyes were big and froggy, just like those of the older man. I assumed the two to be father and son.

The eyes of the younger man were constantly blinking as he stared at me and George. Like his father, he had a .60 caliber Sharps trained on us. He held the weapon in his right hand, leaving his left hand free to pluck bristly black hairs from his beard, a nervous habit he seemed unaware of. The results of the habit were bare patches on his chin and cheeks, making him look as if he had a severe case of ringworm.

"My name is Henry Pottsmouth. This is my son, James," said the old man.

"Headin' back to Missouri from prospectin'. Injuns stole our horses and gear in the Snake River country. Dirty, thiev'n savages."

"Put those buffler shooters down and have some supper," said George, in a voice so calm and quiet that I looked at him in surprise. He hadn't moved from his relaxed position by the fire. He was still chewing on a piece of meat.

"Got pressing business back in Missouri," continued the old man, ignoring George's invitation. "Those horses and hides of yours ought to just about pay our steamboat fare back. Not that I'm a thief. Just unfortunate circumstances forcing me to take what I've got to have."

"Don't have to explain to me, old man," said George, with a friendliness unwarranted by the situation. "I'd do the same thing in your shoes. When a man loses his outfit in this country, he's got to get another."

George reached out and cut another chunk of meat from the dripping roast and shoved it in his mouth, showing no concern for the two rifles pointed at us.

"Can I shoot one of them, Pa?" said the boy.

George looked him in the eyes. "If you do, you'll have to scrape those hides by yourself," he responded, his mouth still full of buffalo meat. "If these hides aren't fleshed out, they'll rot on the way to Benton. Me and the boy will clean 'm all up for you by tomorrow night; that is, if you're not going to shoot us. I don't hanker to the idea of slaving over green hides all day so I can be shot at sundown. Just as soon be shot in the morning and miss the work on the hides. Give me your word that you'll let us go when you leave, and we'll do you a first class job on them hides."

"Not a bad idea," said the old man after thinking on the matter for a few minutes.

"But, Pa," said the boy in an annoyed tone. "You said—"

"Nevermind what I said," replied the old man with more than a little sharpness. "The sooner we get those hides cleaned and get on our way, the better off we'll be. By the time they walk to Fort Benton, we'll already be in St. Louis."

"It's a deal, then?" asked George in the same friendly voice.

"Do a good, fast job on those hides, and we'll let you go," responded the old man.

"Now that that's settled, sit down and have a little supper. Then we'll get to work on the hides," said George to the old man.

Then George said to me, "You're lucky, thanks to me, kid, that you're still alive. Now get those pegs ready so we can stretch out the skins."

But when he reached out to slice off another piece of meat, the old man had another idea.

"Hold up a minute," the old man ordered. He said to his son, "Get the knives and search them for hidden weapons. I'll keep 'm covered."

As James came close, I noticed that he smelled as bad as he looked. He collected our guns and knives and returned them to his father.

"Did you check the leggings?"

"Yeah," said James. "The big one had a knife sheath by his right ankle, but there was nothing in it."

George and I began to stretch out the hides while the two newcomers finished off our roast.

George joked openly with the two thieves and acted as if they were better friends to him than I was. They hadn't found his hidden knife, but I wasn't sure if he intended to use it or not. I personally didn't put much stock in their promise to let us go when the hides were finished, but good old George didn't seem to have a worry in the world.

"After these fellows take off," he said to me, loud enough so they could hear too, "I think we'll just jerk a bunch of this meat, then hike over the mountains into the Snake River country. I know some friendly

Shoshones who'll fix us up with a new outfit. We'll trap around there this fall. Then early next spring we can return to Benton, hopefully with enough hides and furs to buy your passage back to the states."

"Want us to smoke the tongues too?" George asked the old man. "They're worth fifteen cents a pound in Benton."

"Yeah, and if you keep being so helpful, maybe we'll leave your traps behind."

"Thank you kindly," answered George with a smile, as he resumed his labors on one of the hides.

Chapter 22

When it was too dark to work any longer, the old man, gun in hand, followed us back to the fire, where James was tending another sizzling hump roast.

For the first time since the newcomers' arrival, I had time to sit back and ponder what was happening. I didn't know if George was going to try anything with his hidden knife, but if he didn't, I fully intended to attempt an escape during the night and hide out somewhere in the woods. I had no intention of trusting the two thieves to let us go after the hides were fleshed out.

As I thought back on the events of the past few hours, I suddenly remembered the two men saying they had been prospecting in the Snake River country. I had a sick feeling in the depth of my stomach as the thought occurred to me that perhaps these men were the prospectors my friend Ike had been traveling with.

"Were there others in your prospecting party?" I asked, with more than a little reluctance, fearing the worst for Ike.

"Naw, just us and the nigger," answered the old man.

"The big fellow that was hanging around Fort Benton?" asked George.

"Friend of yours?" asked the old man.

"No," said George. "Just saw him hanging around. Looked stronger than a bull, easy to remember a man like that."

"What happened to him?" I asked, trying to sound indifferent, fearing they might not tell the truth if they sensed my true concern for Ike.

"Should I tell 'im, Pa?" asked James as he began to laugh, an uncontrollable belly laugh, almost hysterical. It was sickening.

"Don't see anything funny," said the old man. "The nigger saved our lives. That's nothin' to laugh about." But then he started to laugh too.

"What happened to him?" I asked again, after the laughter had quieted. I was looking at the ground, not wanting them to see the growing rage in my eyes.

"Dumbest nigger we ever saw, wasn't he, Pa?"

The old man nodded, then explained how the three men with their horses and supplies had been driven up a small canyon by six or eight Indians.

"When we got to the end of the canyon and the horses couldn't go any farther, we tied them up in an aspen grove and began firing back at the Indians. Big Ike was a good fighter, fearless and strong. A good shot too; he wounded a couple of them bucks.

"When it looked like they was about to close in on us, I told Ike to keep firing while James and me snuck out the back, climbed up on the cliffs, and started a crossfire. I told him that if he could hold 'm off till we got on top, we'd be able to pick 'm off like flies and drive 'm off."

The old man and James began laughing again. I didn't see anything very funny. Neither did George.

"When we got to the top of the cliff," the old man continued, barely able to control the laughing, "we could see more Injuns coming up the valley. There was no way we could lick that many, even with a crossfire.

"Instead of shooting and showing the Injuns where we was, we decided to put as much distance as possible between us and them. Good ole Ike kept holdin' 'm off, thinkin' all the time we was climbin' the cliff. Probably still hold'n 'm back, wondering why we is taking so long."

They started laughing again.

I looked over at George, thinking now would be a good time to use the concealed knife—while they were laughing. To my total amazement, George was stretched out flat among the green hides, eyes closed, snoring.

I was overwhelmed with sudden nausea as adrenaline began to surge through my veins. I knew for sure that George was up to something, that his friendliness to the two thieves was a ruse, that he had some kind of plan. First of all, it was summer and he had been sleeping without the benefit of blanket or robe. Why had he suddenly buried himself in buffalo robes? Second, I had been on the trail with him for more than a month and knew that he didn't snore. Third, James hadn't found George's hidden knife in the legging.

I wasn't sure what George was up to, but I knew I'd better be alert and ready to help whenever he made his move.

I moved closer to the fire and asked for a piece of meat.

"Should I give him some?" James asked his father.

"Gotta keep his strength up if he's gonna scrape hides tomorrow."

James cut off a chunk of meat and tossed it in the dirt in front of me. I felt like picking it up and throwing it in his face, but I knew it would be best to keep cool and let George do whatever it was he was planning to do. In a matter-of-fact manner, I picked up the piece of meat, brushed off the dirt, and bit off a small piece.

James and the old man feasted for a long time while George appeared to be sleeping. Apparently they hadn't had much to eat for several days. James finally spoke, "Pa, I really don't think you ought to let them go."

"Shut up!" ordered the old man.

"You aren't going to give them their guns back, are you?"

"I said shut up! And go fetch a rope and tie them up. I don't aim to stay awake all night holding a gun on them."

I felt a sudden panic at the thought of being tied up. That would ruin our chances of escaping.

"If you tie us up, our hands will be too sore to work on the hides tomorrow," I protested.

"If you can't work, I'll let James shoot you," responded the old man. Then to James, "Hurry and tie them up."

"But, Pa," said James, "we don't have any rope."

"They've got some, stupid. Find it, and tie up the other one too."

My heart was thundering in my chest. Of course I was concerned about saving my own neck, but more than that, I wanted revenge on the two strangers for what they had done to Ike. I couldn't let them tie me up, not now. I had to do something before it was too late. And if they tied up George, his plan, whatever it was, wouldn't work.

It was dark now and the ropes for the horses and pack saddle were lying in a clump of grass beside a tree about thirty feet from the fire. I had no intention of telling them where the ropes were.

After a few minutes of searching, James still could not find the ropes. The old man pointed his rifle at my face and said, "Tell me where the ropes are, or I'll . . ."

"They're over here under the buffalo robes," said George in a sleepy voice. "The boy is right. We'll be pretty sore tomorrow if you tie us up." He yawned.

"If you think I'm going to stay awake all night holding this gun so you two can be more comfortable . . ."

"Suit yourself," said George, putting his hand over his mouth to suppress another yawn.

James was already rummaging through the pile of buffalo robes, looking for the rope. In the flickering light of the campfire he couldn't see very well, so he was mostly feeling his way through the robes. I wondered what George was up to. He knew as I did that there were no ropes in the buffalo hides.

It wasn't long before I heard a muffled clanking of steel against steel. Then James let out the most terrifying scream I had ever heard. In an instant I realized what had happened.

While the thieves and I had been eating, George had somehow managed to set the bear trap. He had placed it among the buffalo robes where James had been feeling for the ropes. The steel-toothed trap was now clamped tightly on James's wrist.

During the moment of surprise—when the jaws of the trap clanked shut on James's wrist, and while the old man and I looked toward James to see what had happened—George hadn't taken his eyes off the old man.

At the right instant George sat up, the buffalo robe falling to his lap. His right hand darted behind his head, then forward in a swift throwing motion. The firelight reflected for an instant on the double-edged blade of the knife with the elk horn handle.

The old man saw the reflection too, but his rifle was pointed at me instead of at George. Even though his reflexes were fast, by the time the rifle was swinging toward George, the knife had buried itself to the handle at the base of the old man's neck, just below the Adam's apple. His death wasn't instantaneous, however, and George's scramble for safety wasn't quick enough to get completely out of the way of the exploding .60 caliber cannon. The big lead ball smashed a gaping hole through the top of George's left foot, as the old man fell forward on his face, dead.

When he saw his father fall, young James forgot about the pain from the bear trap. Furiously, he began groping among the hides for his dropped rifle. I knew I should tackle him before he could get the gun, but my body seemed detached from my mind. I couldn't move. I could only watch him groping among the black hides, while poor, wounded George was attempting to untangle himself from his own robe.

Again there was the clank of steel, not as loud as before, but just as distinct. James yelled again as he caught his left hand in the jaws of an eight-pound beaver trap.

"Keep squirming around. There's two more traps in there," laughed George, unable to resist an opportunity for humor in what appeared to me to be a very humorless situation.

George's warning had an immediate effect on James, who suddenly froze with the fear of getting caught in another trap. He just crouched there, whimpering his defeat, afraid to move.

I went over to help George. His foot was bleeding badly, but he was in good spirits over our victory. He lay on his back and put the wounded foot high in the air. Soon the bleeding slowed down to a gentle oozing.

"Wish we had some whiskey. Good for cleaning wounds, and I'll soon be needing some pain reliever," said George. After washing his foot the best I could, I cut a strip off the end of one of the saddle blankets, rinsed it in the creek, and made a good bandage.

As I did so, George preached me a little sermon.

"I hope you'll never forget the lesson you learned tonight," he began. "The Bible's right when it says to love your enemies. Did you notice how nice I was to them? That's why they wasn't watching me very close and gave me the chance I needed to take care of things. You got to love your enemies, boy. Otherwise they'll never give you a chance to get back at them." He laughed out loud. Then he said seriously, "That old man wasn't going to let us out of here alive."

The next morning we sent James on his way, unarmed, but with all the meat he could carry. We covered the old man with rocks. Thanks to him I knew what had happened to Ike. I figured my black friend had probably been killed. Maybe, however, he had survived and was hiding out alone somewhere, but my search would have to wait until George's foot had time to heal.

Chapter 23

The bullet hole in Beaver George's foot didn't heal the way we had hoped. First there was the incessant bleeding, then the swelling, and finally the sickening smell of rotting flesh. Soon he was delirious with fever.

I offered to amputate the foot, thinking that might be the only way to save George's life, but he vehemently refused to let me do it, insisting that it was going to heal. When he lapsed into unconsciousness, I decided to amputate anyway, but by the time I had heated the knives and the crosscut saw in the hot coals, he was dead.

I buried Beaver George under a pile of rocks on a grassy hillside overlooking the Wisdom River. I wanted to put a marker on the grave but was afraid that if I did, Indians would rob the grave and scalp the body.

I was alone in a wild, dangerous land, barely sixteen years old. If I could make it safely back to Fort Benton, my horses and hides would sell for more than enough to buy riverboat passage back to St. Louis and civilization.

On the other hand, I wanted to find out what had happened to Ike. The two prospectors who, to save their own necks, had deserted him during an Indian attack, thought he was dead. I had a hard time believing that. After spending an entire winter with the escaped slave, dodging the Missouri law, I had a lot of confidence in his ability to survive. He was as strong as a bear and as cunning as a wild fox. He was a survivor in ways hard for civilized men to comprehend. In my heart I believed he was still alive, possibly alone and in hiding somewhere in the Snake River country. I decided to try to find him.

I loaded the hides, traps, and plenty of jerked buffalo meat on two of the horses and headed for Bloody Dick Creek, which flowed eastward from the Bitter Root Mountains into the southern end of the Wisdom River Valley.

Before he died, Beaver George said the two prospectors probably crossed the Continental Divide through a small pass at the headwaters of Bloody Dick Creek. He said that if I went through that same pass and turned south toward the Snake River, I would probably find the canyon where the prospectors had deserted Ike.

I has asked George how Bloody Dick Creek had earned its name. He said the first trapper to head up the little stream in search of beaver had been badly mauled by a grizzly bear. The trapper's first name was Dick. I can't remember the last name, but I'll never forget George's final comment about Bloody Dick Creek.

"Lots of mean grizzly in the area. Chewed up a number of trappers over the years. If that's the way we go, we'll have to keep a sharp lookout for grizzlies."

As I rode across the sun-bleached prairie looking ahead to the snowcapped peaks of the Bitter Root Mountains, I couldn't forget George's warning about the bears. Below the snowcapped peaks, the conifer forests were lush and thick, untouched by the saws and axes of white men. Great bear country.

I had never worried about wild animals as long as I was with George, but now that I was heading alone into a canyon where grizzly bears had a reputation of attacking people, I felt a real fear—a fear that wouldn't go away.

The sun was still shining when I reached Bloody Dick Creek. Instead of traveling as far as possible before dark, I made an early camp and gathered plenty of firewood so I could maintain a blazing fire throughout the night—a fire that would keep the bears away.

The first thing I did was tether the horses out to graze so they could eat as much as possible before dark, when I would bring them in close to the fire. Next, I gathered wood for the fire.

I didn't sleep much during the night. I was careful to keep the fire burning, as I constantly heard new and strange sounds in the nearby woods. When the dawn finally arrived, I was relieved and tired. My fears vanished with the darkness. After staking the horses out to graze, I decided to take a quick nap under the first rays of the morning sun before resuming my journey.

I don't know how long I slept, but the next thing I remember was a startled snort from one of the horses. Without lifting my head, I reached for the rifle at my side. It was gone!

I looked up into the faces of three grinning Indians, one of whom was pointing my own rifle back at my chest, while the other two tied my hands and feet together with strips of rawhide.

The three Indians started going through my gear. All three were young and athletic looking. All were dressed the same—moccasins, loincloths, and buckskin shirts. Two wore their hair in long, black braids, while the hair on the third hung loosely about his shoulders. They weren't wearing war paint. Each had a knife in his belt and a small medicine bag hanging from a loose thong about the neck. Their bows and arrows were lying in the grass. I couldn't see any horses. I assumed they were tethered off in the nearby woods. The three young braves smelled like I did, of smoke and sweat.

They chattered incessantly as they went through my belongings. I couldn't understand anything they said. I didn't know what tribe they belonged to—probably Shoshone, Bannock, or Blackfoot. All three tribes had notorious reputations for torturing prisoners. Beaver George had told me of their skill in keeping victims alive for days as they scalped, skinned, and burned various parts of the body. My young captors looked like the kind who would want to combine sport with torture. George told me about a band of Blackfeet who had skinned the bottom of the trapper's feet, stripped off his clothing, and given him a half-mile head start before they hunted him down with spears. I wondered if that was what they would do to me. I tried to wiggle my hands free, but the rawhide held tight.

One of the Indians grunted with delight when he discovered the bag of trade items. All three seemed very pleased with the mirrors, beads, knives, and other trinkets. They sat in a circle around their new treasures and began dividing them into three piles, one pile for each of the braves. Next they divided up the hides, then the traps.

Their conversation became louder and more excited when they discovered the old bear trap—the one George had used to catch James Pottsmouth by the hand. Apparently they had never seen such a big trap before. Soon they were arguing, probably trying to determine what kind of animal the big trap was supposed to catch.

Finally, one of them picked up the heavy trap with both hands and carried it over to me. I was sitting with my back propped up against a boulder. He dropped it at my feet and said something to me in his strange language. Even though I didn't understand a single word, I knew he was asking me to settle their argument.

"Bear trap," I said, slow and loud. The three braves just stared at me, not understanding what I had said. Then I thought, "Why should I bother to satisfy their curiosity when they are going to torture me to death?" Then another thought came to my mind. By keeping them interested in the trap, I was postponing my own torture.

I rolled over on my belly, pulling my hands and knees under me, not a difficult task even with my hands and feet tied. I inched along the ground, growling like a hungry bear, then raised upright on my knees, roaring like a mad grizzly. I nodded toward the trap.

The Indians were delighted with my response and gathered around the trap again in lively discussion. One of them pointed toward the mountains and the headwaters of Bloody Dick Creek as he spoke. The others nodded their agreement. Occasionally one of them would nod toward me as they spoke. I vowed that if I ever got out of this thing alive, I would immediately begin studying the Indian languages.

It wasn't long until the three warriors were on their knees trying to set the big trap. The one in the middle pulled at the steel-toothed jaws while his companions on either side tried to depress the spring-steel clamps. It didn't occur to them to use the big set screws to suppress the clamps.

After several unsuccessful attempts to set the big trap, one of the Indians untied my hands and feet while one of the others picked up my rifle, so he would be ready to gun me down in the event I tried to escape. They wanted me to show them how to set the trap. At the moment, they were more interested in trapping bears than torturing white men. I wanted to prolong that state of mind as long as possible.

Taking a lot of time, I tightened the set screws, forcing down the clamps so I could open the jaws and set the pan. Carefully I loosened the screws, then indicated to the Indians that the trap was ready.

The one with the gun grinned broadly, pointed the barrel directly at the center of my chest, and then nodded for me to step forward into the bear trap. I didn't move, hoping he was joking.

He wasn't. His expression changed to a frown. He raised the rifle to his shoulder and nodded one more time for me to step into the trap. I was beginning to believe he really intended to pull the trigger. His companions said nothing to stop him. I had to do something fast, anything.

"Grrrrr." I dropped to my knees, growling and pawing like an angry bear, just missing the trap with my right front paw, and then the left one, as I frolicked about like a crazy bear. The Indians seemed delighted with the dramatics. The one with the rifle lowered it to his waist.

It isn't easy to dance about on one's hands and knees. I was tiring quickly and had to figure out a suitable climax to my dance, one that would please the Indians without catching a hand or foot in that ugly trap.

Spotting a broken ponderosa pine bough, about the size of a horse's front leg, I grabbed it and shoved it into the jaws of the trap before the Indians could object. The steel jaws clanked loudly as they crushed the limb, shattering it into several pieces. The Indians were impressed. They chattered with enthusiasm as they again tied my hands and feet with rawhide strips.

After helping themselves to a generous portion of my buffalo jerky, they retrieved their three horses from the nearby woods. They packed the hides, trinkets, and traps on two of my horses, leaving the third with only a saddle. I concluded that they were going to take me with them. I was relieved, knowing I was not going to be tortured to death, at least not in the near future.

Before helping me onto my horse, they untied my feet, but not my hands. As soon as it was evident that we were heading upstream toward the headwaters of Bloody Dick Creek, I concluded that we were embarking on a hunt for grizzly bears.

Chapter 24

With my hands tied behind my back, I was grateful the black mare picked her footing with care along the rocky mountain trail. Two of my captors rode in front of me, the other behind. The two packhorses trailed behind him, one of them limping from a bruised front hoof.

It was midafternoon when the Indians in front pulled in their horses to inspect a fresh pile of bear droppings in the middle of the trail. I thought for a minute we might stop and look for more signs and possibly find a place to set the trap, but after only a brief stop, we continued the journey up the trail. We hadn't gone more than fifty yards when we came upon another pile of bear droppings. This time we didn't stop.

It was apparent that my Indian friends weren't interested in trapping just any bear. As our caravan continued, it was obvious they knew exactly where they were going. There was a certain bear they wanted to trap, and they knew where he hung out. I figured it was probably a grizzly, and a mean one too—maybe the same one Beaver George had told me about, the one that had attacked the white trappers.

The question that kept bothering me, though, was now that the three Indians knew how to set the trap, why had they brought me along on the bear hunt? With my hands tied, I would slow them down and be in the way. Maybe they figured they would have their sport with me while they were waiting for the bear to get caught in the trap.

My questions were answered sooner than expected. The trail emerged from an aspen grove onto a rocky side hill, overlooking a rugged alpine valley. A pocket of untamed greenery nestled among towering granite peaks. A score of white streams gushed boldly from the cliffs to feed the lush valley floor spotted with ancient ponderosa and fir trees and clumps of aspen. Willow and alder grew along the streams, and there were thick patches of wild raspberries, huckleberries, and serviceberries—paradise for bears. The snake-like streams in the open meadows bulged here and there into glassy beaver ponds. At the lower end of the valley, the meandering streams joined to rumble white and foamy through a deep rocky gorge. A brisk west wind was trying to push some heavy rain clouds over the jagged peaks.

The caravan stopped. The Indians talked excitedly for a few moments before riding down through the rocks into the valley. The packhorse was limping worse than ever and had to be coaxed through the rocks. I had a feeling we had reached the end of the trail, that this was the valley of the killer grizzly.

As we emerged from the rocks into the meadow, I began to notice plenty of bear signs—overturned rocks, rotten logs that had been torn apart, occasional droppings, and claw marks on most of the big trees. Some of the scars were level with my field of vision—and I was mounted on a horse! Big bear.

We stopped in front of a gnarled old ponderosa pine with more claw marks than any of the other trees we had passed. And some of the highest ones were fresh. That, combined with the lack of berries on the nearby bushes, was evidence that we had arrived at one of the bear's favorite hangouts. The Indians were quiet as they looked and listened for any sign of the bear.

When they were satisfied that the beast was not around, one of the Indians rode up beside me and, without warning, gave me a hard shove, knocking me out of the saddle. My hands were still tied behind my back as I tucked in my shoulder and rolled across the meadow toward the big tree.

As I was getting to my feet, one of the braves grabbed my arm and pushed me toward the tree. I didn't know whether to cooperate or resist, because I was unsure what was happening. One of the mounted braves tossed a rawhide rope to the one who was holding me. He quickly tied one end of the rope behind my back to my lashed hands. As soon as the knot was secure, he gave me a hard shove away from the tree.

There was a sickening feeling in my stomach as I watched the Indian climb up into the tree and tie the other end of the rope to one of the lower limbs. The other braves had dismounted now and were removing the bear trap from the packhorse. As they set the trap and secured the chain to a fallen log, I understood why they had brought me along on their bear hunt. I was the bait.

They covered the open jaws of the trap with pine needles and leaves. After mounting their horses, they said some things to me that I couldn't understand, all of them grinning. They were laughing as they began to ride away.

The lame packhorse, limping badly now, pulled hard against its lead rope. The Indians stopped to consider what to do with the injured animal. It didn't take long for them to make up their minds. One of them pulled the poor horse toward the big tree while one of the others whipped it on the rump with a green willow. As soon as the animal was secured tightly to the tree, the third Indian rode up and, without a word to the others, notched an arrow onto his bow string, drew it back full length to his jaw, and let go.

The arrow sank deep into the side of the helpless animal, just behind the front shoulder, into the lungs. It grunted in surprise, jerked back, then from side to side. Soon it was on its knees, then fell to its side—bright red blood oozing from its nose and mouth. One of the Indians stepped up behind the head and slashed open the throat. The blood ran into black pools about the base of the tree, islands of pine needles floating on the dark puddles. The same Indian then reached over the middle of the animal and ran the blade of his sharp knife over the tight belly, spilling the insides onto the ground, filling the air with a sweet, warm smell. The westerly breeze picked up the scent and carried it gently across the meadow toward the woods. Before getting back on their horses, the Indians moved the log and trap close to the dead horse, concealing the open jaws of the trap beside the intestines.

After the three red men had ridden out of sight, I sat down in the grass to consider my situation. The sun was behind the threatening clouds. There was still an hour or more of daylight.

The evening breeze carried the smell of the dead horse across the meadow and into the woods to the foxes, coyotes, wolves, mountain cats, and bears. Especially the bears. After feeding almost exclusively on late summer berries in recent weeks, the smell of fresh horse meat would be very appealing.

I stood up and began walking around the tree, my leash growing shorter as it wrapped around the trunk. The rawhide rope was made from a three-inch-wide strip of bull buffalo hide twisted into rope form. Beaver George had used a similar rope to stake out his saddle horse. I remembered him telling me about a horse he once had that liked to chew on rawhide ropes. After it chewed its way through the second rope, he traded the horse to an Indian.

If a horse could chew through a rawhide rope, I figured I could do it too. I looked in the direction the Indians had gone, wondering if perhaps they were watching me from some distant lookout, possibly from the top of a tree. I couldn't see any sign of them but decided to be cautious and wait until dusk before chewing the rope in two. I started walking the other direction, unwinding the rope from around the tree. If a bear came before I was free, I figured I'd stand behind the dead horse and try to lure the bear into the trap; then at least he would be dragging the trap and the attached log as he came after me. There was no way I could get into the tree with my hands tied. I had visions of the bear chasing me around the tree while my rope got shorter and shorter.

The wind began to blow harder, the clouds becoming thicker and darker. A few minutes later the wind was fierce, and the clouds thundered boldly as they tumbled through the sky, shooting jagged yellow streaks of lightning into the green forest and granite rock slides.

Soon the clouds became quiet as they spread like a heavy black blanket over the valley. As the craggy peaks punctured the soft underside of the blanket, the clouds broke open and began dumping water on the valley below.

When the cloudburst turned my surroundings into nothing more than a gray blur, I began chewing on the rawhide rope, just below where it was tied to the tree. It had a slippery, salty taste. It was very hard at first, but the more I chewed, the softer it became. The muscles in my jaws were soon aching for a rest, but knowing I would soon be free, I continued chewing with the fierceness of a half-starved savage gnawing on a piece of jerky.

I was concentrating totally on the softening rawhide rope when suddenly, without warning, something grabbed my hair and jerked my head back. I gasped with surprise, nearly choking on my own saliva, figuring the bear had come upon me by surprise and would soon be tearing me apart.

It wasn't a bear, but one of the warriors who had come back to check the prisoner and the trap before darkness settled over the valley. Before I could turn around and face him, he shoved a wad of knotted rawhide into my mouth and tied it in place with a leather lashing. Then he was gone, trotting back up the trail. Apparently he didn't want to be around when the bear came. It was almost dark now, and the rain had nearly stopped.

Now my situation seemed hopeless. I was wet, cold, hungry, and very much afraid of the approaching night. I had felt pretty much in control as long as I had a plan of escape, but now that the Indian had taken that away, I began to panic. There was no doubt in my mind that one or more bears would come to feed on the dead horse. I would be defenseless against them.

In desperation I sprinted forward into the meadow, hitting the end of the rope with all my strength. I winced with pain as the rope jerked me over backwards, wrenching my arms. I stayed there a moment, on my back, the cold rain washing my grim face. Feeling the desperate determination of a cornered animal, I crawled to my feet, marched back to the tree, and charged again against the end of the rope. I didn't care about the pain as I was jerked back again. I couldn't fight bears with my hands tied; I had to get free. I lunged against the end of the rope again and again.

I was standing in the grass at the end of my leash, panting, gathering strength for another lunge when I realized that on the last few lunges the rope hadn't jerked me back nearly as hard as the first. Yes, the rain-soaked line was softening and stretching. And if the wet rope would stretch, why not the rawhide strips holding my wrists together?

The rain had stopped, but the grass was still wet. I dove into the soaked greenery, rolling over on my back, pulling my wrists through the wet vegetation—twisting, turning, and pulling against the softening rawhide. Not only did the rawhide begin to stretch, but it became slippery as well. After a few minutes of vigorous twisting, one of my hands slipped free.

It was dark now and the spent clouds were pushing over the eastern mountains. A few stars were sparkling in the last blue of the western twilight. A full moon, low in the southeast, was casting silver edges on the vanishing clouds.

Before leaving the big pine tree, I climbed into the lower branches and untied the other end of the rope so I could take it with me. It wasn't really a weapon, but maybe I could use it to climb to a secure hiding place in the granite peaks.

I thought about taking the steel bear trap too, but decided against it, thinking its weight would slow me down. Still, I didn't want to leave it where it was. After unchaining it from the dead log, I very carefully picked up the trap and carried it over to some small trees, about thirty feet from the dead horse. When the Indians brought me here, they had tied the pack animals to these trees. I figured that when they came back in the morning, the red men might tether a horse or two in the same place. I set the trap in a likely spot where an Indian might stand when tying up his pony. I covered the trap with pine needles. I was very pleased with myself for being so clever. Maybe I would make a good mountain man after all. Picking up the coiled rope, I disappeared into the night.

Chapter 25

The moon was shining brightly as I trotted across the meadow toward the dark woods. Thinking that I might run head on into a grizzly coming to feed on the dead horse, I picked up a round stone, about the size of a large apple.

It wasn't long until I came upon a well-traveled game trail. The trees began to thin as I followed the trail into the rugged mountains. The going was faster now. I wanted to cover as much ground as possible before my escape was discovered. Soon I was high enough to look down on the meadow and the dead horse. There was no sign of the Indians. I hoped they would wait until morning before returning.

As I slowed to a walk, I noticed a rotten smell on the breeze, blowing gently down from the mountains in front of me. Probably from a dead elk or deer. Or was it? I stopped. The smell seemed to be getting stronger with every breath.

In the moonlight, my eyes followed the trail to where it disappeared behind some huge boulders, about twenty feet in front of me. George once told me how foul bears could smell when they had been feeding on dead carcasses. I couldn't hear anything, but suddenly I thought I saw some movement among the boulders.

With its nose high in the air, a huge grizzly stepped into the moonlight. Its glossy coat had a silvery glow. It was sniffing for a scent of what might lie ahead on the trail. Then, as it began to take another step forward, it spotted me.

The bear froze like a statue, front paw still in the air. I didn't move, either. The only movement was the twitching back and forth of the bear's left ear. I tightened my grip on the rock.

I don't know how long we stood there looking at each other, but when the grizzly took another step forward, I threw the rock at him. I was lucky. It was a direct hit, smashing the tender end of his nose. As the grizzly bear let loose with a mighty bawl of pain and rage, I galloped back down the trail as fast as I could go.

I knew better than to run uphill. George had said that bears, with short front legs and long back legs, couldn't run nearly as fast downhill as uphill.

After rubbing his smarting nose in the dirt, the raging grizzly plunged down the hill after me. It didn't take long to realize that even downhill the bear could outrun me. As I raced along, I began to look for a stout tree to climb.

I could hear with increasing loudness the roar of rushing water. The gorge. Most of the trees along the path seemed too small to withstand the battering of an angry grizzly, so I continued to run, suddenly finding myself at the cliff-like edge of the rocky gorge. My ears were filled with the violent roar of water crashing over splintered granite boulders.

To the right, an old gnarled pine, its roots drilled into solid rock, stood firm at the very edge of the cliff, half its limbs reaching toward the hill, the other half reaching out over the empty, dark gorge.

I sprinted toward the tree as the bear crashed out of the brush behind me. As I ran, I could see that the lowest branch was probably out of my reach, so I readied the rawhide rope without slowing my pace. When I reached the tree, I tossed the loop over a branch, just as the bear came up behind me. As I scampered up the rope and out of reach, the bear swung at me with his right paw, his powerful claws tearing through the legging, skin, and flesh of my right leg. Before he could do any further damage, I had pulled myself to safety in the lower branches of the tree.

The raging beast took out its pent-up anger on the tree, swatting, clawing, and pushing. The tree, which had been holding tightly to that cliff for over fifty years, wasn't about to be pushed out of place by a clumsy old bear.

The beast was furious about not being able to reach me. It sat back on its haunches and bawled its fury to the pre-dawn stars. Then it started pacing back and forth beneath the tree, occasionally looking up at me. It sat down again and bawled some more.

The relief I felt at getting safely into the tree was short-lived. The dawn was advancing across the eastern sky. My leg was hurt and bleeding. Soon the Indians would be looking for me; treed by a noisy bear, I would be easy to find. With my injured leg I would have no chance to outrun the Indians, even if I managed to get away from the bear.

I had to figure out a way to get rid of the bear before the Indians found me. Climbing carefully around in the branches, I broke off some dead limbs and threw them at the beast, hoping to drive him away. His only reaction was to appear more angry and bawl louder than ever. Occasionally he'd rub his nose, probably remembering the stone I had thrown at him. He had no intention of leaving.

Suddenly I had an idea, a good one. I uncoiled the rope and tied a loop for roping. The next time the bear stood on his hind legs with a front paw against the trunk of my tree, I dropped the loop over his head. Before he had time to react, I jerked the line tight and made two loops and wrapped the other ends of the rope around a stout limb, one that reached out over the gorge.

The bear twisted and fought like a wild horse. Every time he gained any slack in the rope, I jerked it tighter. It didn't take long until all the slack was gone and the bear was cinched up, moving closer to the edge of the gorge. He suddenly stopped his wild thrashing and leaned back against the rope without moving.

No matter how I tried to jerk him over the edge, I couldn't get him to budge another inch. Unable to bawl, and barely able to breathe, the beast began to realize the seriousness of his predicament. The first morning light made visible the jagged boulders and foamy white water at the bottom of the gorge, about a hundred feet below.

With new determination, the grizzly leaned back into the rope with all his savage strength, cutting off his own breathing. The two loops around the limb weren't enough to hold five hundred pounds of determined bear. The rope slipped an inch, then two. The beast was doggedly increasing the gap between himself and the gorge. After gaining about six inches, the animal eased the tension in the rope just enough to get some air, but not enough to let me take in any slack. The bear learned quickly.

I could see that the cunning beast was gaining the upper hand in the tug-of-war. I decided to take advantage of his breather and get a third loop around the limb. An extra loop would prevent him from pulling out any more rope.

As I leaned forward to make the additional loop, a searing pain stabbed into my wounded leg as I snagged it on a jagged branch stump. I jerked back, overreacting to the pain. All my weight was on my good leg as it slipped out from under me. I scrambled to clutch for anything solid, but feeling sick, I felt my body accelerate out and down toward the bottom of the gorge. I tried desperately to catch myself on the limb with the two loops, but in my tumbling and turning was unable to do so. I did manage somehow to hang onto the rope, which would have slipped through my clenched fists had it not been for the knot at the end.

When the situation finally stabilized, I was dangling at the end of the rope about four feet in front of the surprised grizzly, who was tied to the other end of the same rope. Like a worm at the end of a fish line, or a juicy chicken turning on a vertical spit, I swung tantalizingly in front of the bear's nose. One moment I was facing the angry beast, looking into his snarling face, and the next moment I had turned my back. I held on tightly with both hands, waiting for the beast to reach out and claw me down from my desperate hold on the rope.

It seemed the bear just sat there and watched for a long time. Finally he reached out to swat me. The claws of his right paw grazed the edge of my hip, just enough to get me spinning like a top. As the bear inched a little closer to the edge in an effort to swat me again, a wedge of granite broke free from under one of his front paws.

This minute shift in balance was just enough to start the bear slipping and sliding toward the gorge. The tautness of the rope on its neck prevented the beast from turning to either side. Helplessly, the bear slipped into space. Luckily for me, he came to rest about two feet below my boots.

With five hundred pounds of bear on one end and one hundred and fifty pounds of boy on the other, the rope began to slip. When the bear went down; I went up. I soon discovered that by wiggling my body, I could increase the slippage. It wasn't long until the bear's weight pulled me into the lower branches of the tree. I hooked my left elbow over the big limb and let go of the rope. In a split second, the rope hissed around the limb where it had been looped and was gone, the bear with it.

A minute later I was out of the tree, standing firmly on the edge of the gorge. There was no sign of the bear below. After bouncing off a few boulders, it had disappeared into the churning white foam.

I didn't have much time to contemplate the narrow escape and how close I had been to death. I knew the Indians would be looking for me now that it was light. I had to find a hiding place, and soon. The bear had made a lot of noise chasing me down the mountain and bawling at me in the tree. It was likely the Indians had heard the racket and would know where to come looking for me.

My leg was still bleeding. Because I knew it wouldn't be a good idea to leave a trail of blood, I removed my shirt as a wrap for the wound. Before bandaging it up, however, I smeared as much blood as possible on the rocky edge of the gorge. I suspected that the sight of blood might make it easier for the Indians to believe that I had gone over the edge of the cliff with the bear.

After hastily wrapping the wound, I limped up the hill until I came to some thick brush. I crawled into a patch of wild rosebushes between two big boulders. Through the branches I had a clear view of the gnarled old pine where I had battled the grizzly.

It was midmorning when the three Indians showed up, their horses picking their footing carefully along the rocky trail. First they spotted the fresh claw marks on the tree trunk, then the freshly broken limbs that I had thrown at the bear. At last they saw the blood on the edge of the cliff. They looked up into the tree for a long time to make sure I wasn't still up there.

Finally, two of them dismounted to get a closer look at the blood-smeared rocks. After a minute they stretched out on their bellies, looking over the edge at the boulders and white water below for any sign of me and the bear. I couldn't help but grin as I looked back at the mounted warrior and noticed that his left ankle was wrapped tightly with a strip of buffalo hide. That explained why he hadn't dismounted with the other two. There was no question in my mind as to how he had received the injury—the bear trap, of course, the one I had covered with pine needles, near the little trees.

As the other two stood up and began discussing the situation with their wounded friend, they appeared very disappointed, not knowing what had happened between me and the bear. Apparently they concluded that I had gone over the cliff too. They climbed back on their horses and returned the way they had come.

About an hour after they rode out of sight, I crawled out of my hiding place and fashioned a crutch from a dead aspen limb. My leg was sore and stiff. I looked westward toward the peaks of the Bitter Root Mountains. It was going to be a long, tough hike to the Snake River country, but my spirits were high as I began hobbling up the trail.

Chapter 26

My clawed leg was stiff and sore as I began to hobble up the rocky trail toward the continental divide. Eventually the trail disappeared into a vast expanse of huge granite boulders. I had to throw the crutch away as I jumped and crawled from rock to rock. Soon my wound was bleeding again, a little at first, then worse than ever. I tied my blood-soaked shirt tighter around the wounded leg, but it didn't do much good.

Finally the boulders gave way to a grassy southern slope. The grass was partly dry from the August sun, and there were a few white-tufted yarrow plants scattered here and there. I remembered Beaver George using the plant to stop the bleeding in his wounded foot.

I picked a handful of the fern-like leaves, then dropped into the grass to doctor my bleeding wound. After removing the blood-soaked shirt, I rubbed the yarrow briskly between my palms until I had a wad of juicy green pulp, which I pressed gently into the deep gash. The bleeding stopped almost immediately. The wound tingled as the fragrant yarrow penetrated, forcing the oozing vessels to contract.

Across the meadow I found a spring bubbling out from under a huge boulder. After drinking deeply from the cold, clear water, I washed the dust and smeared blood from the wound. Then I rinsed out my maroon shirt that had been serving as a bandage. The spring water turned orange as it gushed over the swirling shirt, and the buckskin became brown again as the last of the blood was dissolved and carried away.

After stretching the shirt over the top of a warm, sunny rock to dry, I stretched out in the grass and closed my eyes. I hadn't slept or eaten for over thirty hours and was more tired than hungry. I fell into a deep but troubled sleep—seeing visions of the raging bear, the three Indians, Beaver George buried under a pile of rocks, and my friend Ike, deserted by his companions in the Snake River country. I dreamed my old enemy Dick Boggs, Ike's former owner, was chasing after me, a big shiny deputy's badge on his shirt. He was more frightening than the Indians or the bear. I awakened with a new resolve to stay in the Rocky Mountains, never to return to Missouri. And stronger than ever, I had that undeniable feeling, deep inside, that Ike was still alive.

As the summer sun was about half buried beyond the western mountains, I found a sheltered spot among some boulders just below the timber line. There was plenty of wind-twisted deadwood for a fire. I removed some of the fringe from my shirt to fashion string for a small bow. Then I gathered some dead sticks and dry tree moss. After fashioning a peg from one of the sticks, I was ready to start a fire. Looping the bow string around the peg, held firmly between two pieces of wood, I began pumping the bow back and forth, as Beaver George had made me practice many times.

It wasn't long until a thin lacing of smoke was curling skyward. I dropped the bow and picked up the piece of glowing spark. I rolled it gently into the nest of dry moss and puffed ever so carefully. Several tiny yellow flames emerged from the moss. I placed the smoking nest on the ground and piled on some of the smaller twigs. It wasn't long before I had the company of a warm, crackling fire. It was going to be a long, cold night at the high altitude. I felt a warm gratitude to George, who had insisted that I learn to build fires without flint and steel. As darkness settled in, I quickly gathered enough firewood to last through the night.

I spent a warm but hungry night waiting for the dawn, when I could continue my journey and search for food. I was weak from lack of nourishment and knew that if I was to survive in this wild land, I would have to eat, and without a rifle, that wouldn't be easy.

In the gray dawn I let the fire die, and when it was too cold to sit any longer, I resumed my downhill journey. The wounded leg, along with my hunger-weakened condition, made traveling very difficult. Each step was a major undertaking.

By the time the sun was high enough to feel warm, I spotted a thick thistle patch just uphill from an aspen grove. Carefully, I picked about a dozen of the younger plants and began peeling off the outer peel with its needle-like thorns. The inside stalks were crisp and juicy, delicious after a two-day fast.

After eating my fill of thistle, I moved on down the mountain, feeling better. After a while, I came to a little stream. I gulped down enough of the icy liquid to give me a headache, then waded into the stream to pick a handful of rock tripe, a gilled fungus that grows on wet rocks. I had never tasted it before but remembered George pointing it out once, saying it would keep a man from starving. It tasted like salty mushrooms sprinkled lightly with dirt. The saltiness compensated for the gritty taste, and I wolfed down several handfuls before continuing my journey.

As I descended to the lower altitudes, I began to find thimbleberries, salmonberries, and a few huckleberries. These tasted better than the thistle and rock tripe. When I reached the valley floor, I found an abundance of nutty-tasting serviceberries, enough to fill my stomach. I became stronger as my stomach digested the wild foods, but even though my belly was full, I was still hungry—with a hunger that only fresh meat would satisfy. I craved a juicy chunk of roasted buffalo or elk meat, but without a rifle, I knew I wasn't going to get it.

Finding the canyon where Ike had fought with the Shoshones wasn't as difficult as I first thought. Knowing the Indians and prospectors both had horses, I figured all I would have to do is check the mouths of the canyons for horse tracks. After only a few weeks, they should still be easy to spot.

Late in the morning of the second day of the search, I found what I had been looking for—plenty of horse tracks leading in and out of what appeared to be a box canyon. My first reaction was one of caution. Maybe some of the Shoshones were still around.

I climbed the brushy sidehill to a rock outcropping where I had an excellent view of both the canyon and valley. I wasn't in any hurry to enter the canyon. Several weeks had passed since the battle, and a few more hours wouldn't matter. I waited for what seemed like several hours—watching up and down the canyon and valley for any movement and listening for any unusual sound, like a human voice, the neighing of a horse, or the clattering of rocks being pushed out of place by horses' hooves.

Eventually I began to stalk cautiously toward the head of the canyon, trying to stay as high as possible on the hill while staying close to brush and trees for cover. I moved slowly, stopping every few steps to look and listen.

After a while I spotted a thick aspen grove at the upper end of an open meadow. It was a likely spot for the fleeing prospectors to tie up their animals and make a stand. Behind the grove, the canyon became steep and rocky—difficult, if not impossible, for horse travel.

As I walked toward the aspen grove, I suddenly caught the scent of decaying flesh. My first thought was that Ike had been killed after all. I knew the smell couldn't be from one of the Indians because they would have carried off any dead companions for proper burial.

I was relieved when I discovered the stink was coming from a dead horse, half eaten by coyotes and bobcats. I figured it had probably been killed in the battle. Beyond the horse I found several arrows with the stone tips broken off. Fresh splintering signaled bullet holes in some of the trees. I found coals from a cookfire, a bone-handled knife in the grass, and horse droppings near some of the trees—but nothing else. There was no sign of Ike. I didn't really know what to look for. There was no body and no grave. I concluded that Ike had either escaped or been taken captive and tortured at a distant Indian village.

Upon leaving the canyon, I headed south, following the trail left behind by the mounted Indians. Several days later, as I approached the vast Snake River Valley, I found the trail had been washed away by violent afternoon thundershowers. I couldn't tell if it turned to the right, left, or went straight ahead into the huge valley.

Since I was neither mounted nor armed, I decided the only sensible thing to do would be to head for the nearest white settlement. I wasn't sure if I was closest to Fort Benton or Santa Fe. Knowing there were plenty of hostile Indians between me and Fort Benton, especially Blackfeet, and aware that the cold fall weather was approaching, I decided to try for Santa Fe. I would stay close to mountain ranges whenever possible, hoping that I might run into white trappers or prospectors who might take me in. I knew I had to get to Sante Fe or join up with someone who had food and weapons if I hoped to survive the winter.

Several weeks later I reached Henry's Fork, a tributary to the Green River. Weary of hiking day after day across the seemingly endless prairie, I started thinking about fashioning a raft and floating down the Green and Colorado Rivers to the Spanish settlements in California.

It was on Henry's Fork that my story began. I remembered well how the mounted Ute warrior had chased me down the steep hillside into the beaver pond, his horse falling to its death on the pointed beaver stumps, pinning the warrior beneath its lifeless body in a foot of icy water. After saving the brave from a watery grave, reviving him beside my warm campfire, and feasting with him on horse meat, I became his friend—even though neither one of us understood a word the other was saying. An unspoken trust had developed, something hard to explain—but when we left the beaver pond, heading southeast toward the Ute homeland, I felt better about what I was doing than at any other time since Beaver George's death.

I later learned that my Indian friend was named Neuwafe, meaning winter snow. He belonged to the Paw-gwan-nuance, meaning lake shore people, one of the five main bands of Utes. There was little unity or cooperation between the five bands. The Paw-gwan-nuance home village was on the east side of Utah Lake, later called Utah Valley by the Mormons.

There were about a hundred Indians in the village, including the women and children. They lived in about two dozen buffalo hide tepees. When I arrived with Neuwafe, they had just established their winter camp and wouldn't be moving until spring. During the summer and fall, the tribe frequently headed north and east to follow the buffalo herds. The band's horse herd contained more than three hundred animals. Most of the Indians were very suspicious of me at first and very curious about my white skin, but after about a week, they seemed to accept me as a member of the band.

Neuwafe lived in a tepee with his mother, Blackbird, and his little sister, Red Leaf. I learned later that his father had been killed in a raid on an Apache village far to the south. Neuwafe's uncle was chief of the band. Neuwafe was in his twenties, I guessed, but still not married.

That winter was cold and bitter, and except for occasional hunting trips into the nearby hills for elk and deer, and into the nearby marshes for ducks and geese, we spent most of the time in the warm tepee, fashioning weapons and horse gear. I learned how to chip obsidian arrowheads with the pointed end of a deer antler, using a piece of buffalo hide to protect my palm from the glassy splinters. I learned how to use a cookfire to strengthen a green arrow shaft. I learned how to notch a shaft so it wouldn't split, how to secure feathers with pitch and sinew. I fashioned my own bow from chokecherry wood and deer sinew. Whenever the weather was good, I practiced shooting my arrows into a pile of partially dry swamp moss. The arrow points shattered whenever they struck anything hard such as a tree or a stone.

Sometimes Neuwafe and I would go riding on two of the nine horses he had inherited from his father. I nearly always rode a young bay stallion. He was fast and strong, and with time became my horse. Neuwafe didn't really give him to me. The horse just gradually became mine, at least I thought so, as I rode and cared for the animal. At that time, my knowledge of the Ute language wasn't advanced to the point where I could intelligently discuss such matters.

With the coming of spring, the tribe packed up all their belongings in buffalo hide bundles and migrated east toward South Pass and the open prairie in search of buffalo. Neuwafe and I rode side by side. I rode the bay stallion.

Chapter 27

I chewed impatiently on a rubbery sego lily bulb. It wasn't much of a breakfast, but there was nothing else. The last of the pemmican had been eaten three days earlier. The Paw-gwan-nuance band of the Ute tribe was heading northeast past the snowcapped peaks later named by the white men, the Uintahs. A week earlier we had departed from the band's winter camp on the shores of Utah Lake.

In the morning sun, the snowcapped peaks shone brilliantly against the deep blue Utah sky. There was no snow where we were. It was May, and the rolling plains were covered with a new blanket of sweet, green grass.

I was mounted on the young bay stallion, his head down, grazing, his ambitious jaws tearing off mouthfuls of the new spring grass. Off in the distance, tribe members were bustling about camp making last-minute preparations for the first buffalo hunt. Less than an hour ago a scout had galloped into camp with news of a small herd of bison grazing just a few miles away.

Hunters began gathering their packs and rounding up their buffalo horses. As the men emerged from the tepees, armed and ready for the hunt, they didn't mount their spirited buffalo horses but their nearby saddle horses instead. The faster buffalo horses were led to the hunt in an effort to conserve strength for the chase.

I didn't have the luxury of a second horse. I was fortunate to even have the bay stallion. Sometimes I called him Ike, in memory of my powerful black friend who had come up the Missouri River with me a year earlier. With the passage of time I began to believe that Ike had probably been killed by the Shoshones north of the Snake River country.

This was my first hunt with Neuwafe's tribe. I was anxious to prove myself. Most of the men of the tribe thought me clumsy. When I first joined the band, I couldn't ride, hunt, or shoot arrows nearly as well as the other boys my age.

During the migration to the buffalo country, there had been considerable discussion among both boys and men as to whether or not I should be allowed to hunt with the other hunters. Some thought that since my skills were not much better than most of the younger boys, I should have to hunt with them, chasing the calves that followed behind the main buffalo herd.

Neuwafe came to my defense, and it was finally agreed that I would be allowed to hunt with the men on the first hunt. If I was successful, as measured by my ability to kill at least one buffalo, I would be allowed to continue hunting with the men. If I failed to kill a buffalo, or got in the way of the other hunters, then I would have to hunt with the boys the remainder of the season.

I had killed buffalo before, with my .50 caliber Hawken rifle the summer I was with Beaver George. But I wasn't sure how successful I would be with the obsidian-tipped arrows, shot from my chokecherry bow from the back of the galloping stallion.

Most of the boys my age and size were already hunting with the men. I didn't want the dishonor of being assigned to the younger boys. I didn't want to dishonor Neuwafe, who had promised the tribe, when they agreed to let me in, that someday I would become a great Ute hunter and warrior.

I was worried on this beautiful spring morning. I wondered how the big bay would respond. It was one thing to race alongside another horse, or chase a deer into the brush, but quite another, I thought, to close in on a thousand-pound buffalo. Some horses never overcame their fear of stampeding buffalo. Would the bay stallion have the courage to move in close enough for me to be accurate with my arrows? A distance of just a few feet.

I wondered about my own courage. Would my aim be sure, my arm strong? I knew if I wasn't careful, an enraged bull could disembowel and overturn my horse with one quick swipe of his shaggy head. I began to wonder if perhaps I should have swallowed a little pride and been content to hunt with the younger boys for a summer.

I was dressed like most of the other warriors, in a loincloth, leggings, and moccasins. There were twenty arrows in the elk-skin quiver over my right shoulder. I had made every one of them. Each arrow had two black circles painted around the circumference of the shaft, just below the feathers. If I killed a buffalo, it would be easily identified after the hunt by the black marks on the arrows.

My arms and chest were bronzed from long exposure to sun and wind. I was a little taller and a lot stronger than when I first came to this land a year earlier. What set me apart from the Indians, more than anything else, was the sandy hair hanging to my shoulders. I was riding bareback, but most of the older braves had light, padded saddles, stuffed with buffalo hair.

As I joined the other riders, I felt uneasy, knowing I had not proven myself, that I was not accepted among them, that they were still suspicious of my white skin. I knew I was on trial as a hunter and they would be watching me closely. It would be bad for me if I did not kill a buffalo. It would be worse if I displayed a lack of courage, or fear. I desperately wanted to be accepted among them. I wanted their respect and admiration. I was one of them now. My upbringing in the white settlements of eastern Canada and Missouri was nothing more than a cloudy memory of what seemed a very distant past. My plans for the future didn't go beyond becoming a brave and competent Ute warrior.

I fingered through the feathered shafts, making sure they were all there. I made sure the coiled end of my horse's lead rope was tucked firmly under the front of my breechcloth. This was a safety precaution in case I was thrown from the horse during the chase. By hanging on to the uncoiling rope during the fall, I could maintain control of the horse and prevent it from getting away from me.

Soon the scout, Many Horse Hooves, galloped down from a little knoll to meet the hunters. He pointed in the direction of the buffalo herd, grazing peacefully in an open flat around the point of a small hill. We couldn't see them yet.

Crazy Calf, the chief of the band, was in charge of the hunt. His word was final, and everyone seemed willing to do exactly as he instructed.

The herd was small, less than a hundred animals, making it necessary to assign riders to each side of the herd. Given their choice, most riders, usually right-handed, would choose the right side because of the difficulty of shooting arrows from the left. But if everyone followed on the right, the herd would turn and scatter and there would be less success. So some of the riders had to be assigned to the left side to keep the herd going in a steady direction.

Usually the riders on the left wouldn't shoot any arrows until a straggler moved away from the herd, allowing the rider to get between it and the herd for the desired right-handed shot. If a straggler didn't appear, the brave hunter would sometimes ride right in among the stampeding bison, greatly increasing the danger of being trampled or gored.

All these thoughts raced through my mind when I was chosen to ride on the left. I knew they were saving the right side for the best hunters, the ones they could count on to bring down the meat.

At Crazy Calf's command, we stopped at the point of the hill. The buffalo were still out of sight. The braves who had been leading their spirited buffalo horses dismounted from their riding horses and mounted the hunting ponies. The saddle horses were then sent back to the caravan of women, children, and pack animals following close on our heels.

The mounted hunters spread out in a line as if preparing for a horse race. Each man had an equal chance to be first to reach the herd and make the first kill. Crazy Calf, mounted on his dancing pinto at the right end of the line, held his bow high above his head. When he brought the bow down, the chase would begin.

I leaned over my horse's neck, the reins in my right hand, the bow with a notched arrow and a handful of mane in the left. It was going to be a fast start, and my grip on the mane was my insurance that the enthusiastic pony wouldn't leap out from under me.

Crazy Calf's bow went down and the race was on. Almost immediately the buffalo were in view just a few hundred yards ahead. In full stampede, they were going the opposite direction before we had covered half the distance.

Because the bay stallion had never been in a race like this before, he seemed to think we were chasing the calves that were falling behind the main herd. He seemed confused and somewhat hesitant when I urged him past the calves, but when he caught sight of the thundering bulls charging on the heels of the swifter cows, the horse suddenly surged ahead with a new strength and speed, understanding that we were going after the big ones.

By the time I reached the bulls, they were still bunched close together. I urged the horse past them to the faster cows, which were beginning to spread out some. Now that the hunt was underway, most of my fear was gone. The surging muscles of the galloping horse gave me a sense of confidence and power.

I was about to ride in among the racing cows, when just in front of me, a young cow veered out away from the herd. Quickly I urged the pony into the gap between her and the herd. When the cow realized the horse was beside her, she swerved back toward the herd. The fearless pony held its ground and the cow had to straighten out again.

That's when I dropped the reins, freeing my right hand to pull back the bow string. I hoped the horse would remember its training and remain beside the cow. I took quick aim at an imaginary circle behind the cow's upper shoulder and let the first arrow fly.

The cow didn't falter in the least as the shaft sank deep into her side about six inches behind the intended mark. I drew another shaft, remembering that it sometimes took two or three arrows to bring down a stampeding buffalo.

Just as I was drawing back the second shaft, a wounded buffalo directly in front of me lost its footing. Its chest and chin dug into the sod like a plow as it ground to a halt. With the cow on my left and the herd on my right, the pony had no choice but to leap over the dying beast. I was so intent on getting the second arrow into the cow that I didn't see the downed buffalo until it was too late.

The horse's unexpected leap unseated me. Before I could grab for the mane, I found myself falling backward over the horse's flanks. As the horse struck the ground again, I tumbled into the green sod.

My first concern was the loss of a chance to get a buffalo. My hunt was over and I would not be allowed to ride with the men again. Then I felt the jerk under my belt as the lead rope pulled free. I lunged for the disappearing line and held fast. It seemed as if the horse was never going to quit dragging me over the slippery new grass. By the time the horse stopped, the cows were gone and the last of the bulls were charging by. I still had my bow and quiver. Shaken but determined, I leaped upon the bay, spun him around, and lunged after the last bull.

The horse was tired now, but so was the bison. After I slapped him good on the flank with the bow, the horse mustered the speed to move alongside the last buffalo. The first arrow hit too far forward on the shoulder. The second shaft was too far back, like the first arrow in the cow. And the third was a little too high. The arrows didn't seem to slow the old fellow down.

The tired horse was falling behind. Even a few more bow slaps on the rump couldn't coax another drop of energy out of the cup that was already empty. Tears began to swell in my eyes as the buffalo began to pull away. I had tried so hard but had failed to prove myself worthy to hunt with the men.

I relaxed my heels to let the pony know the hunt was over. Just then the front legs of the disappearing bull buckled and the beast ground to a halt, finally rolling over on its side, coughing red saliva. By the time I reached the animal, it was dead.

I slid from the back of the lathered horse and walked around the dead bull, several times. I couldn't pull my eyes from the conquest. Finally the spell was broken by the voice of Neuwafe.

"Won't get up," he said.

He looked pleased that his white friend had killed a buffalo.

Grinning from ear to ear, I slipped out of my leggings and drew my knife to begin dressing out my buffalo.

As Neuwafe turned to ride away, to take care of his own kills, he pointed his bow to the east and said, "The other one's over there, the cow."

As I began to insert my knife into the soft underbelly of the bull buffalo, I heard hoofbeats behind me. It was Red Leaf, Neuwafe's little sister. She had come to help dress the kills.

She was a year or two younger than I was, a shy girl. When I first came to the village with Neuwafe, she seldom talked to me and would never look me straight in the eye. But after a few months, as we got to know each other better through our day-to-day living, we became good friends, much like brother and sister.

Had I not been successful in the hunt, I would have wanted to be alone. But now that I had proven myself as a hunter, I was glad to have someone to share the glory with me. Red Leaf looked different today. Instead of her normal clothing—a trim doeskin dress, almost white, decorated with a few beads and porcupine quills—she wore a ragged, loose-fitting smock. At butchering time, all the Indian women wore their oldest and most ragged clothing.

Her long, raven hair hung loosely about her shoulders. Against the contrast of the dull clothing, her bronze skin looked smoother, her smile brighter, her eyes more intense. Mounted on her buckskin pony she looked older—less like a little sister and more like a woman. I was glad she had come to help me with the butchering.

It wasn't long before our arms were red with blood, almost all the way to the shoulders. A bull buffalo is a big animal, and reaching inside to get it cleaned out was messy business. After it was cleaned and I began skinning, Red Leaf began working over the insides, the parts usually discarded by white men. The stomach would be used as a cooking kettle. The intestines would be turned inside out, with the fat on the inside. Pieces of meat would be stuffed inside like sausages and roasted. It was not uncommon, however, to leave it raw. Children often chewed on two-foot sections of the raw intestine. Meat cooked in sections of intestine is juicy and flavorful. The leg bones are roasted, then split open for the marrow fat. The hooves and soft inside of the horns are fashioned into drinking flasks and containers. In the summer and early fall, some of the unskinned tails are always saved as fly swatters. With rawhide lashings, the long ribs can be fashioned into sturdy sleighs. Most of the internal organs, including heart, kidneys, brains, and liver are eaten fresh, and usually cooked within a few days of the kill. Some of the meat is eaten fresh, but most is jerked into strips and dried in the sun or pounded with fat and berries to make pemmican. Most of the jerky and pemmican is saved for winter.

Next to the meat, the most important part of the buffalo is the hide, which provides cover for the tepee, saddles for the horses, ropes, bridles, moccasins, containers, and warm bedding.

It took Red Leaf and me the remainder of the day to clean both buffalo and haul the meat, hides, and other desirable parts back to the camp. At the same time, Blackbird (Red Leaf's mother) was helping Neuwafe dress his two kills and take them back to camp. Most of the families in the camp had been successful in the hunt, and spirits were high. In the late afternoon, the camps built huge fires in anticipation of an all-night feast.

Chapter 28

As we sat around the fire that night feasting on fresh roasted buffalo, I began to feel that perhaps I ought to spend the rest of my life as an Indian. It seemed like a pretty good way to live, roaming the mountains and valleys, living off the land and the plentiful buffalo herds. It was an adventurous life—racing half-wild horses across the open plains, hunting wild game, fighting occasionally to defend what was yours—your life, your belongings, and your friends.

The Utes had a different philosophy about life and property. They worshiped the land and nature—the sun, the wind, the storms, the animals, the trees, and the earth itself. The earth was like a mother, a provider who fed and clothed and sheltered her children. To an Indian, owning a piece of ground was as foreign a thought as owning a piece of your own mother. It just didn't happen. Plowing or digging a mine shaft was an act of desecration. The land was sacred, a holy provider, not an object of exploitation. Success was not measured in land and gold, but in horses, wives, and courageous exploits.

The Indian life was simple, and in the summer when the breezes were warm and the game plentiful, it was a good life, particularly for a strong young man. As I remembered my life back in Missouri—the hard work to plant crops every spring, the never-ending chores, the strict schoolmasters, the long church meetings, the hate and persecutions of the Missouri mobs against my people—all these memories, by comparison, made the Indian life look very appealing. Plus the fact that I was sure I was wanted by the Missouri law for what I had done to Dick Boggs. No, I didn't want to go back.

That feeling was reinforced as I looked across the fire at Red Leaf. She had discarded the blood-stained butchering smock and was now wearing her usual doeskin dress—white and clean. Her clear eyes reflected brightly the dancing flames as she tended the roasting meat.

I was exhausted from a long day of hunting and butchering, but the sight of Red Leaf in the warm firelight seemed to extinguish the weary feelings, replacing them with a desire to please, to share, to be with this Indian girl. Occasionally, when our eyes would meet, usually for a longer than normal contact, I began to believe she was experiencing similar feelings. I could feel my heart beating in my chest.

These emotions were new to me. I was just sixteen years old, but there was no doubt about it. I had fallen in love. And so quickly. I longed to be alone with her, to hold her hand, to say tender things, to look into those deep, beautiful eyes without having to worry who might be noticing.

As I watched her remove our evening meal from the glowing coals, I suddenly became aware that Neuwafe was watching me. I returned the look. His hands and face were greasy as he gnawed aggressively on a half-cooked, three-foot buffalo rib. He had a knowing, but annoyed, expression on his face. Quickly, I looked away. When I realized Neuwafe knew how I felt about his sister, my face turned crimson.

It made me angry, knowing that I was blushing. So stupid. I didn't understand. Neuwafe was a trusted friend. I hadn't done anything wrong. There was no reason to blush, but I did anyway.

The roast, so carefully prepared by Red Leaf, was a long loin, cut from the top of the buffalo's back. She had been roasting it for several hours in a four-foot section of inside-out intestine. Close to the fire, leaning against a post, was a rack of ribs, golden brown and sizzling in the heat of the fire. In thinking about Red Leaf, I had forgotten my hunger, but as she carefully peeled away the hardened remains of the intestine to expose the steaming strip of meat, my mouth began to water. After months of eating dried meat and sego lily bulbs, the fresh meat looked and smelled so good.

The loin was as moist, tender, and flavorful as any I had ever tasted. No words were spoken as the four of us devoured the entire loin. Then we began slicing off the three-foot ribs and chewing on them. As our stomachs became full, we discussed the hunt: the chase, the killing, the butchering, and the interesting sidelights, like my falling from the horse and still being able to remount and kill the last bull.

I remembered working side by side with Red Leaf—her strong hands, quick smile, eagerness to please. It was a perfect evening until Brown Wolf entered the circle of our fire.

Brown Wolf was a year or two older than I was. He was an excellent rider, a proven hunter, and a brave fighter. He had never paid much attention to me and had occasionally visited our fire to see his friend Neuwafe, or so I had supposed. But as he visited us on this particular night and squatted cross-legged beside Red Leaf, he offered a friendly smile in her direction. I realized for the first time that it was Red Leaf, not Neuwafe, who attracted Brown Wolf to our camp.

I had never paid much attention to Brown Wolf before, but as he sat beside Red Leaf, gnawing on a buffalo rib, I began to notice all kinds of things about him—things I didn't like. His eyes were too close together. His feet were too big. His leggings were stained. I couldn't deny that his shoulders were broad and muscular, his movements graceful and confident.

It bothered me that Red Leaf seemed to be enjoying Brown Wolf's company, returning his pleasantries with poise and friendliness. How could she be so two-faced? Surely she couldn't like him, not after butchering side by side with me all day. More than once she had looked into my eyes and smiled. Our arms and hands had touched many times as we worked together loading the packhorses with hides and meat. Surely these things couldn't have been accidental.

But as I looked across the fire, she actually seemed to be enjoying Brown Wolf's company as he bragged about the four buffalo he had killed during the morning hunt. I was confused, hurt, and angry. When it became apparent that Brown Wolf had no intention of leaving, I stalked off to the tepee to sulk in solitude.

It was a long, restless night. Looking back, it is hard to distinguish between my nighttime dreams and my daydreams. I saw myself in hand-to-hand combat with Brown Wolf. Red Leaf had agreed to marry the winner. I saw myself protecting her from grizzly bears, stampeding buffalo, and the dangerous predators from other tribes. I was always successful in saving her, and she always thanked me with a grateful hug and sometimes kisses.

My white upbringing in the settlements of Canada and Missouri were only distant memories now. I was a Ute warrior, a proven hunter. The most important thing in my life was winning the hand of Red Leaf. I would fight, kill, and die, if necessary. Nothing else was important. And I hated Brown Wolf.

Chapter 29

The summer of 1840 was a good year for hunting buffalo, at least for the Paw-gwan-nuance Ute band. By July we had more than enough jerked meat and pemmican to get the tribe through the coming winter. The packhorses were heavy with meat and hides as the band returned to the shores of Utah Lake in anticipation of a leisurely summer and fall. Some of the young men were planning horse-stealing and slave-trading expeditions, neither of which I knew very much about at the time.

Having proven my abilities as a hunter, with at least one kill in each of the hunts, most of my thoughts now were turned toward Red Leaf. It seemed to me that every day she grew more beautiful. I loved to watch her as she tended the fire, prepared food, or combed her long hair. When she realized I was watching her, she seemed to blush.

Whenever Brown Wolf came around to court, I was overwhelmed with a jealous rage. I never said or did anything to show how I felt, but nevertheless, I was always boiling inside when Brown Wolf stopped by to see Red Leaf.

One afternoon, just after we had stopped to make camp, I noticed Red Leaf rearranging the quill pattern on her best doeskin dress. She seemed unhappy that many of the quills were broken and had to be discarded, weakening the striking nature of the design. There were no more replacement quills in her little buckskin sewing bag.

I remembered earlier in the day, while riding in the nearby hills, coming upon the carcass of a recently killed porcupine. Its soft underbelly had been eaten out by some kind of predator. I remembered stopping my horse and contemplating how the predator might have killed the porcupine without getting quills in its paws and mouth. I remembered Beaver George telling me how sometimes a mountain cat could quickly slip a paw under an unsuspecting porcupine and tear open the soft underside without getting quilled.

I asked her if she wanted more quills. She responded with an enthusiastic nod.

I bridled my bay stallion, leaped upon his back, and pulled Red Leaf up behind me. As we galloped off through the sagebrush toward the nearby mountains, she reached around my waist with her slender, brown arms and held on tightly. I had to believe that she was holding more closely than necessary. She liked me too; I knew she did.

I was on top of the world. The powerful stallion beneath me, the beautiful woman holding tightly to my waist. I felt free, strong, happy, in control. My only regret was that the porcupine wasn't farther away so the ride could last longer. It didn't occur to me that we were being followed.

The porcupine carcass was in a small meadow between an aspen grove and a rocky hillside. The grass was green and lush. There was a gentle, cooling breeze, a refreshing contrast to the late afternoon sun.

When I let the horse out to graze, I left the long lead rope trailing behind as a partial restraint. Red Leaf and I sat down beside the porcupine to pick quills for her little sewing bag. Because she had always been chaperoned by Neuwafe or Blackbird, this was one of the few times up to that point that I had been alone with her.

We carefully selected only the longest and fattest quills, exchanging pleasant small talk as we worked. I learned quickly that when working with quills, it is best to watch one's hands rather than the face of a beautiful Indian maiden if one wishes to avoid bloody fingers.

While licking the blood from one of my sore fingers, a rider suddenly appeared beyond the end of the aspen grove. My first reaction was one of anger toward myself for leaving camp without weapons. I wasn't even wearing my knife.

If the rider was an armed enemy, Blackfoot or Apache, I was in real trouble. Since the rider was headed directly for us, it was apparent he had seen us, and there would be no chance of hiding. My horse was at the far side of the meadow, too far away for us to get mounted before the rider reached us. My horse held his head high, watching the approaching rider.

For the first time, I noticed how clean the meadow was—no nearby clubs or fist-sized rocks. I was about to grab Red Leaf's hand and race for the cover of the aspen grove when she recognized that the rider was Brown Wolf.

At first I felt relief that he wasn't an enemy. At least he wasn't going to try to kill me and carry off Red Leaf. Then I felt anger, the jealous sort. How dare he follow us! How dare he spoil my time to be alone with Red Leaf!

When Brown Wolf galloped up and swung down from his pony, I could see he was angry. He had caught me sneaking time with his girl. He was jealous too.

Brown Wolf stood six feet tall in his moccasins and must have weighed about 175 pounds. He was well muscled, in excellent condition. I had watched him wrestle with the other younger braves and knew I was no match for him in hand-to-hand combat. It appeared, however, that I would have to fight, no matter how poor my chances of winning.

Red Leaf and I stood up to meet him as he swung down from his horse. Before I could figure out how to talk my way out of this explosive situation, he gave me a shove. I surprised myself, and him too, by answering his shove with a bony fist to the jaw. Half stunned, and obviously surprised, he staggered back, almost falling, shaking his whirling head.

I just stood there in amazement, hardly believing what I had done. I made a mistake in giving him time to regain his senses. Now he was angrier than ever and drew his knife. I was in big trouble.

As Brown Wolf stalked toward me, the glistening blade clenched tightly in his fist, I hurriedly looked around for something to use in defending myself. There was nothing.

As I dodged his first lunge, I felt a sharp prickling of pain on the side of my ankle. Glancing down, I noticed that the ankle was pushing against the porcupine carcass. Brown Wolf was circling to make another lunge.

Suddenly I knew how to defend myself. Bending over, I quickly grabbed both hind legs of the carcass and came up swinging. It wasn't very heavy. The insides had been eaten out. But there were still plenty of sharp quills.

I swung the porcupine just like I used to swing pillows at my brother at bedtime. The first blow was aimed directly at his astonished face, and lucky for him, he stopped the blow with his left forearm. There were about a hundred quills in his arm as the amazed Brown Wolf began to back away. This time I took full advantage of his surprise and began beating him with a fury, like I was whipping a fire with a wet blanket. I didn't stop until Brown Wolf had turned tail and was running wildly after his pony.

When he was out of sight, I returned to Red Leaf, who was closing the sewing bag. She had all the quills she needed. The earlier, golden mood of the afternoon had been ruined by the fight. Without speaking, we climbed on my horse and headed back to camp. This time she sat farther back on the horse, barely touching my sides with her hands.

I didn't know what was going through Red Leaf's mind, but I was worried about Brown Wolf. In defending myself, I had humiliated him. He would be the laughingstock of the entire tribe. If he didn't want to leave the tribe in shame, he would have to kill me to save face. I didn't want to fight him again, not now. I had been lucky with the porcupine. I didn't pretend to believe I would be so lucky the second time.

I began to think that it would be better for me to leave than to get into a life and death struggle with Brown Wolf. It would be better to swallow a little pride and live than to be killed. On the other hand, the safety the tribe provided meant a lot to me. I wasn't sure I could make it alone. I certainly couldn't consider taking Red Leaf with me and putting her life in danger. Maybe Neuwafe would protect me from Brown Wolf, but he couldn't be with me all the time. Brown Wolf would get his revenge if I stayed with the tribe.

As we rode through the sagebrush, this time at a walk, I didn't feel like talking with Red Leaf. I didn't want her to think I was afraid of Brown Wolf. I didn't think I was really afraid to fight him, not after all I had been through. It was just that I didn't want to die. What was I going to do?

Sensing my desire for quiet, Red Leaf remained silent during the ride. But as we approached the camp, she said two words.

"Don't tell." Then she said it again. "Don't tell."

I stopped the horse. I didn't know the language well enough to have a heart to heart discussion on why she said that, but her meaning was unmistakable. She didn't want me to tell anyone about the fight with Brown Wolf. It seemed like a foolish suggestion, contrary to everything I had learned from the Utes. It was not only commonplace but expected that men and boys boast of their daring feats. My creativity and daring in defeating Brown Wolf with a dead porcupine would win me untold face and acceptance among the members of the tribe. It was a great victory for me, regardless of what might happen later with Brown Wolf.

"Don't tell."

She certainly was persistent. I tried to think through the consequences of following her counsel, and suddenly I realized that she was right. Dead right. Two ideas popped simultaneously into my mind. The first was that if I didn't tell, Brown Wolf would not lose face in the tribe and therefore would not have to seek revenge. The second idea was that in not telling I would be putting Brown Wolf in a situation where he would have to be nice to me, in the fear that if he wasn't, I might tell about the porcupine fight and shame him. It was like blackmail. I liked it.

I turned around and looked at Red Leaf, wondering how someone so young and beautiful could be so wise. We promised each other not to tell anyone about the fight with Brown Wolf. As I turned back to the front, urging the stallion into a full gallop, Red Leaf scooted closer and wrapped her arms tightly around my waist.

Chapter 30

Red Leaf and I had been right about Brown Wolf. At first he seemed surprised, then confused, when I kept quiet about the whipping I had given him with the dead porcupine. He watched me very suspiciously for several days, obviously wondering what I had up my sleeve, thinking I might be waiting for some special moment to disgrace him in front of the tribe.

After a week or so, I could tell by the look on his face that he was beginning to believe that I had no intention of disgracing him. The hateful fire in his eye was disappearing. He looked at me with some respect. Not much, however, and never with a friendly smile, but it was obvious to me that in the opinion of Brown Wolf, the strange white boy suddenly held a position of respect.

His attitude toward Red Leaf, however, didn't change at all. He still had that hungry-dog expression whenever he looked in her direction. He was in love with her, as I was, and still a dangerous rival for her hand.

About ten days after the incident with the porcupine, the tribe arrived at the home camp near the shores of Utah Lake. Not long after that, Brown Wolf and some of his friends outfitted themselves with food and horses and disappeared into the western desert beyond the lake. The lengthy farewell indicated that they planned to be gone for some time.

From early summer's successful buffalo hunt we had plenty of food to get the tribe through the winter, so I didn't think they were going hunting. When I asked Neuwafe where they were going, he said something about getting horses. I erroneously assumed Brown Wolf and his friends were going into the desert to catch wild horses. I didn't learn until later of the elaborate trading system the Utes had adopted to acquire horses.

The Utes had three methods of obtaining horses. The most difficult was catching wild horses—a dangerous, tiring, and oftentimes fruitless undertaking. Not only were wild horses difficult to find and catch, but once caught they were hard to tame.

An easier method of obtaining horses was to steal them from other tribes, a very dangerous but often fruitful endeavor. A successful raid by three or four braves could sometimes net thirty or forty animals, all broke and ready to ride. If a brave was caught, however, he faced certain torture and death.

The most productive and safest way to get horses was to ride into the western desert and capture horseless Gosiutes and Paiutes, mostly women and children, and take them to Mexico or California, where they could be traded for horses. The young men and boys brought the best prices at the Mexican silver mines. The girls approaching puberty, twelve or thirteen years old, brought top prices at the haciendas, or big ranches. A healthy, attractive girl would sometimes bring as many as six horses.

Knowing how Brown Wolf felt about Red Leaf, I was surprised that he was willing to leave the village, especially when he knew I would be there to pursue my romantic interests with her. Indians were hard to understand.

With Brown Wolf gone, my life suddenly became very happy. Much of my waking time was spent with Red Leaf. Much to the disgust of Neuwafe, through the summer and fall months I frequently took Red Leaf with me to hunt deer or elk in the nearby foothills, catch trout in the streams that fed the lake, or hunt geese in the marshes surrounding the lake. Sometimes we just rode off together exploring the nearby hills and valleys. It was a carefree time, with Brown Wolf gone and plenty of food already stored for winter.

I began to think about marrying Red Leaf, according to Ute custom, and raising a family of my own. I was nearly seventeen years old, a little young for marriage in the white society but not in the Indian society. In fact, the Indian girls usually married much younger.

One of the problems that concerned me was getting my own tepee. A typical tepee required from fifteen to twenty buffalo hides. I had killed five animals during the summer hunt but had given the hides away. At the rate I was going, it would take me three more summers to kill enough buffalo for a tepee. I couldn't wait that long. I had nothing of wealth that could be traded for hides—no horses, no trinkets, no extra knives or guns. I didn't want to continue living in the same tepee with Neuwafe and Blackbird after Red Leaf and I were married.

I began to realize that the Indian life wasn't as carefree as I had supposed. Just as in white society, I needed some material wealth in order to get what I wanted. As I looked around me at the respected braves in the tribe, I realized that the most obvious measure of success was the number of horses owned by a man. All I had was a borrowed horse from Neuwafe. The Utes traded horses for whatever they wanted—guns, knives, trinkets, robes, tepee hides, and even wives.

At least I didn't have to buy Red Leaf with horses, or so I thought at that time. We were in love with each other, and I was confident her brother and mother would be delighted to see her become my wife, even though I did not trade any horses for her. How naive I was, thinking all I had to do was find a tepee so we could move in and live happily ever after.

Many of the dreams of youth must be abandoned in the face of sudden undeniable reality. Such was the case with Red Leaf and me. The dream ended quite abruptly when Brown Wolf returned from his horse-trading escapade in Mexico.

It was near the end of winter when he returned. The tribe was engaged in the annual bear dance, in which the dancers initiate the coming of spring by imitating bears coming out of hibernation. At first the dancers' movements are slow and heavy, as a bear's would be coming out of hibernation. As the dance continues, the pace quickens until at the end the dancers are in a wild fury. Next to the sun dance, this was probably the most important dance in the tribe.

There was a full moon that night. The dance had barely begun when someone announced that a large number of horses were approaching the camp. When the singing and dancing stopped, we could hear the thunder of many hooves on the open prairie. The men raced to their tepees to get weapons in the event we were being attacked. Women rounded up their children like mother hens with their chicks and herded them into tepees.

The alarm was unnecessary. A herd of riderless horses, driven by Brown Wolf and his companions, galloped through the camp. The bear dance became a victory celebration for the young men who had brought home so many horses.

While I had been enjoying a leisurely courtship with Red Leaf, assuming it would probably result in our marriage in the spring, Brown Wolf had been building his own little horse herd by trading slaves to Mexicans. Brown Wolf understood the Ute culture and the value of horses better than I did.

The tribe gathered around to hear Brown Wolf and his companions tell how they had captured a dozen or so Paiute children in the western desert and taken them to Mexico to trade for horses. I was disgusted. I thought I had left slavery behind in Missouri. The Utes were every bit as insensitive to slavery as were the southern plantation owners. Brown Wolf now had eleven new horses as a result of his trade.

Neuwafe listened to the stories with enthusiasm. I was disappointed, knowing he would do the same thing, if he hadn't already done so. Red Leaf, on the other hand, remained in the tepee. I assumed that she was upset over the selling of innocent children into slavery, as I was, but discovered the next morning that she had a very different concern.

We were awakened by the prancing and snorting of horses in front of the tepee. Neuwafe was the first to go out; I followed close behind. As I left, I looked over at Red Leaf. She was gazing at her hands with a forlorn expression, showing no interest at all in the commotion that was taking place in front of the tepee. It was as if she already knew what was happening outside and didn't approve.

I didn't approve either when I saw Brown Wolf holding the lead ropes of eight of his new horses. He had come to barter with Neuwafe for the hand of Red Leaf in marriage.

I couldn't figure out why Neuwafe even bothered to talk with Brown Wolf. I didn't figure there was any way he could trade his sister for eight horses, or any number of horses for that matter—especially to a man she didn't love. She loved me, not Brown Wolf, and Neuwafe knew that.

I couldn't figure out why Neuwafe was inspecting the horses so closely—looking into their mouths and ears, picking up their feet, leading them about. It was as if he were giving serious consideration to the offer.

Suddenly I remembered the look on Red Leaf's face and realized that even though I had spent nearly a year with the Utes, I still didn't understand them, not really. Neuwafe was my friend—we had saved each other's lives. He knew, if anyone did, that I loved his sister. How could he trade her to Brown Wolf for eight horses?

After carefully inspecting each of the horses, Neuwafe squatted on the ground, in deep thought. I wanted to talk to him and ask him what the devil was going on, but I could tell by the stern expression on his face that he didn't want to be bothered, at least not by me. Brown Wolf stood in front of Neuwafe, holding his horses, waiting impatiently for Neuwafe to respond.

It seemed like an eternity. Neuwafe just continued squatting there, looking stern, fingering the end of one of his thick braids. When he finally stood up, he looked directly at Brown Wolf and shook his head and said eight horses was not enough for Red Leaf. That was all. He went back in the tepee. Brown Wolf and I glared at each other for an instant before I followed Neuwafe into the tepee and received a lesson in Ute tradition that I would never forget.

My knowledge of the Ute language had been improving steadily, and between the two of them, it didn't take Neuwafe and Red Leaf long to explain the problem so that I could understand it. What I couldn't understand was why they hadn't bothered to tell me sooner. I suppose they assumed I knew more than I really did.

It was Ute tradition for men to pay for their women. In our society this is sometimes called a dowry. It was a disgrace for the father, or in this case the brother, to give the girl or woman to anyone other than the highest bidder.

Even though Neuwafe had turned down the eight-horse offer, he was now in a position where he would be disgraced if he accepted anything less than eight horses for Red Leaf. Her value had been established. Unbelievable. There was no question that he loved his sister with all his heart, but even so, he was bound by the tradition of the tribe.

The day before, I could have taken Red Leaf as my wife for one or two horses. Today I would disgrace Neuwafe with an offer less than eight animals. And eight was just the beginning. Brown Wolf wouldn't give up easily. Maybe he would be back the next morning with fifteen animals, setting a new minimum price for the hand of Red Leaf.

Again I thought of running off with Red Leaf. But where would we go? To live in relative security, we needed to belong to a band. There was nowhere to go. I was more than willing to gamble my own safety, but I just couldn't see risking Red Leaf's life by running off with her into the hostile wilderness.

It wasn't long until Neuwafe presented to me what in his eyes was the only reasonable solution to the dilemma. I needed my own horse herd, and I needed it quickly so I could be the top bidder for Red Leaf's hand. Neuwafe agreed to help me do it. By going with me, he would be unavailable to consider additional offers from Brown Wolf.

I realized Neuwafe was doing me a huge favor. I would always be grateful to him. On the other hand, there was no doubt in my mind as to how he intended to help me get the horses. I knew Neuwafe would not understand my abhorrence to the Ute custom of trading Paiute and Gosiute children into slavery. On the other hand, how could I turn down his offer to help me take his sister as my wife? I just couldn't sit back and let her become Brown Wolf's squaw.

The next morning Neuwafe and I rode past the south end of the lake toward the western desert. We led two extra horses for carrying the captive children to Mexico. During a sleepless night I had convinced myself that for Red Leaf's sake, just this once, I had no choice but to get involved in the Ute slave trade business.

Chapter 31

Neuwafe and I had been in the western desert about a week when we finally found a small band of Gosiutes, later called "diggers" by pioneers. During the week I had been deeply troubled by my decision to get involved with the trading of Indian children into slavery. Even though I felt forced into the situation, there seemed no other way to get enough horses to save Red Leaf from Brown Wolf. Still, I felt awful, as though I were stepping across an invisible line of corruption and dishonor.

I was about to the point where I was going to tell Neuwafe that I couldn't go through with the trade when we discovered the Gosiutes. We had been working our way along the base of a mountain range containing numerous white cliff rock formations with many caves. We were riding along the foothills, with the cliffs and caves on our left. On the right was a vast expanse of marshes. Neuwafe said the area was an ideal habitat for Gosiutes, who had neither horses nor effective weapons. The caves offered excellent protection from the elements and enemies, and the marsh provided much of the yearly food supply—cattail roots, fish, snails, snakes, frogs. In the foothills they hunted rabbits, squirrels, lizards, grasshoppers, and ants. They dug up sego lily bulbs, camas tubers, and arrowroots. The most common item in the hand of a Gosiute was a three-foot digging stick, sharpened on one end. Above ground, they harvested sunflower seeds, serviceberries, yucca pods, cactus pears, and arrowroot leaves.

Red Leaf had taught me how to identify many of the wild foods during the past summer and fall. I was an interested student because I wanted to learn everything I could about surviving in this wild, harsh land. Eating cooked weeds (as I often called the wild plants) did one thing for me, and that was to increase my appetite and appreciation for rich, red, juicy buffalo meat.

We had just reached the top of a rocky knoll when we spotted the Gosiutes, about twenty in number, scattered across the sagebrush plain below. There were three or four men, half a dozen women, and about a dozen children. It was nearly afternoon and the spring sun had warmed the earth to a comfortable temperature. Most of the Indians were wearing robes or clothing made from rabbit skins and shredded bark. Coming out of a long winter, most of them looked thin and haggard. None of them had any excess fat.

At first I was confused about what the Indians were doing. The older children were scooping dirt out of scattered holes. The women were shaking the dirt in shallow willow baskets much like a prospector pans for gold. The men were digging a pit next to a huge fire. Some of the smaller children were dragging in brush and sticks for the fire.

Since the Indians hadn't seen us yet, we quickly retreated out of sight, tied up the horses, and sneaked forward on foot to a place between two large junipers, where we could survey the situation without being seen.

It didn't take long to figure out that the women weren't panning for gold. They were panning for ants. The children were scooping out the insides of ant hills. As they shook the baskets, the dirt sifted through, leaving behind the ants and ant eggs, which were dumped into the pit by the fire. Before our arrival, the men had filled the bottom of the pit with hot coals and rocks which in turn were covered with a layer of bark and wet grass. The ants and eggs were dumped on the hot bed, then covered with another two layer of grass and bark, followed by more smoking coals and rocks, then more grass and ants. Layer by layer, the pit was slowly being filled. I had heard of roasting pigs, sheep, and even beef in pits, but never ants. I figured the Gosiutes were pretty hungry.

Suddenly I didn't feel so bad about selling Indians into slavery. Certainly they would eat better at the Mexican haciendas and silver mines. The western desert was a desolate land. I tried to tell myself the Indians would be better off with the Mexicans, even as slaves.

To our left the sagebrush plain ended at the base of some white cliffs where there appeared to be a number of caves, obviously the dwelling places of the unfortunate Gosiutes. Neuwafe and I decided to attack from the left, thereby cutting off the most direct route to the safety of the caves.

Our plan was a simple one. Since the Gosiute men were little and scrawny, and without weapons, except for a few digging sticks, we didn't anticipate a fight. Leaving the two extra horses behind, our plan was simply to sweep down upon the helpless and surprised Indians, round them up as cowboys would their cows, scoop up four or five of the older children, put them on our spare horses, and head for Mexico. I was certain they would find the buffalo jerky we were going to feed them much more appetizing than the ant gruel they had worked so hard to prepare for themselves. The horseless Gosiutes would not be able to follow us on foot. Surprise and intimidation would make us successful.

A few minutes later, Neuwafe and I emerged around the left end of the knoll, whooping and hollering as we galloped toward the surprised Gosiutes. As we began to round them up, Neuwafe headed around to the right, while I went to the left. Apparently the Indians had gone through this experience before, for they quickly formed a group at the middle of our imaginary circle—except for one of the boys who scampered past me toward the cliff. I let him go, not wanting to risk losing control over the group for the sake of the one that got away. As I looked over at Neuwafe, he didn't express any opposition when I let the boy go, so I assumed I had done the right thing.

It wasn't until the Indians were rounded up in a group and we were facing them that I realized how bad this thing really was. The terrified children hung desperately to their mother's skirts and legs, knowing they were the intended victims of our raid. The three men stood at the back of the group, their eyes on the ground, their hands empty, having dropped their digging sticks. At first I felt disgust for the men, for their inability or unwillingness to protect their families.

Looking into the faces of the terrified children, however, the object of my disgust became myself. I realized I was no better than the Missouri mobs who had persecuted my people, the Mormons, back in Missouri. I remembered how angry I had been about the looting, the burnings, the beatings. Now I was about to perform similar cruelties and injustices on helpless Indians by tearing children away from their mothers and selling them into slavery. I was every bit as bad as the Missourians, maybe worse, because I was doing this thing for material gain. At least most of the Missourians believed they were driving out the Mormons to protect what was theirs. A sick, helpless feeling welled up inside of me.

Neuwafe dismounted, spear in hand, and strutted boldly among the

Gosiutes, occasionally grabbing a child and shoving it in my direction.

I had just decided to tell Neuwafe that I couldn't do it, that I wouldn't do it, when I noticed a sudden wave of chatter among the captives. They were looking past me toward the cliffs.

As I looked around, I saw the biggest Indian I had ever seen. He was racing straight toward us, a long spear-like weapon in his right hand. The boy who had run away was following behind, trying in vain to keep up with the big warrior. The man's movements were strong and bold as he glided through the sagebrush, quickly narrowing the gap. Even at a distance I could see his huge muscles rippling in the afternoon sun. A cape of rabbit skins hung from his broad, well-muscled shoulders. It flapped wildly behind him as he drew closer and closer.

There was something unusual about the big warrior's head. At first I wasn't sure what it was, but I suddenly realized that unlike any other Indian I had ever seen, this one had short hair. At that moment I also realized that he was darker than any Indian I had ever seen. In fact, he was almost black.

I suddenly realized that it was Ike! My long-lost friend. The man I had helped escape from slavery! He was still too far away to recognize facial features, but that powerful, graceful body was unmistakable. It was Ike, all right. He had survived the Shoshone attack in that distant Snake River canyon. Like me, he had joined an Indian tribe, the Gosiutes, or so it appeared.

Before I had time to figure out what to do next, Neuwafe mounted his pony and thundered past me. He headed straight for Ike. With a firm hold on his spear, there was no doubt about his intention to sink his spear deep into the heart of the big black warrior.

I urged my horse into a full gallop after Neuwafe, hollering for him to stop. Partially from my yelling, but also as a result of recognizing the size and strength of the black man, Neuwafe slowed his horse, allowing me to catch up with him. I dug my heels into the side of my pony and shot right past Neuwafe, without offering any explanation so I would be sure to be the first to reach Ike.

Ike's greeting was less than friendly as I galloped up. He crouched like a cat, ready to spring, his spear firmly in his fists. I realized, almost too late, that he didn't recognize me. In the year and a half that had passed since I last saw him, I had grown taller and broader, and my skin was as dark as any Indian's from long exposure to sun and wind.

"Ike, it's me, Dan Storm," I shouted as I jerked my pony to a sliding halt.

The expression on Ike's face changed from one of fierce determination to one of confusion.

"Ike," I shouted again as my feet hit the ground. "Don't you remember me?"

A look of recognition finally spread across that familiar face, and without a word, he leaped forward to greet me with a powerful embrace.

"It's so good to see you again," I said. "I had a feeling you were alive, but I had about given you up for dead."

Ike didn't say a word, but as I looked into those clear eyes, I noticed a tear streaming down his black cheek. Neuwafe, still mounted on his pony, was about thirty feet away, dumbfounded by the unusual show of affection between me and the black warrior.

Chapter 32

Neuwafe left one of the horses behind for me when he headed back to the Ute camp in Utah Valley. He seemed more than a little disgusted with my joyous reunion with Ike. As much as anything, he seemed put out by the fact that I wanted to mix with the Gosiutes, Ike's adopted tribe. To Neuwafe the Gosiutes were the scum of the earth, good for nothing but to provide slaves for the more powerful Utes. As he left, I told Neuwafe that after spending a few days with my old friend Ike, I would return to the Ute village. I reminded him of my feelings for Red Leaf and promised I would be bringing him many horses to trade for her hand. I didn't have any idea how I would do such a thing, but I had to buy time so he wouldn't be tempted to accept an offer from Brown Wolf.

When Neuwafe was gone, Ike and I walked back to the cliffs. One of the boys was sent to fetch my horse. The Gosiutes gathered around us, chattering quietly among themselves, seeming awestruck that I was his friend and he had saved them from harm. Many of them seemed amazed at my sun-bleached hair and blue eyes. I figured they had probably never seen a white man before.

Just as we reached the caves, the boy returned with my horse. He handed the lead rope to Ike, saying something that sounded like "Boss Man."

"What did he call you?" I asked Ike.

"Boss Man. Don't like Injun names, hard to say."

I couldn't wait to hear Ike's story, how he had escaped the gun battle in the canyon north of the Snake River, how he had come to join the Gosiutes, and how he had become the Boss Man.

Ike waved the Indians away so we could be alone on a grassy slope in front of one of the caves. Ike had never been much of a talker, so I told my story first—how I had escaped from the Blackfeet after the riverboat had exploded, how I joined up with Beaver George in Fort Benton, how we had found out about Ike from the prospectors just before George died, how I had met Neuwafe on the Green River and joined the Ute band. By the time I finished my story, the sun was low in the sky and a cold breeze was beginning to blow up from the marshes.

Ike led me into one of the larger caves. We stretched out on mats of grass near a fire. The cave was warm and cozy; the flames of the fire casting friendly flickerings on the sandstone walls. As Ike was beginning to tell his story, a woman entered the cave and set a basket of little brown cakes between us, then left us alone to talk.

It didn't take Ike long to tell his story, and I'm sure he left out much of the detail. As I said, he wasn't much of a talker.

He said he figured I had been killed or drowned after the riverboat explosion. He joined Henry Pottsmouth and his son, James, on the prospecting expedition in a desperate move to get out of Fort Benton before someone figured out he was a slave without a master and attempted to send him back to St. Louis.

Ike said that when the Shoshones attacked them, he fought to defend the camp while the Pottsmouths moved up on the ridge to ambush the Indians from above. When he realized the Pottsmouths had deserted him, Ike simply surrendered to the Indians, thinking that if he continued to fight, they would get him sooner or later anyway. At the time he wasn't aware of the wicked tortures commonly inflicted on captives in these kinds of situations.

His captors, however, seemed curiously interested in his black skin and Negroid features. Ike was a novelty to them, so instead of torturing them, they took him to their village on the banks of the Snake River to show him to other Indians.

"Used to figure white men was hard on slaves. They's nice, next to Injuns," explained Ike. "Injuns think nuthin' o' tyin' a slave to a post out in the weather, the same as a dog. Sometimes they'll throw 'm some scraps, if they think about it. They forgot a lot."

While Ike was talking, I was munching on brown biscuits. They were heavier than any biscuits I had ever tasted—kind of crunchy, like coarse corn bread, but slivery as though they contained wood shavings. The flavor was really different. Swallowing would have been tough if it weren't for the saltiness.

Ike explained how he and a Gosiute boy had escaped from the Shoshone camp during the night, and how the boy had led him to the Gosiutes. After driving off some Shoshone slavers with a staff, Ike assumed a leadership role, at least when it came to battle and defense of the tribe. It was an easy role for him to assume since he was so much bigger and stronger than any of the other men in the tribe.

I noticed that Ike was somewhat thinner than I remembered him. All the Gosiutes were thin. Apparently they didn't eat as well as the Utes.

The woman came back into the cave, this time bringing us what looked like a big glob of blackberry jam on a piece of cottonwood bark. It was blacker than any jam I had ever seen, almost like tar. Ike spread some on one of the biscuits and handed it to me. It wasn't like any jam I had ever tasted. Not sweet, it had a strong peppery flavor. But it certainly improved the taste of the biscuits.

"What is this black stuff?" I asked. Ike reached out and scooped a big gob with two of his fingers and shoved it in his mouth, licking his fingers clean before returning his hand to his lap.

"Guess," he responded, grinning broadly.

"Serviceberry jam?" I asked, knowing Indians ate a lot of serviceberries. I had never tasted serviceberry jam.

"Nope."

Suddenly I remembered the ant hills that the Indians had been digging up when Neuwafe and I found them.

"Ants?"

Ike nodded. I had guessed correctly. I ate my next biscuit plain, without the ant jam.

"What kind of biscuits are these?" I asked, my mouth half full.

"Grasshopper cakes. Been eaten 'm all winter. Sometimes there's nothing else."

"Grasshopper cakes!" I exclaimed, spitting out the un-swallowed portion.

Ike explained that grasshoppers were the winter staple. More than anything else, it was grasshoppers that kept the tribe from starving during the long winter months. He said that in the fall, at the time of the first frosts, the Indians would gather huge piles of grasshoppers during the morning hours when the insects were too cold to hop. The hoppers were roasted in pits. And those not eaten were immediately stored for winter, at which time they were ground into flour and made into cakes.

I crawled over to my saddle next to the cave opening and pulled out two big strips of buffalo jerky from a hidden pocket, tossing one to Ike.

"Try some Ute food. Buffalo jerky."

Ike finished his before I swallowed my first bite.

"Got any more?"

I gave him two more pieces, which he wolfed down like a hungry dog.

I explained to Ike how in just a few months the Ute tribe had killed enough buffalo to keep the whole tribe in jerky through an entire winter. He was amazed.

"If they had horses, the Gosiutes could do it too," I said.

"We have a legend," began Ike, thoughtfully, "about a Gosiute warrior who caught a wild horse many summers ago. The people had seen horses before and thought they were big dogs.

"They fenced the horse in a cave so it wouldn't run away or be stolen. It wouldn't eat grasshopper cakes, raw fish, or roasted rabbit meat—foods generally relished by dogs. The horse starved to death.

"Today, when my people catch a horse, they eat it right away."

I looked toward the entrance of the cave. For the first time, I wondered what had become of my horse.

Sensing my concern, Ike said, "Don't worry. I told them not to eat your pony."

I asked Ike if he wanted to come back to the Utes with me and become a buffalo hunter. I was sure they would accept him into the tribe, as they had me.

To my surprise, he wasn't interested. Instead he invited me to join him and the Gosiutes. He said I could be co-chief with him, that we could get horses for the Gosiutes, teach them how to defend themselves against enemies, and maybe even trade for some guns. He added that he would like to get some seeds and try farming.

It was apparent that Ike had found a place where he belonged. In spite of the bad food, he seemed intent on remaining with the Gosiutes and improving their lot. The Gosiute life didn't look very appealing to me, but I suppose that being an Indian chief was pretty heady stuff for a former slave.

I told Ike that maybe I would join him, but if I did, I wouldn't be alone. I told him about Red Leaf and my intention to make her my wife. I explained the problem with the horses, how I needed ten or more for a dowry. I confessed that I had come with Neuwafe to steal the children, so we could trade them for horses. I added that I didn't know if I could have gone through with the slave trading, and that I was glad he had stopped us.

"Before I do anything else, Ike," I explained in all seriousness, "I've got to get some horses before Red Leaf becomes Brown Wolf's squaw."

We were silent for awhile, Ike downing several more biscuits after dipping them in the black jam. I quietly finished my strip of jerky. Finally Ike surprised me by saying he knew where there were a lot of horses.

He said he had seen a large herd, at least fifty in number, about a half-day's journey to the south. They had been grazing around a spring, under the watchful eye of six or seven braves, possibly Comanche or Apache. Ike had spotted them three days earlier while hunting rabbits. He didn't know if they would still be there, but even if they weren't, their trail would be easy to follow.

"You and me, we go steal some," he suggested.

I began to protest. I didn't want him risking his life to help me get horses for my own personal needs.

But he didn't let me finish. "You need horses to get girl. I need horses for Gosiutes. We both get horses."

I reached out and shook his hand. "It's a deal, partner," I said.

We decided to leave first thing in the morning.

Chapter 33

When the sun came up the next morning, Ike and I were already heading south. I was riding the horse and Ike was walking briskly at my side. After an hour or so he rode and I walked. For weapons, I carried a bow and a quiver full of arrows. Ike had his long staff. For food, we had buffalo jerky and grasshopper cakes. We also had a rawhide rope.

Back in Missouri, horse stealing was a serious crime, but the Indian cultures of the Rocky Mountains had a different attitude. It wasn't a crime unless you stole from your own tribe or friendly neighbors. Stealing from enemies and strangers was perfectly legal, but very risky. Captured horse thieves were usually killed.

Horses and women were a man's most prized possessions, usually in that order. Later, when more white men came to the Rocky Mountains, guns and firewater sometimes became the most sought-after items. But in 1840 the horse was king—the measure of wealth, the symbol of success and prosperity. And rightfully so. The tribes with horses, like the Utes, were the tribes that prospered. Those without horses, like the Gosiutes, barely survived.

"If they catch us, they'll kill us," I said to Ike, wanting to make sure he understood what we were getting into.

Ike didn't respond immediately, as if he wasn't bothered by my comment. I realized that I sometimes misjudged the big black, thinking he understood less than he did because of his ignorance of good English. But he was not a child. He was not dumb or slow by anybody's standards. In fact his close call with the Shoshones and his hand-to-mouth existence with the Gosiutes had probably brought him very close to the line that separated life from death. He probably had a better appreciation than I did of the risk we were facing. Finally he spoke.

"This ain't near as skeery as when Massar Boggs and his dogs was hunt'n us."

I agreed with him. It was a lot better being the hunter instead of the hunted.

I tried to think ahead, to make some preliminary plans on how to steal the horses, but I couldn't. There were too many unknowns—mostly geographic in nature, like the lay of the land, natural barriers, the best escape route, and so on. It simply was impossible to do any planning until we could see where the horses were.

It was good to be back with Ike again, to know after all those questioning months that he was alive and well. But I was far from being content. My thoughts continually returned to the Ute camp and Red Leaf. I missed her so much—her warm smile, those bright eyes, her gentle touch. She loved me and I loved her, with all my heart. I was incensed at the thought of her belonging to Brown Wolf or anyone else. I was determined to be successful in the horse raid. This was the first time I had been away from her for more than a day or two.

I vowed to myself that I wouldn't come back without the horses. But when we reached the valley where Ike had seen the horses, they were gone. They left an easy-to-follow trail, however, leading east and north. We looked around for any clues that might identify the Indians who were driving the horses, but could find nothing other than the cold coals of a fire. Without wasting any time, we began our eastward journey.

The trail was easy to follow, even over rocky formations where the animals left sufficient droppings to show where they had been. The horses were only a day or two ahead of us, but we could tell by the long distances between grazing signs that the animals were being pushed hard.

After three days of pursuit, we didn't seem to be getting any closer. With only one horse between us, it didn't appear that we would be able to catch them—at least not until they reached their destination. Ike seemed content with what we were doing. He wasn't in as big a hurry as I was. Someday those horses would reach their destination, and when they did we wouldn't be far behind.

The trail continued in an easterly direction through rugged mountain passes, across desolate flat lands, and over sweeping sagebrush prairies. I knew that eventually we would reach the Green or Colorado River. How soon, I had no idea.

Sometimes I wondered what kind of life Red Leaf and I would lead once she became my squaw. At first, I had just assumed that we would get our own tepee and live with the Utes. Life as a nomad had plenty of excitement and adventure for a fellow without commitments. But when I thought about raising a family, the white man's way seemed to be better. A log home with a stone fireplace seemed much more appealing than a drafty tepee. My idea of home was a house surrounded by barns, corrals, fruit trees, gardens, and grazing herds of cattle and horses.

Sometimes I longed for white man's foods. Buffalo jerky was a lot better than grasshopper cakes, but sometimes I craved a thick slice of homemade bread covered with butter and honey, a rare beefsteak with fried potatoes and onions, or a piece of chocolate cake with a cup of fresh milk.

As much as I hated school back in Missouri, I now longed to read a book or a newspaper. I would teach Red Leaf and my children how to read. I would read to them from the Bible and the Book of Mormon.

Sometimes I wished I could stay in my dreams rather than come back to harsh reality. This horse stealing was dangerous business. Neither Ike nor I had any previous experience. The Indians outnumbered us three or four to one. If we succeeded, they would certainly pursue us. How could we outdistance them, or hide from them if they had horses too?

On the fifth day, from the top of a treeless ridge, we spotted what we figured was the Green River, winding like a giant snake among the rugged sandstone cliffs. It was full and brown with the first of the spring runoff from the distant mountains.

The trail of the horse herd headed straight for the river. I was disappointed that we hadn't caught up with them before they had crossed to the other side. I was more than a little worried about crossing such a big river during the spring runoff.

We were following the trail down the middle of a draw, almost to the river, when we were surprised by the neigh of a horse not very far away. Ike quickly put his hand over the nose of our horse to prevent it from neighing back. We tied the horse to a tree and climbed the rocky side hill to get a better look. I was sure we had finally caught up with the horse herd.

Based on the sign we had been following, we figured the horse herd contained about fifty animals. But when we reached the top of the ridge, we looked out over a huge meadow where hundreds of horses were grazing, many more than the number we had been following. The meadow had natural fencing on three sides—the river on the far side, and jagged rock formations across the bottom and up the near side. Across the open end, or top of the meadow, was a string of about a dozen tepees.

There were children and dogs running about the tepees. Strips of red meat were drying on willow racks. Several buffalo hides were staked out on the grassy turf, flesh side up. Apparently this was the base camp of the Indians we had been following. Not only were there more horses but also more Indians than we had figured on. We had no way of telling what tribe they belonged to. The men wore their hair in braids like the Utes, but I supposed braves from many tribes could have the same custom.

During the night, with the help of a full moon, Ike and I scouted the cliffs surrounding the meadow, looking for some kind of back door, possibly a sloping canyon, that could be used as an escape route for stolen horses. Our search was in vain. There was no way for a horse to get out of the meadow except past the tepees. Up close, the river looked uncrossable. The swollen, brown water raged swiftly past the camp, threatening to carry away any man or beast that attempted to cross it into the rocky gorge beyond the bottom of the meadow. Perhaps it had been crossable in the fall when the water was low, but not now. Besides, there appeared to be nothing but cliffs on the other side. We figured it best to stay away from the river.

After much discussion we finally came up with a plan—so bold and daring that we figured it might just work. It was a simple plan, nothing fancy or tricky.

Chapter 34

Just as it was getting dark the next evening, Ike and I slipped down from the rocks into the lower end of the meadow. When we were sure we couldn't be seen from the Indian camp, we walked quietly among the horses until we found two we could catch and mount. It didn't take long. Most of the horses seemed fairly tame, not frisky, but still tired and hungry from the long winter.

Our plan was to wait until the moon came up, then try to stampede the entire herd past the tepees and sleeping Indians. Hopefully the tethered horses near the tepees would break their tether ropes and join us, leaving the Indians no way to follow.

Ike and I both felt uneasy about the plan. It appeared too simple, too easy. Perhaps the horses would refuse to go past the tepees. Maybe Ike and I would be easy targets for alert archers. If we didn't get all of the animals, how would we outdistance the Indians who mounted the strays and came after us?

Neither of us had any alternative suggestions, however, so we decided to plunge boldly ahead and hope for the best. If we became separated, we agreed to meet back at the Gosiute camp.

In the pre-moon darkness we began to round up the animals at the lower end of the meadow so we would be ready to begin the stampede as soon as the moon came up.

Ike and I waited until the moon was full above the eastern hills. Some of the Indians still stood around the fires, but most had retired into the tepees for the night. I felt very uneasy, a sickening feeling in my stomach.

One thing that bothered me was the tameness of the horses. In order for our plan to work, the horses had to stampede. Tame horses were harder to get going. Apparently they had been driven and handled so much in recent weeks that the usual spunk and spirit one would expect in a herd of Indian ponies just wasn't there. The only concern they seemed to have was the new green grass sprouting out of the soft soil. I wished I had my Hawken rifle, so I could fire a few shots to get them running.

Suddenly the quiet of the night was shattered by a loud, piercing scream. It was Ike, shouting at the horses. I joined with a scream of my own, digging my heels into my horse's ribs. The horse herd began galloping toward the line of tepees, picking up more and more grazing animals as they gained momentum. It was far from the wild-eyed stampede we had hoped for, but still, the horses were running, and in the intended direction. I began to feel that we might be successful after all. And, as far as I could see, there were no stragglers. All the horses were joining the running herd. So far, so good.

Looking ahead to the Indian camp, in the light of the dying fires I could see Indians scrambling out of their tepees with blankets and ropes in their hands. They began to form a line across the end of the meadow. Ike and I continued our yelling and screaming, urging the horses to run faster.

The first sign of failure was when a small group of horses, anticipating the line of blanket-waving Indians, began to veer off to one side. There was no way Ike and I could keep them all together. I realized then that we would be leaving some horses behind, enough to enable a large group of Indians to pursue us. But there was no turning back now. We had to drive as many as possible through the barrier of tepees and shouting Indians.

The Indians knew exactly what to do. They were standing behind the line of campfires waving buffalo robes to fan the fires back to life. The blazing light reflected wildly on the waving robes.

The entire herd began to veer toward the river. Ike and I did our best to turn them back toward the tepees, but there was no turning back. The horses were determined not to run through the flaming line of flapping robes.

Ike and I followed the herd, not willing to break through the line of Indians without the herd as a buffer. Upon reaching the river, the stampeding horses headed back down the meadow, turning their backs on the line of blanket-waving Indians. Ike and I continued with the main herd, figuring that when we reached the bottom of the meadow we would dismount and scamper into the rocks. There was no question that the Indians would be coming after us.

I was wondering if they would wait until morning to look for us when I became aware of hoofbeats approaching from the rear, farther out in the meadow.

Though several strays had broken away from the herd, it didn't seem natural that they would try to catch up with us again. I looked around.

In the moonlight I had no trouble recognizing the riders on the approaching horses. Apparently some of the Indians had mounted the tethered animals near the tepees and were coming after us. Five or six, it appeared. They were farther out in the meadow in an attempt to prevent us from escaping into the cliffs. I yelled at Ike to get his attention, then pointed at the approaching Indians. I urged my horse to run faster. The Indians continued to narrow the gap.

Upon seeing the Indians, Ike urged his horse forward in the narrow gap of meadow between the racing herd and the river. He waved for me to follow him. My inclination was to stay away from the river to avoid being trapped in the corner where the river and cliffs came together at the bottom of the meadow.

When I hesitated, Ike motioned again for me to follow him. He seemed to know exactly what he was doing and insisted that I follow him. I urged my horse into the gap between the herd and the river, not understanding why, but trusting Ike's judgment.

We were almost to the end of the meadow when Ike pointed to a spot just ahead of us where the main current of the river pushed close against the shore, undercutting the grassy bank. It wasn't until Ike held his nose with two fingers to indicate he was going swimming that I realized that he intended to ride his horse over the bank into the raging current. Quickly I glanced over my shoulder at the pursuing Indians who had now caught up with us on the other side of the thundering herd.

As much as I dreaded the thought of going into the river, I realized it was too late to consider any other alternative. The only one left was getting caught and killed by the Indians. With a sudden jerk, I pulled my horse's head toward the cut-away bank. The horse's first reaction was to stop, but it was too late. It lunged forward into space, just as Ike and his horse hit the water ahead and to the right.

The plunge unseated me, but I managed to grab the horse's tail before it swam out of reach. The water was icy cold. I looked for Ike and spotted him directly ahead, lying flat over the back of his horse, guiding it downstream into the main current. My horse was following.

As we were swept past the bottom of the meadow, where the horse herd had ground to a halt at the water's edge, I could see the mounted Indians trying to push through the milling horses in a vain effort to get into position to shoot arrows at us before Ike and I disappeared out of sight into the raging canyon.

We were swept into the blackness of the canyon before the Indians had a chance to shoot a single arrow. The river narrowed between the cliffs and ran faster and faster. We piloted our horses the best we could to avoid the occasional boulders that stood in our way. The towering cliffs on each side made escape impossible.

Occasionally the moon came into view as the river wound its way among the cliffs. We looked ahead the best we could for a break in the rock walls that could offer a possible escape route.

Suddenly the river grew quiet, but it didn't seem to slow down. Ahead we could hear what sounded like distant thunder. It wasn't thunder, though, because it didn't stop, but gradually grew louder and louder. It was the sound of water crashing over rocks, possibly a waterfall, but white water for sure—an uncontrollable force that would beat us and our horses into pemmican.

As we were swept around a bend, the river suddenly widened, shallow and quiet before the worst rapids, exposing a sandy beach and wooded valley on the west bank. A few minutes later, with blue lips and chattering teeth, Ike and I led our horses onto the beach. After running up and down the beach a few times to get warm, we gathered materials for a bow drill to make a fire. I removed some of the fringe from my buckskin shirt to fashion the bow string.

Soon my soaked buckskins were steaming from the warmth of the fire. Ike and I were chewing on the last of my wet jerky while the two horses were grazing nearby. Ike was in good spirits, pleased that we had succeeded in stealing two horses, a gain of one since we had to leave my old horse behind.

As far as I was concerned, we had failed. I knew Neuwafe wouldn't take less than ten horses for Red Leaf.

I realized how stupid I was to think I could just ride up to an Indian camp and run off with all the horses I wanted. Indians were used to people trying to steal their horses and weren't about to make horse stealing easy. I had learned that lesson the hard way.

Still, I had to have horses. I was opposed to trading slave children for horses, and I had never even seen a wild horse, let alone caught one. Stealing still seemed the best way to go. But how? It was clear those Indians didn't intend to make it easy for us. I wondered if we could go back to the meadow and watch until the Indians tried to move the horses, then make a move. Still, it seemed like a risky undertaking, doomed to failure.

It was a restless night for me, thinking of Red Leaf and trying to figure out a better way to get horses. On the other side of the fire, Ike seemed to be sleeping peacefully.

At first light we explored the little valley on foot. We discovered a game trail and followed it to the top of the plateau. I was annoyed with Ike's cheerfulness. He seemed to be thoroughly enjoying our little adventure. On our way back to camp, at a place where the trail passed between two large boulders, Ike pushed over a dead tree to block the trail.

"What did you do that for?" I asked. "We'll have to move it when we bring the horses out of here."

"Don't want horses to get away while we gone."

"Gone? Where are we going?"

"Get more horses."

"We're not going back there!" I exclaimed, pointing in the general direction of the Indian village.

"I show you how we get horses." Ike knelt down and began to sketch his plan in the sand. This time the plan made sense. I was sure it would work. We began making preparations to return to the Indian village.

Chapter 35

At dusk, Ike and I were high in the rocks, where we had an excellent view. The Indian village looked peaceful enough, no different from the day before. The dogs and children were playing as usual. Apparently the Indians were no longer alarmed by our attempted raid on their horses. They probably figured the raging river had carried us to watery graves.

All the Indians seemed to be near the camp. None were out in the meadow with the grazing horses. Surveying the landscape, we could see the grassy bank where our horses had leaped into the river the night before. We could see the sandy beach at the bottom of the meadow where the cliffs met the river, the same place where the stampeding horse herd had come to a halt.

As soon as it was too dark for anyone in the tepees to see us, we crawled down from the cliffs into the meadow as we had done before. Each of us caught a horse and led it quietly over to the sandy beach at the bottom of the meadow. Ike took both of the lead ropes and walked into the water, trying to get the horses to follow. When they pulled back, I slapped their rears with a long willow branch. Reluctantly they followed Ike into the river. As soon as they were swimming, Ike removed the ropes. After giving them several good, hard slaps on the backs with the wet ropes to keep them swimming toward the middle of the stream, Ike headed back to shore. By the time the horses tried to turn back, it was too late. The swift-moving current had carried them into the chute of no return.

Our plan was a very simple one. Any horse we could get into the chute would be carried to our canyon where we had escaped the river the night before. No horse with any sense would continue swimming past the little valley with the sandy beach. All would want to join the other horses already grazing in the lush meadow.

Our challenge was to get as many horses as possible into the river before the moon came up, without the Indians knowing what we were doing. At all costs we had to avoid spooking the horses or making any noise that would attract the attention of the Indians.

We were fortunate to have a beach at the bottom of the meadow. The task would have been infinitely more difficult if we had been forced to jump the horses from a bank. But leading them into the gradually deepening water at the beach wasn't nearly so hard.

One thing on our side was that most of the animals were accustomed to crossing streams. River crossings were common in the everyday life of the nomadic wanderers. A horse that had been with a wandering Indian tribe for any length of time had crossed numerous streams and rivers.

Most Indians had little patience for a horse that resisted plunging into raging rivers or leaping over difficult rock formations or fallen trees. The most common means of persuasion was a small pine tree with the branches removed about an inch from the trunk. After sharpening the branch ends, the Indian would begin to whip the reluctant horse on the rear until it plunged forward. Apparently most of the horses in the meadow were accustomed to this kind of treatment and offered little resistance to our efforts to get them into the river.

Soon our teeth were chattering from going in and out of the icy water, but as we continued to work, we became enthusiastic about the success we were having. By the time the moon rose over the mountain, we had pulled or driven thirty-two animals into the river. Catching two more, and mounting them, we followed the horses into the raging chute.

When we reached the valley where the wet horses were grazing quietly in the meadow, we heaped twigs on the uncovered coals of our old fire and soon were warming ourselves in front of a blazing fire.

I couldn't help but wonder what the Indians would do when they discovered that some of their horses were missing. They would probably circle the meadow looking for tracks that would indicate where the horses had escaped. The first time around they would probably pass up the beach where we had driven them into the river because that was the usual drinking place where tracks from drinking horses would be expected to accumulate. Since they would find no other tracks leaving the meadow, eventually they would have to conclude that the horses had disappeared down the river. They would follow, possibly in the river, but more likely along the cliffs until they discovered our little valley where the horses had emerged from the river. If we were lucky, they wouldn't discover the little valley until late the next day.

At any rate, we didn't intend to wait around any longer than necessary. As soon as our steaming clothes were hot enough to keep us from shivering and our teeth from chattering, we rounded up the horses and began driving them out of the canyon. We pushed over dead trees at several narrow places in the trail in an effort to make it as difficult as possible for the Indians to follow us.

Chapter 36

It was early on a frosty morning in late April 1841, when Ike and I stampeded our newly acquired horse herd through the Ute village. A few minutes later, I was standing in front of Neuwafe's tepee, holding the lead ropes to fifteen horses. I hadn't yet seen Red Leaf, but I didn't expect to see her until the dowry had been accepted.

Neuwafe emerged from the tepee—a stern but pleased look on his face. A buffalo robe was wrapped around his shoulders. Without a word, he began a careful inspection of the horses, picking up feet, inspecting teeth, running his hand along their backs and necks and up and down their legs.

When he was finished, he just looked at me a minute, without words. Then he took the lead ropes out of my hand and led the horses away toward the pasture. That was all. Neuwafe had accepted my dowry. I had permission to take Red Leaf as my wife.

However, I was feeling that somehow it hadn't seemed natural or complete. It was too matter-of-fact, too much like buying a horse, or a piece of meat.

I half expected Red Leaf to come out of the tepee. Surely she had been observing the transaction between me and Neuwafe. But still, she didn't come. I began walking toward the river, trying to sort this thing out in my mind. There was something missing, something in the Ute culture I didn't understand. I knew that if I pushed my way into the tepee and took Red Leaf as my woman, neither Neuwafe nor anyone else in the tribe would object. But that wasn't enough. She had to choose me too. Instead, she stayed in the tepee.

Maybe she didn't like the idea of being bought and sold with horses. Then it occurred to me that I hadn't really purchased the woman but merely the permission to marry her from her guardian or brother. What was I supposed to do now? Any Ute would have known what to do in the culture they grew up with. But for me, a white man from a different world, it was hard to understand the things the Utes took for granted. I wished the Utes had a marriage ceremony similar to that practiced by white men. That would have been easy—a preacher saying a bunch of words from the Bible, and each partner exchanging rings and saying, "I do." That I could understand. The Utes didn't have a marriage ceremony. Still, there had to be more than the exchange of horses. But I couldn't put my finger on what was wrong.

While walking across the meadow away from the tepees, I remembered a courting custom among the Utes that had always appeared silly to me—and more than a little unnecessary.

I recalled my first spring with the Utes, two years earlier, when fresh meat was scarce. I remembered watching a young brave bring a freshly killed elk into camp. The two front quarters were on one horse, the two back quarters on the other horse. Without unloading them, he tied the horses to a tree near the tepee of a young woman he had been flirting with.

I remember watching closely, wondering if he would give us some of the fresh meat. We had eaten nothing but jerky for weeks. The whole camp was hungry for fresh meat.

After tying the horses to the tree, the young brave entered his tepee. I supposed at the time he had gone to get some members of his family to help skin and butcher the quarters. Perhaps he wanted to sharpen his knife on the family sharpening stone.

I couldn't understand when he didn't come out of the tepee. I watched for several hours, and still he didn't come out. I was surprised that other members of the tribe didn't gather around the fresh meat, still loaded on the horses. The morning sun grew warmer and warmer, threatening to sour the fresh meat if it wasn't soon taken care of. It seemed I was the only one in the camp who was aware of the meat. The two horses were incessantly pawing the ground in their impatience to be relieved of the heavy loads.

It must have been almost noon when the young woman who had been courted by the brave untied the horses and led them to the front of her tepee. Her mother and sister helped her unload the quarters, skin them, and cut up the meat. They shared some of the meat with us and other families.

I didn't see the young brave again until he joined his sweetheart and her family for supper that evening. He stayed the night, bringing his belongings the next day as he moved in with his new bride and her family. Now, two years later, he had accumulated a respectable pile of buffalo hides, nearly enough to make a tepee of his own to share with his wife and baby girl.

On one occasion the previous fall, Brown Wolf had tied up a horse carrying a freshly killed doe near Red Leaf's tepee in the hope she would dress it out and cook him a delicious meal. Had she done so, I'm sure Neuwafe would have accepted Brown Wolf's eight-horse dowry. Instead, Red Leaf refused to go near the deer. The next morning the deer was gone. No one knew for sure what had happened to it, but it was rumored that Brown Wolf, in a frustrated rage, had thrown it in the river.

All of a sudden it was clear to me what I must do. After explaining to Ike why I had to go hunting for a few days, and asking him to wait around until I returned, I gathered up my weapons—my bow and arrows—sharpened my knife, and headed toward the foothills of the big mountain, later called Timpanogos.

Chapter 37

Hunting with bow and arrows is a lot different from hunting with a rifle. When Beaver George and I were heading to the Snake River country from Fort Benton, armed with our Hawken rifles, shooting an occasional deer or elk was a simple matter. Whatever we could see within several hundred yards, we could shoot. When you saw the game, the hunt was practically over.

Bow hunting is totally different. When you see the game, that's when the real hunting begins. A rifle is a better weapon for a man in a hurry. The bow, in order to be successful, requires a supreme patience, appreciated fully only by those who have done it.

I was in a hurry to get game and would have preferred a rifle, but since I didn't have one, I was forced to do it the Indian way. I had to forget about being in a hurry. With enough jerky in my possibles bag to last a week, I was determined to keep hunting until I was successful.

I rode to a wooded area at the foot of the big mountain. Red Leaf and I had ridden our horses through the area the previous fall and had seen plentiful deer and elk signs. There was still a lot of snow higher on the mountain, so I figured most of the animals would still be at the lower elevations. There were several south-sloping grassy side hills in the area where the grass was just beginning to green up. I was sure there would be plenty of deer and elk around.

It was almost dark when I arrived at the desired hunting area. In addition to the horse I was riding, I brought along a packhorse. After staking the horses out to graze, Indian style (the lead rope tied to the front foot), I built a small fire to keep me warm during the night. I was grateful for a nearby spring with clear, cold water. Most of the streams at this time of year were murky with the spring runoff.

I chewed slowly on my scant ration of jerky in an effort to make it last as long as possible. I looked into the flickering flames, thinking about Red Leaf. Things would have been a lot simpler had she come out of the tepee that morning to talk with me, to give me the assurance that she still loved me, that she would be my wife. That would have been a lot easier than playing this game with the meat. The Utes had some strange customs.

I wondered about our future together. Sometimes the carefree, nomadic life of the Utes seemed best—moving from valley to valley in the beautiful Rocky Mountain country, chasing the plentiful buffalo herds.

Other times I thought about the life I had left behind—warm log cabins, bread, vegetables, beef, and the comforts of civilized living. Maybe the white society wouldn't accept Red Leaf or our half-Indian children. Perhaps it would be best to stay with the Utes, visiting Ike and his Gosiute tribe from time to time.

At dawn I began to hunt, leaving the horses tied to trees near the cold campfire.

The key to successful bow hunting is seeing the game before it sees you. With a rifle, this doesn't really matter. A good marksman can drop an animal on the run.

The best way to see an animal before it sees you is to move slowly, Indian style—one step, two looks, one step, two looks. It was an impossible task without practice, especially for a man used to being in a hurry. One has to forget time and blend in with nature, noticing the different varieties of mushrooms and fungi, especially the broken pieces that have been nibbled on by the deer or elk. Examining tracks, sniffing the wind, straining to hear every sound. Never in a hurry.

It was late in the morning when I heard an unnatural sound—the thrashing of some branches. It stopped. A minute later it started again, somewhere ahead of me in a thick grove of young aspen trees. If it were the late summer or fall, I would have guessed a deer or elk was rubbing his horns against a tree. But in the spring, the deer and elk didn't have horns. Had I been in the lower, marshy areas, I would have suspected the noise to be coming from a beaver dragging a young sapling to his pond. As far as I knew, there were no ponds or streams in the area.

Slowly, I moved ahead, pausing between each step to look and listen.

The brush was thick, and I couldn't see more than thirty or forty feet ahead of me. The morning breeze was steady from the right; no danger of the animal smelling me.

As I came over a little rise, I suddenly saw the top of a tree thrashing against its neighbors. I couldn't see the bottom of the tree, or the source of the thrashing.

It occurred to me that I might be stalking a bear, one that was sharpening his long claws in the bark of the thrashing tree. I would have to get close to see the animal. Surprised bears sometimes become angry, more inclined to attack than to run away. I would have to take that chance.

I moved closer and closer. At about thirty feet I began to get an occasional glimpse of brown hide through the thick leaves. I couldn't see enough to tell what kind of animal it was. Sometimes the noise would stop, but after a few moments of silence, the thrashing of the treetop would begin again.

The woods were so dense now that it appeared impossible to move farther ahead without making the kind of noise that would alarm the animal. The ground was covered with the leaves of the previous fall. The once damp and quiet leaves were becoming dry and noisy in the spring sun.

I was standing next to the butt of a fallen log. It was clean and free of limbs, having been there a long time. I waited until the tree began shaking again—when the animal would be less likely to notice my movement or noise. Then I stepped quietly up on the fallen log.

To my relief, the animal was not a bear. It was a young bull elk, rubbing away its shaggy winter coat on the underside of a horizontal branch extending from the thrashing tree. Even though I was close enough to shoot, there was too much brush between me and him. Surely the arrow would be deflected.

As the elk rubbed his back on the branch, I began moving sideways along the fallen tree, hoping to find a more open line of fire between me and the animal. Whenever he stopped scratching and looked around, I held perfectly still.

He was a beautiful animal, possibly a two-year-old. His head, neck, and shoulders were a glossy dark brown. His sides and rump were a creamy tan under the remaining shagginess of winter he was trying to rub away. The fuzzy stubs on his head in the next few months would grow into huge antlers, giving the elk the most majestic appearance of any animal in

North America. His eyes were clear and black. He was alert and healthy, although somewhat thin after the long winter.

Suddenly the elk jerked his head to attention, apparently startled by a strange sound or smell. Perhaps he had heard the scuff of my moccasin against the log or caught a hint of my scent. I couldn't detect any breeze, but at only thirty feet, my scent might have drifted in his direction without the help of a breeze.

He hadn't seen me, though. With no definite idea as to where I might be, he looked first in one direction, then another—head high, ears forward, nostrils quivering. I knew if I made the slightest move, he would spot me and disappear into the brush.

I don't know how many minutes I stood there without moving, but soon both feet began to go to sleep, and my left arm, holding the bow and the strung arrow, began to ache. He was not in a position where I could shoot, so I continued to wait, fighting the discomfort and pain of not being able to move.

After what seemed like hours—though it couldn't have been more than fifteen or twenty minutes—the elk walked away from the tree. He stopped to look around five or six steps to my right, where I had a clear line of fire. At ten yards it was an easy shot, but I couldn't risk him seeing me draw the arrow back. I continued to wait.

At a moment when he turned his head to look away from me, I quickly drew the arrow back and let it fly. Just as the young bull was turning his head back in my direction, the obsidian-tipped arrow sank into his side. It hit him a little higher and farther back than I had intended. I had been aiming for the heart but had been too hasty and had missed. The young bull bounded back toward the tree where he had been rubbing his back and stopped.

Again I held perfectly still as he looked around, still not knowing what had happened or where I was. I knew if he saw me and bounded off through the brush, I might never find him. I was hoping that the arrow had at least penetrated the lungs. If the jagged, razor-sharp edges of the point did their work properly, he would soon drown in his own blood.

Just as my feet were beginning to go to sleep again, the elk lay down with his head still up, looking this way and that; he was trying to figure out what was happening, but I knew I had him. Soon he would be too stiff to get up, even if he saw me.

After waiting a few more minutes, I drew another arrow from my quiver. The movement caught the attention of the wounded animal. He watched as I strung the arrow. He tried to get up but couldn't. He was dying. I wished for a rifle so I could shoot him between the eyes and put him out of his misery. I waited a few more minutes until he could no longer hold his head up. Then I cautiously moved forward to dress him out.

The next morning I loaded two of the quarters on each horse and headed back to the Ute camp.

Chapter 38

Upon arriving at the Ute camp about the middle of the day, I tied the two horses carrying the four elk quarters to a small cottonwood tree near Neuwafe's tepee—the same tree where Brown Wolf had tied his horse with the deer on it a few months earlier. I wondered if he had really thrown the deer in the river after Red Leaf humiliated him by refusing to dress it out and cook it for him. I wondered if she would humiliate me too. I hadn't seen her since Ike and I had brought back the horses. Maybe she was having second thoughts about being the squaw of a white boy. I decided I wasn't going to sit around watching and waiting like the love-sick Brown Wolf had done.

Ike, who had waited for me while I was off elk hunting, was now ready to return to his Gosiute band. He had been keeping a close eye on the horses in the event their former owners might have followed us.

We rode out in the big meadow beyond the camp to catch fifteen of the horses. After these were gone, there would be four left for me. I had already given fifteen of the animals to Neuwafe.

My plan was to help Ike herd his horses home—maybe not all the way, but at least far enough so stragglers would stay with the herd rather than drift back to the Ute camp.

As usual, Ike didn't say much, but I figured he was pretty excited about bringing horses home to his Gosiute band. Now his people would be able to travel and hunt buffalo. Their standard of living would increase substantially. They would have to learn to fight too, because traveling bands of Indians were constantly exposing themselves to enemies and horse thieves. They had to be able to defend themselves. I figured Ike would be a good teacher, not so much because of his words, but because of his ability to act.

He was brave, strong, and smart. I was sure he and his Gosiutes would thrive. Sometimes I thought that maybe Red Leaf and I would join Ike and his Gosiutes. The Utes were superior in numbers, strength, wealth, and fighting ability, but Ike was a good chief. Maybe I could help him build his band into a strong people and be some kind of a co-chief with him.

As we drove the horses past the Ute camp toward the open prairie, I looked toward the little cottonwood tree where I had tied the packhorses. They were gone.

I spotted the horses standing quietly in front of Neuwafe's tepee. The elk quarters were on the ground. Red Leaf and her mother were busily skinning them. I wanted to gallop over and give Red Leaf a big hug—to be with her, to talk with her about our future life together. She had accepted me! We were as good as married, and I hadn't even talked to her in weeks! How different were the Ute ways when compared to white civilization. I wasn't even supposed to see her now. I was supposed to wait until evening when she would have a meal prepared for me.

Well, I couldn't just ride by without some kind of acknowledgment. I shouted toward the tepee and waved. Red Leaf and her mother waved back at me, giggling back and forth to each other things I couldn't hear.

My face began to turn red, and I wasn't sure why. I turned back to the horses, glad I was heading out on the prairie with Ike, glad I had something to keep me busy during the afternoon.

At first the horses didn't want to leave the lush meadows and the quietly grazing Ute herd, but after an hour, they resigned themselves to being herded into the western desert. After several hours, I said good-bye to Ike, thanked him for being my partner in the horse-stealing endeavor, and headed back to the Ute camp and my new bride.

I'll never forget the wedding feast prepared for me and Red Leaf. By white men's standards it was not fancy. Because it was spring and the winter's food supply had been pretty much exhausted, there weren't very many kinds of foods available.

Still, Red Leaf made the most delicious stew I have ever tasted. Beginning early in the afternoon, she filled an old buffalo stomach half full of the most tender cuts of the elk loin and covered them with water. While the meat was simmering, she added several handfuls of wild onions she had found on a south-sloping hillside next to a spring. Then she added the last of the sego and camas bulbs that had been stored in a pit behind the tepee.

Next she split open the leg bones and scraped the marrow into the simmering stew. After flavoring to taste with salt, she let it simmer the rest of the afternoon and into the evening.

When I arrived shortly after dark, the aroma of the bubbling stew had extended well beyond the confines of the tepee. I hadn't eaten since early morning, having been out on the prairie helping Ike drive his horses to the Gosiute camp.

My only regret as I approached the tepee for the wedding feast was that I didn't have a tepee of my own for Red Leaf and me to share. Before reaching the tepee, I stopped for a minute to contemplate what I was doing. By marrying a Ute, I would become one of them, more so than I had been before. With a Ute wife it would be difficult to go back to a white civilization that might look down upon our children. Did I really want to spend the rest of my life in this wild land of the Rocky Mountains?

I looked up at the snow-covered peaks of the great mountain, Timpanogos, barely visible in the fading twilight. I took a deep breath of the crisp, still night air, and listened to the night sounds—the muffled voices from the nearby tepees, the lapping of river water against the bank, the snort of a horse in the grazing herd, the growling of a dog catching a strange scent on the night air, another snort from a startled horse. Perhaps a coyote or wolf was trying to sneak past the horses in an effort to find food scraps near the Indian camp.

I entered the tepee and received a warm greeting from Neuwafe and Blackbird. Red Leaf had her back to me as she gathered wooden bowls from a rawhide container. I squatted cross-legged next to Neuwafe and watched the movements of my new bride. Her buckskin dress was whiter than any I had ever seen and decorated tastefully at the shoulders and waist with blue and red beads, sun-bleached bird bones, and porcupine quills. Her glistening black hair hung loosely about her shoulders. Her feet were bare.

Finally, she turned to greet me, first looking down into the fire, then somewhat timidly into my face. It was the first time we had been face to face since all this business with the horse stealing and elk hunting had begun.

There was a look of peace about her, a look of fulfillment. With the passing of only a few weeks, she had begun to look more like a woman, less like a girl. The color in her cheeks, the fulness of her lips, the gracefulness of her movements. But most of all, her face. If I ever met face to face with an angel from heaven, I knew it couldn't look any better to me than Red Leaf did on that night.

There was nothing formal or extraordinary about the feast. Red Leaf filled the first bowl with steaming stew and handed it to me. It was customary among the Utes for the men to eat first, the women later. I had never found any objection to that custom before—but on this, our wedding night, I decided to begin eating only when Red Leaf was ready to eat with me. It seemed like the right thing to do.

She handed the second bowl to Neuwafe, who immediately popped a big camas bulb in his mouth, grunted with pleasure, and began to chew. Red Leaf handed the third bowl to her mother, then dished up her own.

When she finally looked up at me, there was a sudden look of surprise in her face, a look of concern. Apparently, she had never seen a man wait for a woman at mealtime before. She seemed worried that maybe I didn't like her stew, that for some reason I was rejecting it.

Realizing that an attempted explanation might only make matters worse, I smacked my lips and tossed a big chunk of elk meat in my mouth. With a smile of relief, Red Leaf, without taking her eyes off of me, raised her own bowl to her lips and sipped the steaming gravy.

I didn't have to pretend the stew was good. It really was the best I had ever tasted. The meat was so juicy and tender, it hardly needed chewing. The camas bulbs were crisp and chewy. Best of all was the marrow gravy, flavored just right with the onions and salt.

Instead of utensils, we ate with our fingers—fishing out the bulbs and pieces of meat, occasionally taking a deep drink of the rich gravy. The firelight reflected warmly on our chewing faces as we went to work on the stew.

After finishing my fourth serving and licking the bowl and my fingers clean, I put down the bowl and leaned back on the buffalo robe behind me. Neuwafe finished off his sixth serving a minute later. The women put away the bowls and to my surprise, suddenly disappeared through the tepee entrance into the night.

A wedding party without the bride wasn't much of a party, it seemed to me. Still, everybody else seemed to know what was going on, so I figured I would have to go along whether I liked it or not.

Neuwafe pulled a long pipe and tobacco pouch from under his buffalo robe. After tapping the end of the pipe on a fireplace rock to break the old ashes free, he packed it full of fresh tobacco and lit it with an ember from the fire.

Every spring, just before leaving on the summer buffalo hunt, Neuwafe and most of the other men in the tribe would prepare little individual garden pots—often only three feet wide and four feet long. They would plant tobacco in the little pots. When the tribe returned to the shores of Utah Lake in the late summer or early fall, the men would harvest their little stands of tobacco.

After puffing contentedly for a few minutes, Neuwafe offered the pipe to me, something he had never done before. I gratefully accepted, puffing carefully the strong, sweet smoke.

After each of us had smoked several times, with very little conversation, Neuwafe handed me a little leather pouch with a long, looping drawstring. Similar to the medicine bag he wore at all times, it was attached to a thong that wrapped around his neck.

I opened the bag. It was empty. I looked up at Neuwafe, who handed me a little white tooth. He explained that it was from a beaver, the smartest of animals. A small beaver could cut down mighty trees, making them fall in the right places. A beaver always had plenty of food for winter. I put the beaver tooth in the bag.

Neuwafe handed me a claw. He said it was from a bear, that bears were brave fighters, especially when their lives or those of their loved ones were in danger. That's the way a man needed to be. I put the bear claw in the pouch.

Next, Neuwafe began to lay long hairs, one at a time, across my knee. There were black and white ones, but most of them were in varying shades of brown. When he finished, there were thirty-four hairs on my knee. One from each of the horses Ike and I had stolen, he explained. That was a remarkable deed, one I should never forget. I wrapped the bundle of hairs together in a single knot, and placed it in the pouch with the tooth and claw.

Next he handed me some human hair that he had clipped from Red Leaf, his sister, now my wife. He had taken care of her after their father's death. Now it was my duty to care for her, to love her, to protect her, never to forget her. Before putting Red Leaf's hair into the pouch, I looked Neuwafe straight in the eye to let him know I fully intended to take good care of his sister.

I began to close my pouch, thinking Red Leaf's hair was the final item to be carried in the pouch. But Neuwafe held out his hand, motioning for me to wait, that there was something else.

Opening his own pouch, he tipped it to the side. A light-colored stone rolled out onto his palm. He tossed it to me.

The stone was heavy and smooth, about the size of an elk dropping. It glistened in the firelight. Solid gold. A nugget. The biggest I had ever seen. In amazement, I looked up at Neuwafe. He motioned for me to put it in the pouch, saying the Mexicans and British would trade food and horses for the little gold stones. I figured I probably understood the value of the gold nugget better than he did. It was probably worth several hundred dollars, more money than I had ever seen at one time in my life. A small fortune.

If a white man had handed me the nugget, my reaction would have been to ask him where he got it. But getting it from Neuwafe was a gift for my medicine pouch on the night of my wedding to Red Leaf; I felt it would be rude to ask him where he got it. But I wouldn't forget. Someday, when the time was right, I would ask him. It would be good to know where gold nuggets could be found.

After my pouch was closed and the drawstring looped around my neck, Neuwafe began to explain the religious significance of the pouch, how if I wore it at all times, and remembered the significance of the enclosed items, I would find favor with Sin-O'-Wap, the greatest of the gods.

He explained that all the items in the pouch would be good medicine for me, but if I wanted the strongest medicine of all, the kind enjoyed by all great warriors, I would have to get it directly from Sin-O'-Wap. And that only happened after days of fasting and meditation, usually alone on some distant mountain peak. Someday soon I should seek that most powerful of medicine directly from Sin-O'-Wap.

So confident and calm were Neuwafe's words that chills ran through my back and neck at the thought of communing with a supernatural being. I hadn't felt that way since the first time I heard Parley Pratt preach Mormonism in Canada when I was twelve.

Neuwafe was just beginning to tell me about his own vigil to seek out Sin-O'-Wap, when we suddenly became aware of shouting outside the tepee, the thunder of horses' feet, and more shouting. After grabbing bows and arrows, we leaped for the doorway. Apparently enemy raiders were trying to steal Ute horses.

Chapter 39

After strapping the quiver of arrows to my back, I leaped upon the horse that I had been riding during the afternoon. It was tied near the tepee. The sliver of a moon didn't offer much light, and my eyes were still not adjusted to the darkness, but knowing the horse was familiar with the lay of the meadow, even at night, I urged him into a full gallop, in the direction of the stampeding herd.

There was no time to lose. The sooner the raiders were intercepted and distracted from the stampeding horses, the fewer horses would be lost. I could hear the thundering of hooves on both sides as other Utes joined me in the attempt to cut off the runaway herd.

By the time my eyes adjusted to the dark, I found myself in the middle of the galloping Ute horses. I figured I was somewhere near the front of the herd. Gradually, I began to pull my horse in, while waving my bow in the faces of the horses immediately behind me, in an attempt to slow them. I figured the other Ute riders were doing the same—at least those who weren't fighting the raiders. At this point I hadn't seen any of the enemy.

While leaning to the rear and waving my bow in the face of a horse, I suddenly noticed another rider, farther back. Rather than trying to slow the horses, as I was doing, he was whipping them with a rope in an effort to hurry them up. Certainly he had to be one of the raiders. He had been so intent on his task of whipping the horses that he hadn't spotted me.

Giving my horse his head, I slid an arrow from the quiver and notched it on the bow string. Turning around, I drew back the arrow and let it fly in the direction of the rider. Shooting an arrow from the back of a galloping horse is no simple matter, especially when the target is moving directly behind you. It's hard enough to sink an arrow into the side of a buffalo galloping at your side.

It was too dark to follow the flight of the arrow, but an instant after I let it fly, the rider and horse were swallowed up in the sea of galloping horses.

Again I began to pull my horse back while waving the bow in the faces of the horses behind me. Soon I noticed other riders, my fellow Utes, doing the same. A few minutes later the herd came to a halt and we began herding them back toward the camp. It was impossible to tell how many had been lost, but it didn't appear the raiders had escaped with many more than those they had been riding.

Suddenly I remembered the rider who had gone down in the galloping herd. He was probably dead, but I wanted to find out. So I steered my horse away from the herd and toward the spot where I calculated the horse had gone down.

The fallen horse was exactly where I thought it would be, but there wasn't any sign of a dead Indian. Then I spotted my arrow, sunk deep into the dead horse's chest. Apparently the Indian hadn't been hurt and was on foot somewhere nearby. I called back for help.

A minute later, Neuwafe and two other riders were at my side. When they saw the dead horse with an Indian bridle still on its head, they knew what had happened.

We had just begun our search for the fallen raider when one of the braves found him a short distance from the dead horse. Apparently he had broken his ankle in the fall and had managed to crawl only a short distance. After we tied his hands behind his back, we loaded him onto the horse of the brave who found him and led him back to camp.

When we reached the camp, we were greeted by a blazing bonfire. Most of the people had come out of their tepees and were standing in small groups here and there discussing the attempted horse raid. The horses had been herded into a makeshift corral for safe keeping through the remainder of the night. Several groups of riders were roaming the nearby woods and meadows in the event that any of the raiders had stayed behind.

The prisoner was dragged from his horse and carried to a tree near the fire. He was lashed to the tree in a standing position, which forced him to put his weight—at least some of it—on the broken ankle, now red and swollen. I was sure the injury was painful, but he didn't show it on his face.

His expression was intense, his jaw firm. He looked young, probably sixteen or seventeen years old. Maybe this was his first raid. I wondered if he was from the tribe that had been camped on the Green River, the tribe Ike and I had stolen the horses from. Perhaps he and his companions had followed the trail of the thirty-four horses from the Green River to the Ute camp, and they had come to get their horses back. I wished I hadn't gone looking for the fallen rider. I wished the boy had escaped into the night. Someone said he was Comanche.

Already some of the older women and children were spitting on him and jabbing him with pointed sticks. This was nothing compared to the tortures in store for him, and he knew it. The fate of captured horse thieves was common among all the tribes—a slow, painful death, usually involving skinning and burning.

One time I had watched with amazement as Neuwafe and his companions skinned a captured Blackfoot warrior. They were nearly half finished before the poor man died, and not once during the entire ordeal did the man cry out. My admiration for the Blackfoot warrior grew with leaps and bounds as I watched him endure the horrible ordeal. At the same time I felt growing contempt, not so much for Neuwafe and his friends but for the way of life in which such behavior was expected.

I hoped the boy would be brave like the Blackfoot. If he could be as brave, the Utes would find little satisfaction in his death. If he cried out in his misery, the Utes would only find more pleasure in his torture. If his cries became annoying to his captors, they would cut his tongue to keep him silent as the torturing continued. Whatever he did, the torture would continue until he was dead. I wanted no part of it.

I headed for the tepee, where Red Leaf was waiting for me. It was our wedding night, a time to be happy. But how could there be happiness when nearby an Indian boy was being tortured to death?

As I walked slowly toward the tepee, I realized I could never really be a Ute Indian. Their culture could never be my culture—not completely. There were parts of their lifestyle that I loved—the carefree wandering, the buffalo hunts, the freedom, the love and respect for the land and animals. But they had other ways that I hated—the torturing of prisoners, including women and children; the selling of children into slavery; the general lack of concern for human suffering. I wanted no part of that.

I fingered the medicine bag that Neuwafe had given me earlier in the evening. It was important to me. There seemed to be so much meaning in the beaver tooth, the bear claw, the hair, and even the gold nugget. The medicine bag had been mine for a few brief hours, yet it seemed a part of me, a sacred possession.

I thought about my new bride, Red Leaf, her gentle ways, the love we had for each other. Some of the things in my life with the Utes I wanted to continue forever. How could I be part Ute and part something else? I was confused and unhappy as I entered the tepee to greet Red Leaf.

Chapter 40

When the Ute tribe headed east for the summer buffalo hunt, Red Leaf and I stayed behind. We still didn't have our own tepee, at least not one made from skins. But I had fashioned a wickiup of bark and brush piled upon a frame of tepee poles. The dwelling was comfortable and warm but not mobile like the hide tepees.

There were several reasons we were not going with the tribe on the buffalo hunt. The first was a desire to spend more time alone with Red Leaf, to get to know each other better, to spend some time discussing our future together. Most of the time we talked in Ute, but sometimes in English. I wanted her to learn my language too.

The second reason for not following the Utes to buffalo country was my desire to spend some time by myself, to sort out in my mind who I was and what I wanted to be. It was difficult to express these feelings to Red Leaf. She had never known anything but the nomadic life among the Utes. She couldn't comprehend anything beyond that and couldn't understand why I would want to consider anything different, especially when I told her about Missouri mobs. She showed a lot of interest when I told her about men's homes, riverboats, and cook stoves—things. But when I tried to describe books, politics, religion, she just shook her head, unable to comprehend, even slightly, what I was talking about.

Sometimes I thought about the young Comanche, the one who had died so bravely the night Red Leaf and I were married. I wondered if he had parents, brothers and sisters, and possibly a young squaw who mourned his death. I wondered if they would seek revenge. I wouldn't have blamed them if they did.

The Ute women and children stayed close to camp the first few weeks after the horse raid and guarded the horse herd closely in the event the boy's friends and family might come for revenge or attempt to steal more horses. Brown Wolf and two of his companions went in pursuit of the raiders and the six horses they had stolen. None of the stolen horses were mine, so I still had four.

By the time the tribe was ready to leave on the summer hunt, the attempted horse raid was pretty much forgotten, except for one thing. Brown Wolf and his two companions had still not returned.

I had given a lot of thought to Neuwafe's suggestion that I seek out the Ute god Sin-O'-Wap. Through fasting and meditation, I wanted to receive my own medicine dream, my own revelation from the Great Spirit. The Mormons encouraged the same kind of thing—the search for a personal relationship with God through fasting and prayer. Maybe the Mormon God and the Great Spirit were the same. Maybe if I sought him out, he would show me through some kind of sign the direction my life should take.

The more I thought about it, the more the idea grew on me. As I looked at the snowcapped peaks of Timpanogos rising majestically above the valley floor, as I contemplated the graceful, flowing movement of my horses as they frolicked across the grassy plain, as I looked into Red Leaf's face in the light of the evening cookfire and saw the kindness there, the lack of guile, the love she had for me—I knew there had to be a God in heaven or a Great Spirit. And I couldn't see any reason he wouldn't speak to me, or at least give me some kind of sign as to what I ought to do with my life. If I could prove to him that I was sincere and open to what he wanted to tell me, surely he would answer me. Yes, I would seek him out.

The tribe had been gone about a week when one night I told Red Leaf about my plans to climb to the higher elevations of Timpanogos to seek a medicine dream from Sin-O'-Wap. I said I would be gone at least three days. She didn't object, although I knew she wouldn't like being left alone. However, she had plenty to do. I had killed an elk several days earlier. The hide was stretched out in front of the wickiup, ready to be scraped. Most of the meat, still waiting to be jerked, was hanging on willow racks to dry.

Early the next morning, before daylight, I quietly rolled out from under the buffalo robe I shared with Red Leaf and slipped into my buckskins. Red Leaf was still sleeping. I didn't want to wake her. After making sure the medicine bag was in place about my neck, I stepped out into the cool dawn and looked up at the gray silhouette of the towering Timpanogos.

There was a chill in my spine as I contemplated the upcoming vigil. I wondered if Moses felt as I did the first time he climbed Mount Sinai.

I noticed the horses grazing quietly in the nearby meadow as I started walking toward the mountain. I didn't bother them because I had decided to walk. The grass was wet with the morning dew and soon my moccasins were soaked.

Although I was not in a hurry to get to the mountain, still not sure exactly how I was going to conduct the vigil, I hurried anyway in an effort to keep warm.

The land was fresh and alive with the new growth of early summer. The birds were building nests, the does had fawns, the wildflowers were just beginning to bloom at the higher elevations, and the grass was green and lush.

About midday I climbed upon a rock outcropping to rest. The mountain was steep now, and because I had not had anything to eat, I needed frequent rests.

Looking down upon the rich valley, I saw the dark green groves of pine trees, the lush meadows, the long snake-like strings of cottonwood trees lining the streams that worked their way across the valley to the beautiful blue lake. Rising above the valley were the snowcapped peaks of the distant mountains off in the western desert.

Closer to the mountain I could see the open meadow where my horses were grazing, the brush wickiup, the brown spot I knew to be the elk hide stretched out over the grass. I couldn't see Red Leaf. She was probably in the wickiup.

I had been gone for only a few hours, but as I looked down from the mountain on our little brush home, I felt a sudden longing to return, to be with Red Leaf, to help with the elk, just to be with Red Leaf every moment during this best time of the year. I began to feel a little silly about my intended vigil. In white society I would be scorned or laughed at for undertaking such a task. Who was I to think I could just climb up on a mountain and communicate with the Great One who created it all? Why would he bother with me? I was nothing but a dot in the vast creations of the world.

Trying to shove the doubts from my mind, I climbed down from the rock and continued the upward journey, now tedious and difficult. My head ached from the lack of nourishment, my stomach growled incessantly for food, and the late morning sun beat down on my head. Long ago the chills had stopped tingling in my spine, and I realized that the vigil was not going to be easy.

It was several hours later, in midafternoon, when I spotted smoke. I had turned to face the valley before sitting down to rest when I noticed a gray pillar against the blueness of the lake. The smoke was coming from my wickiup, which was alive with yellow and white flames.

Immediately I was on my toes, searching for any sign of movement to indicate that Red Leaf was outside and safe. The distance was so far, it was hard to distinguish detail. Then, suddenly I spotted definite movement, but not next to the wickiup. Out in the meadow, the horses were running, like ants creeping over a green mat. I counted them. Six, not four. Apparently my four horses were being chased by two riders, probably the ones who had set fire to the wickiup.

I lunged forward, racing down the mountain, tears streaming down my cheeks at the hopelessness of the situation. Red Leaf needed me now, but it would be several hours before I could reach the camp, probably too late. Who were those mounted riders? Probably the Comanches. What would they do to Red Leaf? Maybe she was already dead. Would they torture her like the Utes had tortured the Comanche boy? How could I have been so stupid, to leave her alone and unprotected in this wild, cruel land?

Chapter 41

By the time I reached camp, our wickiup was reduced to nothing more than a pile of warm ashes. There was no sign of Red Leaf, our horses, or any of my belongings. Kicking among the ashes I found the half-cremated remains of the elk carcass from which Red leaf had been making jerky. I cut away a huge chunk of the roasted meat and wolfed down a few bites, having long forgotten my fast, knowing I would need strength for what I supposed to be a long journey ahead.

A few minutes later, I was trotting along the trail of the four horses that carried Red Leaf and her captors. The trail headed south and east toward the mouth of the canyon later named Spanish Fork by the Mormon pioneers. My legs were weary and my feet bruised from the race down the mountain. But knowing I would have plenty of time to rest when it was too dark to see the tracks, I refused myself the luxury of a needed rest.

As I loped along, I hoped Red Leaf would have the good sense to be agreeable with her captors—even friendly to the point where they would be persuaded to keep her as a squaw rather than torture or kill her. This was the only sensible way she could buy time until conditions were right for me to get her back. But as I thought about it, I realized that she probably would not be agreeable to them. That was not her nature. I remembered her independence in shunning other suitors, especially Brown Wolf, when she had humiliated him by refusing to touch the slain deer he left near her tepee. I remembered her boldness in racing horses against me across the grassy prairie, and her lack of fear when I left her alone at the wickiup while hunting or embarking on my vigil to Timpanogos. She was brave, strong, and certainly not inclined to give female favors to uninvited warriors. Figuring she would fight her captors, I forced myself to run even faster.

Without weapons and horses, not only would it be tough to catch up with Red Leaf and her captors, but there didn't seem to be much I could do if I found her. I thought about heading west to Gosiute country, getting a horse from Ike, and getting him to come with me in the search for Red Leaf. I knew he would do it.

But valuable time would be lost if I went after Ike. Perhaps a storm would come along and wipe out the trail. Then we would never find her. No, I had to stay on the trail, traveling as fast as possible. Eventually I would catch up, and when I did, I would somehow figure out a way to free her—if it wasn't too late.

It was in the afternoon of the second day when I came upon the place where Red Leaf and her captors had camped the first night. There were cold ashes from the abandoned fire, pawed-up turf, and fresh manure where the horses had been tethered to nearby trees.

Looking about for anything that might have been left behind, I suddenly discovered four stakes that had been driven into the ground to form a four-by-eight-foot rectangle. The earth and grass in the middle of the rectangle was matted and packed. Rawhide thongs were still tied to two of the stakes. There was blood on one of the thongs, but none on the ground that I could see.

My heart was thundering with a rage I had never felt before as I looked at the four stakes and imagined the cruelties that had been inflicted there on my Red Leaf.

With a tight grip on the handle of my knife, I longed to kill, maim, and even torture Red Leaf's captors. My earlier aversion to the cruelties inflicted by Indians on other Indians had vanished. For the first time since I had come to the Rocky Mountains, I felt the things I had often despised in my red brothers. I hungered and thirsted for vengeance. I longed to inflict the most cruel tortures possible on Red Leaf's captors. The mildness of white man's justice, of fair trials and jail sentences, seemed revolting and inadequate. Indian justice was better—swift and cruel revenge.

Beside one of the stakes I discovered the largest Indian track I had ever seen, almost as big as Ike's. It was different than any I had ever seen in that there was no stitching on the inside. Apparently the moccasin was made from a wraparound pattern requiring stitching on only one side.

Whoever the big Indian was, and whatever he belonged to, I figured I would kill him the first chance I got. I didn't find any other human footprints, just plenty of horse tracks.

Just as I was leaving the abandoned camp, I heard the clatter of hooves on stones up the trail. They were coming toward me; I could hear more than one animal.

I scampered into the rocks above the trail, a club in one hand and a knife in the other, waiting for the approaching horses. I had no idea who might be coming. It couldn't be the main Ute tribe. They had gone east and north well over a week ago. It couldn't be Red Leaf's captors, either. There was no sensible reason that they would turn around and come back, not after stealing Red Leaf and the horses.

The first to come into sight was a bay mare, with ears forward, trotting down the trail without rider, saddle, pack or halter. Immediately behind her, another horse came into view, a roan stallion carrying an Indian rider whom I immediately recognized as Brown Wolf. There was a quiver of arrows on his bare, broad-shouldered back, a bow in his right hand, reins in the left. He was alone with the two horses, returning from his raid on the Comanches. Apparently his companions had been killed or were returning on a different trail.

I had to get one of those horses from him. In the Ute camp he had been my enemy. He wanted Red Leaf too, and had it not been for me, she would probably have become his squaw. I had humiliated him in hand-to-hand combat by driving him off with a porcupine skin. Then I had outbid his eight-horse offer for Red Leaf with an offer of fifteen horses. Would he give me the horse just because I asked for it? I had nothing to trade. Or would he take the opportunity for revenge and try to kill me? It occurred to me that it might be wise to just leap upon him, by surprise, and kill him.

Instead, I just stepped out into the trail and nodded a cool greeting. He pulled his horse in and looked around in surprise, as if he expected me to be leading a bunch of warriors ready to attack him. He didn't trust me any more than I trusted him.

The only thing I had in common with Brown Wolf was the love both of us had shared for Red Leaf. While there was probably no way he would just give me a horse for my own benefit, perhaps he would be inclined to help Red Leaf. Hopefully his love for her was not yet forgotten.

I motioned for him to follow me down the trail to the abandoned camp. I showed him the four stakes, the blood-stained thong, the track belonging to the big Indian, and explained what had happened. He listened quietly, an occasional grunt to indicate he understood. When I finished telling what had happened, I asked him for a horse.

He looked at me for a minute, then jerked free a short rope that had been tied to the side of his saddle. He quickly fashioned a loop in one end, caught the bay mare, slipped the loop over her tongue and lower jaw, motioned for me to climb up while he held her still.

I leaped upon the mare, thanked Brown Wolf with a grim nod, slapped the mare on the rear with the free end of the rope, and headed up the trail.

I hadn't gone far when I heard a noise behind me. Turning to look back, I saw the roan stallion and Brown Wolf following me. Apparently his love for Red Leaf was more than I had supposed. The young brave who had been my mortal enemy a short time earlier was now my companion, sharing a common purpose—to save Red Leaf and destroy her captors, especially the Indian with the big foot. It would be good to have Brown Wolf on my side. Suddenly the chances of successfully rescuing Red Leaf were a lot better than they had been.

Chapter 42

Brown Wolf and I didn't say much to each other as we followed the trail left behind by Red Leaf and her captors. We pushed the horses hard across the open stretches but usually dismounted on the steep inclines in an effort to conserve their strength. The bay mare was the quickest to tire, while the roan stallion always seemed eager to push ahead. We were headed east toward the Green River.

Late in the morning we came upon the second camping place of Red Leaf and her captors. We were gaining on them. There were plenty of moccasin tracks in the sand around the cold ashes where the fire had been, including the big track. Brown Wolf figured they were probably Comanches because of the wraparound style of the moccasin pattern. I remembered the rectangle of stakes at the previous camp, and looked for a similar pattern. To my relief, there was none.

Red Leaf's captors made no effort to hide or disguise their trail. They knew the Ute tribe had gone north and east to hunt buffalo, and they apparently thought they had captured all my horses. They knew that on foot I could not keep up with their forced march. I was grateful for my good luck in stumbling upon Brown Wolf.

During the afternoon the lay of the land began to look familiar. I guessed that Ike and I might have passed this way when we had stolen the thirty-four Comanche horses.

The wind was at our back all afternoon, blowing up a storm from the west. Our unspoken concern was that the storm would wipe out the trail we were following.

We were winding our way along a small stream, broken here and there with beaver ponds, when it started to rain. Just a sprinkle at first, but by nightfall we were in a downpour.

Not wanting to attempt building a fire while it was so wet, we crawled under the protective branches of a big fir tree and buried ourselves in a warm blanket of pine needles, enjoying snatches of restless sleep while waiting for the dawn.

Our biggest worry, of course, was how we would be able to follow the trail once the heavy rain had washed it away. I figured we were probably getting pretty close to the Green River. How would we know if Red Leaf and her captors followed the river upstream or downstream, or crossed to the other side? Even though they couldn't be more than a half-day ahead of us, finding their trail again would be tough.

I wondered what kind of night Red Leaf was having. Was she protected from the rain? Was she still being abused by her captors? To what extent had they tortured her? Was she still alive?

In the darkness of the night I removed the medicine bag from my neck and fingered the contents. I always liked to feel the smooth weight of the gold nugget. It wasn't much good to me now. I would gladly have traded it for a good hound that could follow the trail even after the rain. I would have gladly spent it for a rifle, powder, and lead.

As I felt the sharp end of the beaver tooth, I remembered the numerous beaver dams and lodges scattered along the little stream we had been following. One lodge in particular seemed to stick in my mind. We had come upon it just at dark. It was hard to remember details, but I remembered being surprised at seeing a lodge so large. It was almost twice as big as any I had ever seen before. I wondered if a lot of beaver were living inside, or perhaps just a big beaver, a king of beavers. If Beaver George were still alive, he would have delighted in this stream with so many lodges and dams.

As I rubbed the little bundle of horse hair between my fingers, I remembered the Comanche village on the bank of the Green River, the one at the upstream end of the big meadow surrounded by natural boundaries. The thrill of stealing so many horses had been intoxicating.

It suddenly occurred to me that Red Leaf and her captors might be heading for that same village. The familiarity of the neighboring bluffs and hills indicated that we were headed in that general direction. It made sense that the Comanches, in an effort to get their horses back, would be the ones to attack my camp, steal my horses, and carry off my wife.

The next morning our worst fears were realized. The tracks we had been following had been completely washed away by the storm. I told Brown Wolf about the familiar surroundings and how I suspected we were heading in the direction of the Comanche village where Ike and I had stolen the horses. Brown Wolf agreed with me that we should continue toward the Green River and check out the village by the big meadow. As we mounted our horses in the early dawn, an alarmed beaver slapped his tail on the surface of a nearby pond and disappeared below the surface as he swam toward the entrance of the huge beaver lodge.

Soon Brown Wolf and I found the route Ike and I had used to drive the horses along after stealing them. As we hurried along, I wondered what we could do to free Red Leaf if we found her, or what we would do if we didn't find her in the village.

Chapter 43

At first light the next morning, we were hiding in the rocks overlooking the Comanche village. Many horses were grazing in the protected meadow. The grass was taller now, and the river calmer. The first smoke of the morning cookfires was coming from several of the tepees. Several women were stirring up an outdoor cookfire, but it appeared the men and children were all inside the tepees.

Suddenly Brown Wolf's arm shot forward, pointing to a tepee at the far side of the camp. There was smoke rising from the top, but no sign of movement. Then I saw the curled-up form on the ground about twenty feet in front of the tepee, near a stout post. As I looked closer, the form took human dimensions—a small person, a woman or girl, lying on her side in a buckskin dress, curled up on the ground, knees almost touching her chin, her long black hair covering the side of her face. I figured she was probably tied to the post with a rawhide leash, a common method of confinement for Indian slaves.

We couldn't be sure it was Red Leaf, so we watched and waited. If it was her, we could probably sneak into camp under the cover of darkness and cut her free. I couldn't see any dogs near the tepee.

The curled-up form still hadn't moved when the sun began shining over the eastern hills. It seemed we had been waiting forever, and if it turned out to be Red Leaf, I didn't know if I could wait around until dark to go to her rescue. On the other hand, maybe it wasn't Red Leaf, but perhaps just another slave child to be taken south and traded to the Mexicans for horses.

Our attention was suddenly diverted from the still form as the flap of the tepee was thrown back and the biggest Indian I had ever seen stepped out into the morning sunshine. He looked even bigger when he flexed his well-muscled arms above his head to stretch. At the sight of the Indian, the adrenaline began surging through my veins. I remembered the huge moccasin tracks we had been following. If this was the Indian who had made the big tracks, then the still form on the ground had to be Red Leaf.

There was a knot in my throat. The hair on the back of my neck was bristling. I glanced over at Brown Wolf. The intensity of his grimace was almost scary—as if his stare alone was powerful enough to consume the village. His lower lip was quivering, and there was perspiration on his brow.

The big Indian walked over to the post. With hands on hips, feet apart, he began saying something to the woman on the ground. We couldn't hear what he was saying, and we probably couldn't have understood the words, anyway.

The girl on the ground responded to the Big Indian by getting to her hands and knees and crawling away. With her long hair hanging over her face, and as far away as we were, it was impossible to tell if she was Red Leaf.

Without warning, the big Indian kicked the girl in the side, sending her sprawling through the air. She finally jerked to a halt at the end of the leash that connected one of her wrists to the stout pole. Before she could scramble to her feet, he kicked her again, then abruptly turned around and walked back to his tepee.

I turned to Brown Wolf to discuss what we should do, thinking perhaps we shouldn't wait until nightfall to execute our rescue. Brown Wolf was already on his feet loping back toward the horses. I followed. I wished Brown Wolf was more talkative, but on the other hand, I appreciated his decisiveness. He moved with the confidence of a man who knew exactly what he was doing.

To my surprise, Brown Wolf mounted the bay mare, and indicated that I should get on the stronger and faster roan stallion. As we rode quietly at a slow trot toward the village, Brown Wolf explained his plan so I would know what to do. He knew what he was going to do and expected me to go along.

At first I was angry at his assumed leadership, his unwillingness to consult with me. After all, Red Leaf was my wife, not his. But as he explained his plan, I swallowed my pride, realizing that what he said made sense and just might work. Besides, I couldn't think of anything better.

He explained that when we came in sight of the village he would gallop straight for the captive woman until he was close enough to see her face. If it was not Red Leaf, he would turn around and race back. The Comanches would certainly take chase, but since we hadn't done any harm, they probably wouldn't follow us very far.

If the captured woman was indeed Red Leaf, Brown Wolf would yell his loudest war cry as he galloped through the camp and into the big meadow, shooting arrows at any who got in his way. He said the Comanches would come after him, knowing he was cornered in the meadow.

While he was playing cat and mouse with his pursuers, hopefully drawing the attention of the entire village, I was to ride quietly to Red Leaf, cut her free, pull her up behind me, and take her away.

Once he saw that Red Leaf and I were free, he would desert his horse, climb up into the cliffs, and hopefully outrun the Comanches in a foot race across the plain. Brown Wolf was a strong runner, the fastest in the Ute village. Once he reached the plain, he would probably be able to outrun them. The big question was if he would get that far.

I figured Brown Wolf would probably be captured or killed, that the chances of him getting away from the Comanches would be slim once he allowed himself to be cornered in the meadow. I felt bad that I had resented his bold leadership, but I didn't say anything. Brown Wolf wasn't the kind of person one could just apologize to. I did, however, tell him about the river, how after passing through the gorge at the bottom of the meadow it became shallow at the mouth of a little valley, where one could ride a horse to the plain above. I suggested that he might want to do as Ike and I had done and make his escape in the river. He didn't say anything, but I knew he would remember.

As soon as the tepees were in sight, Brown Wolf drew an arrow from his quiver, notched it on the string of his bow, then urged his mare into a fast gallop toward the big Indian's tepee. I reined the roan stallion behind a juniper tree and watched through a break in the branches.

Brown Wolf didn't veer to the right or left, nor did he slow down, until he reached the woman. Apparently he called to her, because she began to get to her feet to face him. That's when he let out a shrill war cry. The woman was Red Leaf.

The big Indian charged out of the tepee just as Brown Wolf urged his mare toward the meadow. When he saw the big Indian, Brown Wolf reined the galloping mare straight for him, forcing him to back away in surprise. Dropping his reins to the horse's neck, Brown Wolf drew the bowstring back to his chin and let the arrow fly at point-blank range as his galloping horse brushed by.

As Brown Wolf galloped into the meadow, the big Indian stumbled about like a drunken man, the shaft of Brown Wolf's arrow protruding from one side of his chest. When he finally fell to the ground, Brown Wolf had pulled the bay mare to a halt just out of arrow range and was shouting insults to the startled Comanches who were scrambling from their tepees.

Soon four or five Comanches had mounted their ponies and were heading after Brown Wolf. Villagers were gathering at the edge of the big meadow to watch the chase.

I eased the roan stallion out from behind the juniper tree and into an easy gallop toward Red Leaf. After covering more than half of the distance, still none of the Comanches had noticed me. So far, so good. All I could see were the backs of heads as they watched the chase in the meadow. Brown Wolf had sunk another arrow into one of his pursuers, and they had retreated a short distance to wait for reinforcements. A dozen more riders and runners were charging to the rescue. Brown Wolf was shouting more insults at them as if he intended to kill them all.

Red Leaf was sitting on the ground, knees to her chest, head down as I rode up. I had expected that she would be waiting for me on her feet, with open arms, ready for me to cut her free. I had imagined pulling her up behind me without having to dismount. Instead, she just sat on the ground, burying her head in her knees. I would have called out to her to tell her to get to her feet, but I thought the sound of my voice might draw the attention of the Comanches.

When I was finally close enough to speak quietly, so only she could hear, I called her name. She didn't respond. I called again—still no response.

I dismounted and knelt beside her. We were losing precious time. She turned away, burying her face in her hands. This was no time to be upset.

I cut the rawhide rope that bound Red Leaf to the post and grabbed her arm to pull her toward the horse. She jerked away, and in a sobbing voice ordered me to leave her.

I grabbed her arm again, jerked her around, and took a firm hold on both of her wrists. Pulling her face up to mine, I began to tell her that we must hurry. I knew she must have suffered much pain recently, but we could deal with that later. For the time being, there was no way I would leave without . . .

For the first time, I saw the face she had been covering with her hands—and understood why she was resisting my efforts to rescue her.

The significance of her refusal to leave began to sink in. What kind of love did this Ute girl have for me? Surely, in all our courtship and brief marriage I hadn't even scratched the surface of how much she really cared for me.

Red Leaf would rather die than be a burden to me. What kind of love was that? She would rather give up her own life than bring inconvenience to me. I pulled her close, wrapping my arms tightly around her shoulders and back, and as the tears streamed down my cheeks with a new understanding and feeling in my own heart, I told her that we would either flee together or stay and die together, but that I would not leave her.

I told her that her blindness didn't change anything. If anything, I loved her more. The ugly, black sores where her eyes had been would heal, and we would have a good life together. But first we must get away from the Comanches. I knew that one of them had just seen me and was now calling to others.

I leaped upon the roan stallion and reached down to take Red Leaf's hand. This time she didn't resist. I pulled her up behind me and urged the stallion into a full gallop. Fortunately, all the Comanches with horses were out in the meadow chasing Brown Wolf. We had a chance to get a good head start before they came after us.

Chapter 44

The roan stallion galloped tirelessly over the grassy plain toward the distant mountains. The afternoon sun glistened brilliantly upon the sweat-soaked hide, alive with liquid lines and swelling bulges as the steel-hard muscles labored with perfect rhythm.

Occasionally I looked back in an effort to see how many Comanches were on our trail, and how far away they were. But the terrain was too level, and there were too many juniper and pine trees blocking my vision. I figured that in the event Brown Wolf was caught and killed, the entire troop of Comanche warriors would be free to come after me and Red Leaf. If Brown Wolf managed to escape onto the plain or down the river, the Comanches would have to split their forces.

In any case, I felt we had a pretty good lead on them. The roan stallion was fast and strong and didn't need any coaxing to keep going. It was exhilarating to feel the strength of the horse beneath me. That, combined with the warmth of the afternoon sun and Red Leaf's arms about my waist, would have given me a sense of well-being and confidence had it not been for the nagging worry of Red Leaf's blindness. How would that change our future life together? How could she live the nomadic life of the wandering Utes? Perhaps I would build her a log cabin. Perhaps I should take her back east to white civilization. I pushed these thoughts out of my mind, realizing that first we had to get away from the Comanches.

I pulled the stallion back to an easy lope when we reached the pine-studded foothills. As the trail began winding its way up a steep, rocky ridge, I dismounted and ran ahead, giving the sweating stallion somewhat of a breather. As strong and as fast as he was, it wouldn't be easy for a horse carrying two people to keep ahead of the Comanches.

When we reached the top of the ridge, I looked back over the grassy plain. It didn't take but a moment to spot four galloping horses, our Comanche pursuers. The fact that there were only four gave me hope that Brown Wolf was still on the loose and that the rest of the Comanche warriors were still going after him. The thing that bothered me most about my pursuers was that they were closer than I had hoped. Maybe a mile back, but no more.

I looked up at Red Leaf, sitting quietly on the horse, shoulders hunched forward, elbows straight, palms on the horse's back, as she used her arms to prop herself in an upright position. There was a weariness about her that didn't fit her young body. I offered her a piece of jerky, but she said she wasn't hungry. I wondered when she had last had a good sleep or good nourishment. Her face was swollen and dirty. The black sores where the firebrands had burned her eyes were open and oozing a clear liquid, almost as if she were crying.

The wounds needed to be cleaned and bandaged. She needed rest and nourishment, not a long hard ride on the back of a galloping horse—but at the present there was no alternative.

I leaped back upon the roan stallion behind Red Leaf and urged the stallion into a full gallop up the rocky trail. Soon the terrain leveled again and the horse ran even faster.

The June sun was already behind the western peaks when we reached the little stream where Brown Wolf and I had seen the beaver ponds. Remembering some thick clumps of willow a few miles downstream, we hurried even faster in an effort to reach the willows before dark. The ground wasn't as rocky now, and the horse didn't have to pick his footing with as much care as earlier.

Suddenly, the horse broke stride and began stumbling brokenly to a halt. As I dismounted to see what was wrong, the stallion shifted his weight away from his left front foot. I picked up the hoof. Red blood was oozing slowly from a crooked gash behind the arrow-shaped frog, or center part, of the hoof. Apparently the animal had stepped on a sharp stone.

I let go of the hoof and tried to lead the horse ahead. Reluctantly it tried to follow, attempting to keep its weight off the injured hoof. The swift, strong stallion had suddenly become useless to us.

Helping Red Leaf to the ground, I took her by the hand and started running. We hadn't gone more than fifty feet when she collapsed. She was too weak. It had been difficult for her to ride the horse, but running or even walking was too much for her now. I took her in my arms and started running ahead—keeping a sharp eye out for a good hiding place.

A short time later we rested at the place where Brown Wolf and I had camped during the rainstorm the night before, next to the big beaver lodge. I looked back toward the headwaters of the little stream. The four Comanches were working their way down the ridge toward the valley floor. They would soon be upon us, and there was no way I could outdistance them carrying Red Leaf. She looked almost unconscious on the grass at my feet. She so desperately needed rest and care, but the cover was sparse. There just weren't any good places to hide from the rapidly approaching Comanches.

In desperation and frustration, I fingered my medicine pouch as I looked about for some kind of clue as to what we should do. The gold nugget, with enough value to buy three or four rifles, was useless. With a good rifle I could put up a good fight. I didn't even have a bow and arrows. Only a knife.

I felt the beaver tooth, then thought about the huge lodge in the stream. Beaver George had taught me all about beaver lodges—the underwater entrance, the inside ledges where the beavers were safe from their natural enemies.

Suddenly I had an idea. Making sure the Comanches were far enough down the ridge to be out of sight, I dove into the icy water of the beaver pond and swam to the lodge. I circled the mud-plastered mound of sticks, feeling beneath the surface until I found what appeared to be the entrance. Taking a deep breath, and using the sticks from the lodge as handles, I pulled myself under the water until I was facing the entrance. After jerking some of the sticks away in an effort to enlarge the opening, I forced my way back into the black tunnel, scratching my ribs and shoulders on sharp sticks as I pushed my way into the dark lodge.

It wasn't completely dark inside. Some daylight filtered through the air hole in the ceiling. A ledge just above the water level, about eight inches wide on two sides, came together at the back of the lodge to form the flat, mudslick floor of a little cave about four feet deep and fifteen inches high. Two beavers were huddled at the back of the cave.

It wasn't much of a hiding place. And it certainly would be crowded with the four of us—Red Leaf and me and the two beavers.

Red Leaf was reluctant to enter the water, but with the Comanches approaching, there was no time for discussion. While she waded into the knee-deep pond next to the shore, I splashed water on the sandy bank to wash away our tracks.

When I turned to Red Leaf, she was already shivering. We swam the fifteen feet of deep water to the lodge. Then I guided her into the underwater entrance. It was easier for her to get through the opening because of her smaller size, although twice her dress snagged on pointed sticks.

When I followed her in, I pulled two large sticks with me, which I placed over the opening to help prevent us from sliding into the water. We situated ourselves on opposite sides of the opening, facing each other, our heads toward the two huddling beavers, who remained at the back of the den.

The same openings that allowed light to filter through the matted ceiling allowed sound to enter too. At first, the only sound was the distant rushing of water over the dam at the lower end of the pond, but soon we heard hoofbeats and voices, obviously the Comanches. Even though I couldn't understand any of the words, it was obvious from the excited nature of their conversation that they had discovered the roan stallion.

Red Leaf was still shivering, and there was little hope of getting warm and dry in the damp, cool beaver lodge. Our buckskins were soaked and would remain so through the night. I had hoped the Comanches would continue their journey downstream, thinking we had gone in that direction. Had they done so, we could have abandoned the lodge and found a warmer and drier place to spend the night. As it was, however, the Comanches figured we were hiding near the horse. Instead of moving on, they began searching for us behind every bush and rock.

Chapter 45

It was almost dark when we heard some splashing in the outside pond. Suddenly the stick-and-mud roof of the lodge began to creak and crunch as an Indian climbed on top. He began shouting to his companions on shore. They shouted back. I drew my knife.

If that Indian had the courage to swim into the dark underwater tunnel in search of an enemy, I would be ready for him. I didn't think he would try to dig in from the top. The maze of sticks and mud would be impossible to dig through.

My suspicions were confirmed when the Indian plunged into the water and began working his way around the outside of the lodge, feeling for the underwater entrance. I was ready with my knife, and knew I had the advantage. But I also knew that in fighting off or killing this Indian I would be giving away our hiding place, and we would be trapped with little hope of escape.

The Indian had already entered the tunnel and was wiggling toward us, when a new idea suddenly entered my mind—an idea that might maintain our secrecy. After slipping the knife back in its sheath, I reached forward and grabbed one of the beavers by its front paw. Before it had a chance to bite, I jerked it forward and shoved it into the watery opening. The second beaver followed close behind, unaware of the Indian wiggling into the entrance.

I don't know who was surprised most, the Indian or the beavers, but when the beavers attempted to come back into the lodge, I slapped them on the noses, heading them back in the direction of the Indian, who by this time was scrambling backwards to get out of the entrance. Soon all was quiet. The Indian and the beavers were gone. And the Indian didn't come back, apparently concluding that we couldn't possibly be hiding in the same lodge with those two feisty beavers.

Soon it was dark, and to our grave disappointment, the Indians made camp in the natural clearing at the edge of the pond. We could hear the occasional sound of their voices and see faint flickerings from their fire through the ventilation holes in our thatched ceiling.

By this time I was shivering too. We worked our way around the cave-like area where the beavers had been so we could huddle side by side and share each other's warmth.

When I wrapped my arms around Red Leaf, I was surprised at how cold she was. In her weakened condition, her body had simply not been able to generate enough energy to keep her warm in the water-cooled beaver den.

Though I held her close and whispered words of affection and promise in her ear, her only response was to squeeze my arm gently as she continued to shiver. She seemed delirious with the cold. The shivering even seemed to prevent her from whispering coherently. I would have given anything for a warm buffalo robe and a bowl of elk stew for her.

While I was holding her close trying to warm her, she suddenly began to cough—a deep raspy bark. Holding my hand over her mouth, I tried to muffle the cough in an effort to prevent the sound from carrying beyond the lodge to the Comanche camp.

After what seemed like hours, the coughing and shivering stopped. But still she didn't seem any warmer.

Never before or since have I experienced such a long night. Twice I fell asleep, but only for brief periods.

Once, I was awakened suddenly by splashing and a scream as Red Leaf in her delirium, had writhed out from under my grasp and accidentally slipped into the icy water leading to the exit tunnel.

As I helped her out of the water and back into my arms, I realized that her situation was desperate, that her life was in the balance. And there was nothing I could do to help.

The most difficult trials of my life flashed through my mind—the death of my parents, the Missouri mob beating me at Gallatin, running from Boggs's dogs, the fall of Far West, the exploding riverboat, my battle with the killer grizzly, cutting the horse in half to save Neuwafe, galloping over the bank into the raging waters of the Green River and disappearing into the black gorge, standing on the slopes of Mt. Timpanogos watching the Comanches burn my wickiup while they carried Red Leaf away.

None of those experiences were half as difficult as holding Red Leaf in my arms, feeling the strength and life ebb from her young body while I was unable to help. Sick from the cold, choked with emotion, and desperate with the frustration of not being able to do enough to help Red Leaf, I dozed the second time into a restless sleep—not a normal kind of sleep, but only a brief escape from the overpowering misery of our situation.

I awoke from this second sleep, gradually increasing my awareness from a state of half-consciousness to a growing panic. Red Leaf was too cold, too still. When I fully awakened, she was dead.

I continued to hold her for a long time, the tears streaming across my cheeks into her long black hair. I didn't want to let her go—my first and only love, my wife, the woman who was going to be the mother of my children, the girl who had preferred to give up her life rather than hinder me with her blindness.

Chapter 46

When the first rays of the gray dawn began filtering through the tangle of sticks and mud, I slipped into the water and wriggled out of the beaver lodge into the open water. I came out with the lodge between me and the Comanches. I had gently tucked Red Leaf's body into the nook where the two beavers had huddled. I planned to come back and bury her after the Comanches were gone.

Emotionally spent, all I wanted was to get away and lose myself in the vast wilderness. There was nothing left. No love, no hate. Not even a desire for revenge on the Comanches. Only a subconscious instinct for survival.

Peering around the lodge, I could see that three of the Comanches were still wrapped in their blankets, while the fourth was huddled over a new fire, trying to coax it to life. Beyond the Comanche campfire, their four horses and the roan stallion, still limping, were grazing quietly in the meadow.

Moving very slowly so as not to make ripples on the surface of the pond, I pushed toward the opposite bank, keeping the lodge between me and the fire builder. Crouching at the edge of the pond, I watched the Indian until he turned his back to me. Then I worked my way carefully downstream, trying to keep as much cover as possible between me and the red men. I held perfectly still whenever the Indian was facing my direction.

I was only a few yards past the beaver dam when the other three Indians crawled out of their blankets and gathered around the fire. I dropped down behind the dam, out of their line of vision.

I realized I was too late getting started. As the camouflage of darkness rapidly disappeared, there was not enough cover for good hiding. My instincts wanted me to survive. Emotionally, I didn't care if I survived or not. Maybe it wouldn't be so bad joining Red Leaf in the happy hunting ground, or wherever else she might be. I didn't feel anything, not even fear.

I peeked over the top of the dam, deciding not to make my next move until I knew what the Comanches were going to do. I expected they might be preparing to get on their horses to go in search of Red Leaf and me. Instead, they were engaged in a vigorous discussion as they looked at the beaver lodge.

A moment earlier, there had been no feelings left in me. But as I watched the four Comanches plotting an assault on Red Leaf's resting place, the hair began to rise on my neck. I remembered Red Leaf's scream as she slipped from my arms into the icy water. Apparently the Comanches had heard that scream too and were planning to discover what was in the beaver lodge.

Dropping their bows and arrows on the ground, the four warriors began cutting spears from dead willows. After sharpening points on the new weapons, the Comanches waded into the cold water, shoving their spears in front of them and swimming to the lodge. All of them climbed on top of the mound, none daring to enter the underwater entrance.

While two of the braves stood poised above the water opening, waiting to spear whatever emerged from the lodge, the other two climbed on the top of the lodge and began working the pointed ends of their poles down through the tangle of sticks and mud.

In my mind's eye I could see Red Leaf's lifeless body lying quietly on the floor of the beaver lodge. They couldn't hurt her anymore. Still, I didn't like the thought of those crude spears puncturing her body. I also realized now would be a good time for me to sneak away, while the attention of the Comanches was on the beaver lodge.

But the thought of those crude spears breaking through the ceiling of the lodge and sinking into Red Leaf was more than I could stand. Besides, I realized it was just a matter of time until they got her, either through the entrance or by making a hole in the roof. I could only guess how they might mutilate the body. Certainly they would scalp her, steal her dress, jab her with their spears in their frustration at not catching me.

There would be no gain in swimming to the lodge to fight all four of them at once. At this point I wasn't afraid to die, but certainly didn't want to give them the satisfaction of an easy victory.

Remembering the bows and arrows that had been left behind on the shore, I crawled toward the meadow side of the pond, keeping out of sight by staying below the top of the dam. Upon leaving the protection of the dam, I slithered on my belly through the tall grass along the edge of the pond. There were a few times when the Comanches could have seen me had they looked toward shore, but they were so intent on shoving the spears into the lodge that they probably wouldn't have noticed me had I stood up and walked toward their bows.

I was flat on my belly, about to reach their bows and arrows, when the Comanches suddenly cried out with a united war whoop. I scrambled toward the bows and arrows, thinking they had spotted me. To my surprise, they hadn't seen me, not even when I lunged forward.

As I notched the first arrow, they were excitedly examining the blood-streaked point on one of the spears, the blood that had inspired them to shout a moment earlier.

Before they had a chance to try for more blood, I let the first arrow fly, striking one of the warriors square in the side, just below the armpit. I had the second arrow and drawn before the other three Comanches realized what was happening.

The first Indian fell forward into the pond and thrashed around for a few moments in the reddening water before going under. The second arrow hit one of the warriors in the hip just as he dove out of sight behind the lodge.

By the time I notched the third arrow, the Indians were out of sight on the far side of the lodge. At thirty feet, they were easy targets for my bow, but I could easily dodge their crude spears. I had them pinned down. Their only advantage was in numbers—three of them to one of me, and one of them was wounded.

I paced up and down the bank, waiting for them to show themselves, or possibly make a break for the opposite bank. I cut the strings on the other bows. In case they managed to get on shore, I didn't want any other weapons available for them to use against me.

After seeing my first two arrows hit their mark, the Indians were in no hurry to take any chances. No matter where I walked along the shore, they made the appropriate adjustments to keep the lodge between me and them. They seemed content to wait for darkness when it would be easy for them to get to shore and disappear into the night.

The bow and arrows gave me a definite advantage in the daylight, but when darkness fell, the advantage would be neutralized. I was beginning to think that maybe I ought to quit, untie their horses, and leave while I still had the advantage. That's when I noticed movement in the willows on the far side of the pond. An Indian was notching an arrow on his bow string. My first reaction was to dive for cover, thinking the Comanches had reinforcements.

But there was something familiar about the new Indian. Yes. It was Brown Wolf. Not only had he escaped from the big meadow, but he had managed to pick up and follow the trail left behind by Red Leaf and me.

He let the arrow fly. One of the Comanches screamed, and the other two dove into the pond, where they had little defense against arrows coming from both banks. Soon all was quiet.

I dropped my weapons, waded into the pond, and swam into the lodge. A few minutes later, with Red Leaf in my arms, I returned to the shore where Brown Wolf was waiting, his face like stone.

His love for Red Leaf had never faltered, not even when she married me. I wondered if I would ever understand the depths of this red man's heart.

I nodded for him to take her from me, to carry her to her final resting place.

We located a grassy spot at the foot of a steep bank. After using stout poles to scrape out a shallow cave, we laid her gently in her grave—on her back with arms folded across her stomach. We smoothed out her dress and straightened her legs, back, and neck to make her look as comfortable as possible.

I couldn't think of an appropriate burial sermon. Neither could Brown Wolf. After kneeling beside her and just looking at her for a while, we dug our poles into the bank and pulled the dirt down over her.

I started looking about for a flat stone to fashion into a marker where I could carve her name. But Brown Wolf stopped me. He said if the Comanches found her grave, they would dig her up and scalp her. Instead of putting up the marker, we camouflaged the grave with brush and stones. I took a good look around at the formation of the hills, the lay of the stream. If I ever came back this way, I wanted to be able to find the grave.

I didn't know, however, if I would ever come this way again. The Indian in me had died with Red Leaf. I wanted to go back to Missouri, to find the people I had abandoned when I fled to the Rocky Mountains—the homeless Mormons. I wondered if they found a place to settle, perhaps in Illinois.

I remembered the first time I had heard Parley Pratt preach in Canada, when I was twelve. He had said something about the Mormons establishing the kingdom of God on earth, a kingdom of peace with a Christian government. I couldn't remember any of the details on how such a kingdom would actually be set up, but I felt that maybe I could help in making such a thing happen. I had my fill of killing, hatred, and revenge.

Brown Wolf and I divided up the Comanche horses, each taking two. I unbridled the roan stallion so that once his hoof healed he would be free to join the wild horses.

Brown Wolf headed north, intending to find the Utes before they returned from the summer buffalo hunt. I headed west, wanting to say good-bye to Ike before heading back to Missouri.

About the Author

Until someone else steps forward, it appears *The Storm Testament* series author Lee Nelson is the only man in modern times to kill a bull buffalo from the back of a galloping horse with a bow and arrow.

No, Lee is not a lunatic bent on suicide, but a best-selling author intent on gathering authentic research. Digging through dusty journals, starting fires without matches, and even chewing on raw buffalo is part of Nelson's research in writing historical/adventure/romance novels unparalleled in authenticity and originality.

Lee was born high in the Rocky Mountains in Logan, Utah, later graduating from high school in California. After studying at the University of California at Berkeley, he served a mission for the LDS Church in southern Germany. Lee has a bachelor's degree in English literature and an MBA, both from Brigham Young University.

Lee Nelson has more than thirty published books, including ten historical novels in *The Storm Testament* series.

0 26575 75443 8